I0739138

Ballet Noir

Caroline Miller

Ballet Noir

This is a work of fiction. Names, characters, businesses, places, events and incidents are either the products of the author's imagination or used in a fictitious manner. Any resemblance to actual persons, living or dead, or actual events is purely coincidental.

A Rutherford Classics Book

All rights reserved

Copyright (c) 2016 by Caroline Miller
Printed in the United States. No part of this book may be reproduced, stored in a retrieval system or transmitted in any form or by any means without the prior written permission of the publishers, except by a reviewer who may quote brief passages in a review to be printed in a newspaper, magazine or journal. For information contact Rutherford Classics at www.rutherfordclassics.com

Second printing

ISBN: 978-0-9981697-6-7 (softcover)
         978-0-9981697-7-4 (e-book)

PUBLISHED BY RUTHERFORD CLASSICS
www.rutherfordclassics.com
Library of Congress Control Number: 2016936636

Publisher's Cataloging in Publication

     Ballet Noir/Caroline Miller

213 pages--1. Paranormal--Fiction. 2. Romance--Fiction. 3. Adventure--Fiction. 4. Mystery--Fiction. 5. Contemporary--Fiction. 6. Necromancy---Fiction. 7. Alchemy--Fiction. 8. Dance--Fiction. 9. Ghosts--Fiction

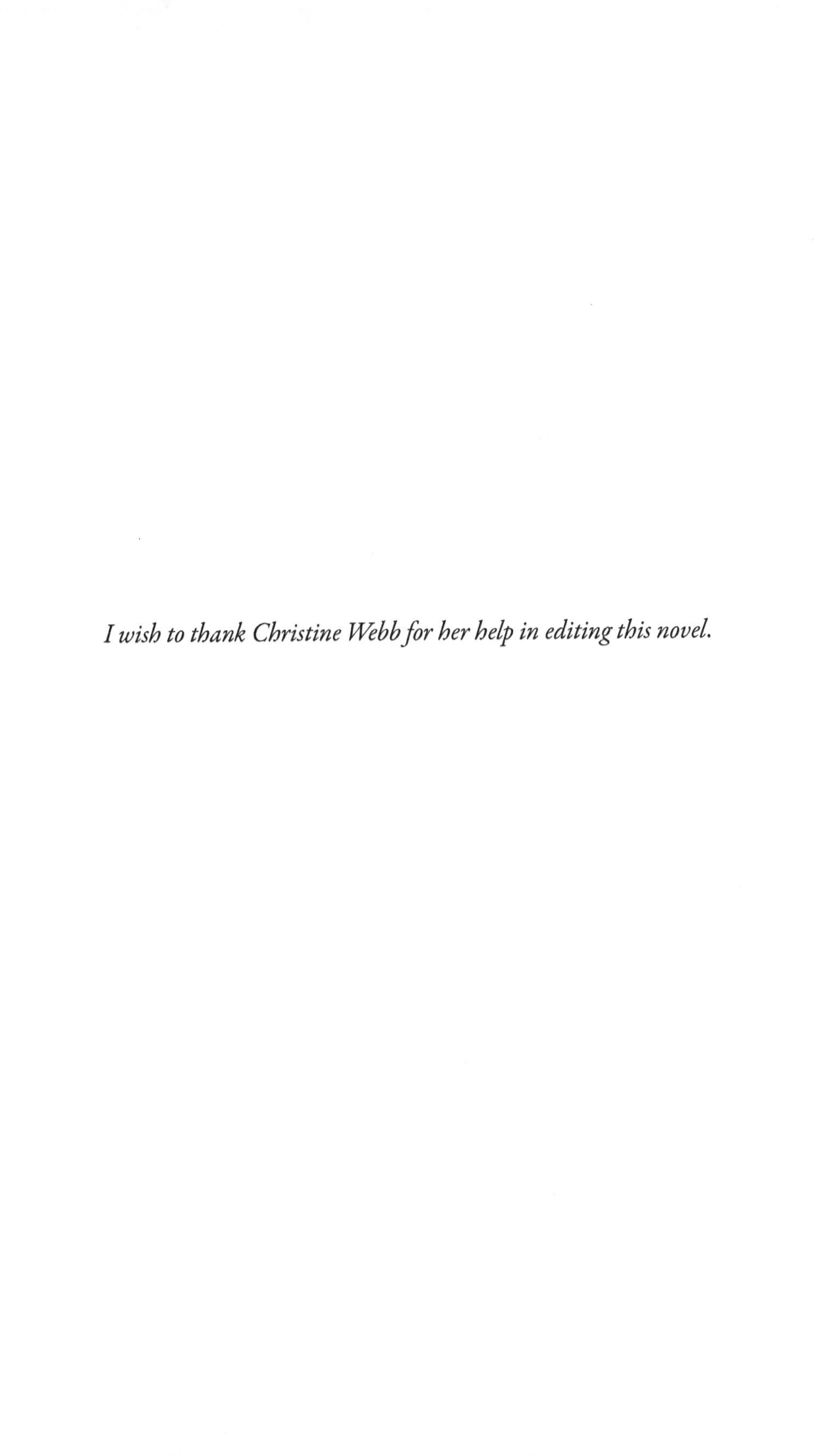

I wish to thank Christine Webb for her help in editing this novel.

Ballet Noir

CHAPTER I

I heard the cries again, just as I had on the three previous nights of our ballet tour. The year was 2009, and these cries were similar to those I'd experienced as a child whenever someone I loved had died. The first time was a week after my grandmother departed. For months afterwards, I'd refused to sleep without a light burning in my room. Then I'd heard them again when I was nine. That time they came after my best friend died of leukemia, the day after I'd visited her in the hospital. My final haunting came when I was twelve. The year was 2000, the turn of the century and was made memorable because it marked the loss of my beloved dance teacher, Madame Yelena Natilova. She'd been run down by a car at the age of sixty-four.

These recent hearings came while I was performing before an audience at the Prague National Theatre. I was dancing the role of Odette and I heard them during the final scene in *Swan Lake.* No one on stage or in the hall seemed troubled by them. The dancers swirling around me kept pace with the music and the audience, anticipating my theatrical death, sat in rapt attention. What I heard came from beyond the footlights and seemed to be exclusively for me.

When the curtain rang down on our final performance in Prague, the audience broke into joyful applause. David Harden, as Prince Siegfried, and I advanced toward the edge of the stage with the full corps de ballet behind us.

"Not bad, Tara Bentley," my partner whispered in my ear. "Not bad at all."

He stepped to one side to allow for my solo bow, and I did the same for him seconds later. Next, we entwined fingers and with our free hands, we tossed kisses to the audience. The patrons went wild and I should have been ecstatic, but my eyes kept scanning the upper balconies for some rational explanation of what I'd heard. Finding none, I felt alone, like a caged animal cut off from the rest of my species.

If I'd hoped to gather my thoughts, alone in my dressing room, I was mistaken. As it was closing night in Prague, members of the corps kept running in to congratulate me, ecstatic that our performance in the first city of our tour had gone so well. I was kept so busy hugging them and sharing compliments that by the time my best friend, Susan Kepler, showed up I'd barely begun to remove my makeup.

Susan was my age, twenty-one, but shorter and with a rounded figure which forced her to be conscious of her weight, particularly as our Artistic Director, Alec Borden of the Seattle Ballet Company, liked his dancers so thin, they barely cast shadows. Her nervous energy saved her. Her speech and gestures were rapid as was her capacity to share gossip. Among members of the company she was known as the Town Crier.

"Aren't you dressed yet? Alec has a taxi waiting for us. He doesn't want anyone late for the cast party at the Grand Hotel Bohemia. Especially, not you. He sent me to hurry you up."

Standing behind me, she peered at her reflection in the mirror.

"Do you think this dress makes me look fat?"

"Don't be ridiculous," I laughed. "Of course you don't. Why do you always need reassurance?"

"And why are you always late?" She reached from behind me to put the lid on my cold cream jar. "Come on. You don't want to hold everyone up."

Her cheerful disposition helped me to feel normal and not like someone losing her mind. For a moment, I considered telling her what I'd been experiencing. Maybe she'd have some explanation or at the very least, she might order me to bed with a bowl of chicken soup. But I hesitated. She wasn't good at keeping secrets. Besides, she looked so happy. She had a right to feel that way. We all did. Our little company, after much struggling, was being noticed at last. I guessed there was another reason for her glowing countenance, as well. She hadn't said anything, but I suspected she was in love.

"I think I'll skip the party," I shrugged. "I'm tired and we have to catch the train for Budapest at 8 in the morning. Then it's rehearsals and three performances at the State Opera House. Then there's Vienna, Milan and Venice."

"Stop that. You're making me exhausted just listening to you. You're the prima ballerina. You have to show up." She bent down to speak in a conspiratorial whisper. "Besides, someone will be there Alec wants you to meet."
I spun around. "Who? Why didn't Alec tell me?"

"I don't know," Susan shrugged. "You'll have to ask him."

As I stood up, she handed me my black dress and helped me with the zipper.

"You do look a little tired," she admitted as she stood back to look at me. Reaching for my powder puff, she dabbed a bit more color on my cheeks.

When she was done, I brushed away the excess and, grabbing my coat and purse, allowed her to pull me out the door.

David Harden, waiting in one of the taxis, waved us inside. Susan headed toward him, with me in tow, and climbed in beside him, already chattering about her hopes for the rest of our tour. As she was capable of an extended monologue, I allowed myself to drift off and was sound asleep when the cab came to a halt in front of the hotel. I remember how cold the night air felt as we stumbled toward the entrance.

Susan was the first to spot the drinks-table and steered us toward the flutes of champagne. Handing David and I a glass, she then proceeded to elbow the other guests out of her way so that she could deliver us, like a pair of express packages, to our Artistic Director.

When we found him, he was talking to a woman taller than he was by several inches. Adding to her sense of height was the floor-length gown and matching red turban that she wore. A few strands of lustrous black curls had broken free beneath the headgear. I judged her to be in her late fifties, but she was lithe and had the posture of a dancer. Certainly, her violet eyes glittered with a critical air as she surveyed the three new arrivals, suggesting she knew her ballet and held firm opinions.

"Ah, well done, Susan." Alec smiled as he waved us closer to him with the tip of his fingers so he could make introductions. "Madame Lazaremko, this is Tara Bentley of whom we were just talking."

Alec narrowed his eyes as he looked at me -- a warning that I was to be on my best behavior. Whoever this woman was and whatever her background, by his glance, he wished me to know that she was in a position to benefit the company.

Madame Lazaremko held out her hand.

"How do you do, Miss Bentley? Your performance tonight was impressive. You danced Odette with perfect innocence. I must congratulate you."

I took the hand that was offered and thanked her for her compliment, though uncertain of her sincerity. The hand I took was cold, which didn't surprise me, as it mirrored her demeanor. I decided to keep the conversation simple and asked if she was fond of ballet. When her cheeks reddened, I knew I'd made a faux pas.

"Come now, Tara." Alec broke in to smooth over my mistake. "Everyone knows Madame was the prima ballerina with the Bolshoi for many years. How long has it been since you retired?" He turned to look into the woman's violet eyes. "Can it be fifteen years, already? What a loss for the theater. I recall the news of your triumphant exit as if it were yesterday."

His flattery dramatically reduced the tension in the air. Madame's shoulders relaxed and when she spoke, her voice, rich with its deep, Russian accent, sounded more wistful than annoyed.

"I'm afraid it has been a while. Miss Bentley can hardly be expected to remember. But she might recognize my stage name: Ludmila?"

Now it was my turn to blush. Of course I'd heard the name. Ludmila was considered one of the great Russian interpreters of the Swan roles, as was my teacher who had died.

"F-forgive me," I stammered. "I know your reputation well. Madame Yelena Natilova gave me my early training and spoke of you many times."

The woman sniffed when she heard the name.

"I doubt she knew much of my work. I was a mere girl with the Bolshoi when she defected."

Alec stepped in for a second time sensing a renewed chill.

"Ludmila is here on behalf of the tour's sponsor, Tara. She brings news that his support might be permanent if we do well in Europe. Of course, we're all anxious to meet our benefactor so that we can express our gratitude."

When Madame Lazaremko said nothing to his implied question, Alec hurried on with the introductions.

Susan was quick to step forward, flushed with excitement and, being aware of who Ludmila was, gave a slight curtsy which the woman acknowledged with the nod of her head. David, not one easily impressed, shook Madame's hand, but damaged any good impression he might have made with his handsome face by allowing his eyes to drift longingly toward the buffet table. When he followed up on Alec's question about the identity of the man behind our tour, naturally, the reply he received was curt.

"He wishes to remain anonymous for the moment. Understand, nothing is promised until the tour is a success. Let us see how the reviews treat you."

Alec's lips twitched with nervousness when he heard her but he maintained his cheerful air.

"Yes, yes. We've plenty of time to discuss the future. Why don't we sit down and get to know each other better?"

He assembled a few stray chairs around an empty table, but finding only three, he suggested Susan and David make themselves useful by bringing us food from the buffet.

Susan looked disappointed, as though she were eager to make the acquaintance of this prickly woman. Gladly would I have changed places with her.

Madame Lazaremko made me uncomfortable. Beneath her arrogant posturing, an air of sadness clung about her. I didn't understand it, didn't know how to deal with it, and felt annoyed that Alec had given me the task of entertaining her.

After the pair had gone, the three of us sat down and Alec again took up the conversation.

"You mentioned you'd be joining us again in Milan. Is there the slightest chance our benefactor will be there? I mean, if all goes well."

Madame waved his question away with a slight impatience.

"His appearance would be of no importance. I assure you, he will rely upon my recommendation, entirely. He has too many other interests to occupy him."

"I see. What might those interests be, if I may ask?" Alec was doing his best to learn what he could about our sponsor, but he was thwarted at every turn.

Madame scanned the room, appraising the other occupants, a clear sign she intended to say nothing more about the matter. Alec tossed me a desperate glance.

"Do you live in Prague, Madame?" I offered weakly. "It's my first time abroad and I think this is a beautiful city. All the buildings look like wedding cakes."

My remark was no doubt foolish, but at least it gave no offense.

"You may call me Natalya or Ludmila, if you prefer," Madame said, turning her gaze in my direction. "And I will call you, Tara. That's how Americans address one another isn't it? By their first names?"

Glad that I still had a head attached to my body, I ventured another remark; this one a compliment about her dress. The effect was like water on a desert flower. She blossomed and told me her gowns were made by a designer in Milan. She spoke highly of her work and, knowing that our company would be performing there, she offered to write down the designer's name and address.

Relieved that the conversation was taking a turn for the better, Alec made an excuse to leave us for a while, no doubt hoping we two women would bond over fashion. Madame barely noticed his departure, but I felt abandoned and in a state of fury, I watched him go.

What more was I to say to this woman, I wondered. Madame and I were dancers, but beyond that, we had little in common. The only other commonality between us was my teacher Yelena Natilova, so I asked her what she knew of my teacher as a girl. The woman opposite me at first looked surprised and then frowned.

"I was a girl, a member of the corps when your teacher was in her prime. She took no notice of me. Perhaps she didn't care for young people. Or perhaps, she saw me as a future competitor. Who knows?"

"That surprises me," I countered. "Madame seemed to adore children. She could be strict, but I was six when I started taking lessons with her and, with her swept up silver curls and silver arm bangles, I thought she was magical, like a fairy godmother."

Madame Lazaremko drew her lips into a thin line, then shrugged.

"People can change, I suppose. I describe her as a prima ballerina, a person we junior dancers never addressed unless she spoke first. Like a British queen, yes?"

For a moment both of us gazed about the room, neither of us able to carry the conversation forward. I was angry with her for what she'd said about my teacher, but as I studied her profile, I had to admire her frail beauty and the grace with which she carried herself, the prime recompense for having lived the life of a dancer. Though I was young with many performances ahead of me, I saw in the gloom of that overthrown prima ballerina a hint of my future. In mid-years, would my life be over? Would I spend it longing for my past?

"The public adored her."

Jolted from my ruminations, I tossed Madame a quizzical expression, this last remark seeming so different from the first. When she expressed herself more fully, I understood that her contempt was unchanged.

"We Russians referred to her as our 'Little Angel,' but when she defected, when she turned her back on us, we did the same to her. All except one."

Naturally, I asked whom she meant and she needed no coaxing to tell me the tragic story of a young male dancer who had fallen so deeply in love with Yelena Natilova that when she defected, he'd tried to kill himself by plunging his car over a cliff. He recovered from his injuries, but he never danced again.

I couldn't contain my horror.

"I don't understand why he'd want to kill himself. If he loved her, why couldn't he be happy that she'd found freedom?"

Madame's glare was glacial.

"Perhaps you are too young to understand these things."

"But this dancer was young. What did he understand that I don't?"

"His soul was too great for his body. Don't compare him with others. There is no one like him. And Yelena Natilova threw him away as if he were nothing. She left without a word of goodbye. He thought she loved him, but she loved only her career."

The bitterness in the woman's voice was unmistakable, which made me wonder if Madame Lazaremko didn't have some feelings for the young man herself.

"What was his name? I'd like to know. Perhaps she mentioned him to me."

"His name was Vladimir Reznikov. He could have been greater than Nijinsky. And so handsome. Every girl in the corps de ballet was in love with him."

"So what happened to him? If he could no longer dance, what became of him?"

"He went to live with his mother and her family in Tuscany. His father was Russian, so she left Vladimir behind to study with the Bolshoi. Unfortunately, his father died of tuberculosis not long after she left, so the son was left on his own. Perhaps if she'd stayed in Russia, his life might have been different. Who knows?"

"Is he still alive in Tuscany? Do you ever hear from him?"

Madame waved a braceleted arm in the air to show her impatience.

"Are you so interested in this story for a reason? Have you a lover, possibly?"

Her question took me by surprise, as if she'd reached across the table to slap my face. My personal life was no concern of hers and I might have told her so if I didn't know Alec would be furious if I offended her. Or maybe I was embarrassed that at twenty-one, I didn't have a lover. There'd been a dalliance at seventeen with a boy my age, but it was brief as both of us were experimenting and not really infatuated with one another. Eventually, we went our separate ways.

When I sat staring into my lap, Madame answered for me.

"I know how it is. You love only the dance. Why not? It's an honest, if not tyrannical lover. One could choose worse."

A faint smile crossed her lips and for a brief moment, I felt a rapport between us. We both knew the pain and sacrifice dance demanded. It *was* a tyrannical lover and age never slaked our passion for it.

"Yes, I do love to dance," I answered softly. When she heard me, she nodded.

"I know. I can see it in your work. You remind me of myself when I was young." She leaned toward me to speak in confidence. "Alec knows his business, Tara, but never forget you possess the talent. Many will attempt to humble you. Don't listen to them. You and I are a rare breed. We push ourselves to the edge of the precipice, abusing our bodies to achieve movements beyond the body's design. We suffer, yet we also succeed. Not many will surrender to that degree – certainly not your partner, that Prince Siegfried. He's a good dancer and that is enough for him. He will never be great. You could never burn with passion for him, I think. Am I wrong?"

My cheeks must have glowed like candied apples. I thought she had done David an injustice but I couldn't help being flattered. Still, she was right about one thing. I had no interest in him and told her I thought he was attracted to Susan.

Madame leaned back in her chair, gazing at me the way a cat might stare into a fishbowl.

"Ah yes, little Susan. She's charming. But so small. She's another not destined for greatness."

Again, I took umbrage with what she said.

"In my opinion, she's a beautiful dancer. I wish I had her grace."

"If that were so, then she'd be dancing the role of Odette and you'd be among the corps." Madame allowed her eyes to scan the guests again looking bored. That was the moment Alec chose to return.

He came toward us, rubbing his hands together as if he hoped for good news.

"Well, well, you two seem to be getting on well. What have I missed? Anything interesting?"

Madame rose as he was about to sit down and so he righted himself again, his eyes searching mine for some explanation.

"Is there anything I can get you, Ludmila? Another glass of champagne?"

"I've an early flight in the morning," she replied with a diffidence that implied she didn't care if we believed her or not. "I'll say good night." She held out her hand for Alec to take. "We'll meet in Milan. By then, let us hope there will have been several good reviews."

Whether she really hoped for our success or not, I couldn't tell from her tone of voice, but she made a speedy exit, turning her back on us at once and disappearing among the guests. Alec tossed a few words after her about a new ballet he was choreographing, but if she heard him, she gave no inkling.

When he turned toward me, his eyes were the size of pinpricks.

"What happened just now? I was watching the pair of you from across the room. You seemed to be getting on okay. Why did she take off like that?"

"I don't know." I shook my head. "She was talking about undying love for a while, then she said some stuff about Susan that I didn't agree with. If there was something specific you wanted me to talk about, you should have given me a clue."

When he heard me, Alec rubbed a hand through his hair and sat down.

"Yeah, I know. I suppose I should have, but I wanted you to act natural, not get upset about meeting a dancing legend. It probably wasn't anything you said. You know the Russians. They're a moody lot. Ever read their books?"

"I like their novels, but she's another piece of work altogether."

"You don't have to like her," Alec said, pointing a finger at me. "Just make nice. A lot is riding on her good opinion. You're lucky she takes an interest in you."

"Yes, that's part of the puzzle. Why should she? I'm a kid from Seattle. How could she have heard of me or about the company? Aren't you the least bit curious about that?"

Alec looked blank, as if my questions hadn't occurred to him. Either way, he didn't seem bothered. Spotting a journalist across the room, he stood up as if intending to introduce himself. But before he left, he wagged a finger at me.

"Never look a gift horse in the mouth, Tara. That's my advice."

Susan joined me at the table after he had gone. She was balancing two plates piled high with canapés.

"This stuff is good," she said, setting one dish in front of me. "And so is the bread."

She bit into a French roll and I watched as the crumbs tumbled down the front of her dress. While she brushed them away, I sampled the items she'd brought as I realized I was hungry.

"These deviled eggs are wonderful. You should have brought more," I said, as I bit into a golden cushion.

"Don't worry," Susan pointed to the buffet table. "There's more."

Susan sat watching as I wolfed down my food, her eyes full of questions.

"Well?" she demanded when she could no longer contain her curiosity. "Did she like us? Are we going to get more money? She didn't say anything about me, I suppose?"

"As a matter of fact she did mention you." I put down my fork and looked at her, intending to choose my words carefully to leave a good impression, but Susan squealed before I could get a word out.

"What? Oh God, don't tell me she said anything bad. I don't want to know if she hated me. She didn't, did she?"

I wiped my chin with my napkin, knowing what I intended to say.

"As a matter of fact, she said your dancing was charming."

"You're kidding?" Susan fell into a spasm, clutching her arms across her bosom as if she'd burst if she didn't hold on to herself. "She said that? She really said that?"

"She really did."

"Oh, I wish I could have heard her. But if I'd have been here, she might not have said anything, or I'd have said something stupid." Susan paused to look me in the eye. "To be honest, she's a little bit intimidating, don't you think?"

"I do and I wish you'd have warned me about what I was getting into."

"How could I, Tara?" Susan squirmed. "Alec swore me to secrecy. Did you find out anything about our sponsor? He's rich, obviously."

"I think she intends to take her secret to the grave," I smiled.

"Still, you talked about something. Your lips were moving. I could see that from across the room."

"Well, she did ask me one personal thing..."

"Come on, Tara. You can tell me. I won't say anything."

That was a lie, even if she meant it to be true. I knew she'd tell David and he might tell Alec, but I didn't care. I wanted Susan's reaction.

"She asked if I had a lover."

"What?" Susan pursed her lips and made a sound like a horse whinny.

"Don't assume you know everything," I replied as I struck a Mata Hari pose. That won me another snicker.

"Maybe she's got a son she wants to fix you up with," Susan went on.

"Ugh! How'd you like to have her as an in-law? No, I tell you, the conversation was weird. She even mentioned some guy she cared about a hundred years ago."

"That's interesting. Who was he? Did she say?"

I told her Vladimir Reznikov's story and of his connection with my teacher while Susan sat with her elbows on the table, her chin propped in her hands.

"Do you suppose Madame Lazaremko still loves him? Could he be our mystery guy?"

I shook my head to indicate I didn't know. The thought had escaped me, but suddenly, it made sense.

"Whoever he is, he owns a villa in Tuscany. That doesn't make him sound poor, does it?"

"No, it doesn't." Susan nodded. "I wonder if there's a way to find out more about him."

"What him?" Prince Siegfried, alias David Harden, had managed to creep up on us unaware. Susan repeated our conversation, and I didn't object when she added embellishments. She told a good story.

David wasn't curious about the past lover. What he wanted to know was if it meant the promise of more money.

Susan snorted.

"If you think Alec would give the money to us if it did, you can forget it. He wants to produce a new ballet."

"A ballet?" David's eyes narrowed. "Where did you hear that? Honestly, sometimes I think you live with your ear to a keyhole."

Susan jabbed at his ribs with her elbow and he pretended to crumble.

"Hey! I didn't say being a snoop was bad."

CHAPTER II

Despite the good food and champagne of the previous night's party, I slept erratically. Twice, I awoke to the same wail or moan of my earlier dreams. No longer able to discount these happenings as fatigue or jet lag, I called home, heedless of the hour, just to make sure everything was all right. My parents were reassuring and I was glad to hear their voices and that they sounded so well; but when I hung up, I couldn't shake the fear that something terrible was about to happen, particularly as the cries no longer confined themselves to my dreams but had penetrated my waking life. Still not knowing what else to do, I packed my bags and prepared to leave for the train station.

Most of the company had gathered on the platform and were craning their necks for a glimpse of the train that would speed us on to Budapest. The chatter and excitement all around should have lifted my spirits, but I remained despondent and imagined that the foul September weather was a portent of some darker business that lie ahead. Already our transportation was half an hour late.

Alec took it upon himself to speak to the stationmaster about the reason for the delay and returned a few minutes later to say a dead cow or a tree had fallen across the track. As he couldn't speak the language, he was obliged to rely on sign language, so his interpretation wasn't really reliable. In any case, he suggested we go back into the station to keep warm while we waited. Everyone did as he suggested, but I lingered on the platform. The gloomy weather suited my mood more than a crowded waiting room.

As I stood, submitting myself to the elements, a chill breeze slapped across my cheeks and more than once, I struggled to confine the wisps of my auburn hair beneath my beret. I cursed out loud, then realized I wasn't alone. Someone was on the platform with me at the opposite end from where I stood. A man, presumably, as the figure was over six feet tall and wore a voluminous garment crowned by a broad brimmed hat such as a man might wear. The edges of his cloak flapped around him like raven's wings, giving him the melancholy appearance of a character from a gothic novel. He was too far away from me to distinguish his features, yet I continued to stare because, for some reason, I was fascinated by him.

"Anyone you know?" David came up beside me with Susan at his side. They'd come looking for me when they didn't find me inside.

"Looks like a ghost," Susan murmured as her eyes followed mine. She tugged at my arm to get my attention.

"Come on. I think we should go inside."

With David on one side of me and Susan on the other, I allowed myself to be led away like a bemused child, but I looked back over my shoulder once or twice to see if the stranger would follow. He didn't.

The room we entered was overflowing, as I'd expected. Passengers draped themselves over chairs and tables or stood in corners complaining that the train's late arrival was an inconvenience. Alec used the time to check with his crew, making sure everyone had his or her ticket. He was headed in my direction when, suddenly, he stopped and listened. Had he heard it, too, that same eerie wail that had set my hair standing on end? Apparently he had, along with everyone else in the room, for all around me, people began to collect their belongings. What had set my teeth on edge was nothing more than the whistle of the approaching train.

I felt like a fool, but was unable to shake the residue fear that had left me quaking. I couldn't go on like this, disturbed by every noise, every footstep, but what was there to do? If I told Alec, he might send me home and I didn't want that. Perhaps I should seek out a doctor. Maybe the long flight had left me with an ear infection. I doubted it as I had no other symptoms and there was nothing wrong with my balance. Nonetheless, I wanted to confide in someone.

"What's the matter, Tara?" Susan stood beside me, looking worried. "You've been acting strange all morning. Is it cramps? Do you need an aspirin or something?"

I shook my head and told her it was nothing. Together we stepped into the flow of passengers who were shuffling toward the train, and, like them, once we'd boarded, I occupied myself with the task of finding my seat and stowing my gear. David and Susan settled into seats on either side of me so that I felt comfortable enough to close my eyes. Maybe all I needed was a few more hours of sleep.

I must have dozed off because when the train's whistle announced our arrival in Budapest, my lids were reluctant to open. Susan had to shake me more than once to make sure I was awake. Struggling to my feet, I felt anything but rested and, noting that I looked tired, David took hold of my case along with his duffle bag.

Many people were already standing in the aisles and buttoning their coats as they peered through the windows to watch the train crawl into the station. A few others, those headed further east, remained in their seats, their eyes closed as if trying to ignore the hubbub around them.

When a line formed in the aisle, David and Susan squeezed me between them like protective parents. As we inched our way toward the exit, I had time to notice moisture clinging to the windows. Apparently, the temperature in Budapest was cold. I fastened the top button of my coat as I'd seen others doing.

Alec was waiting for us as we stepped on to the platform. Most of the dancers had already been herded into taxis. He was holding the last one for us.

"Why do you three always bring up the rear? Come on. If we hurry, we'll make it in time for tea."

The car that was waiting for us must have been idling for some time because a pool of condensed water had collected beneath the tailpipe. The driver looked impatient as he got out of the car to stow our belongings in the trunk. Alec jumped into the front seat with the driver, while David, Susan and I piled into the back. Alec gave the man an address he had written down on a slip of paper. The man looked at it, nodded and seconds later, we were whizzing through traffic on our way to our new lodgings.

Twilight was falling as I cleared a patch of mist from the car window so I could see outside. Despite the darkening sky, I could make out broad boulevards and occasional statues -- bronze men and horses in heroic poses, chests thrust forward and hooves prancing. A few glass towers stabbed acrimoniously at the horizon, but mainly it was dominated by baroque and gothic architecture.

Happily, the trip was short. We reached the boarding house where we would be staying not more than twenty minutes after having left the station. The structure was similar to the others that lined the street; a red clapboard building of four or five floors, depending upon whether or not one counted the basement. The paint was peeling in places and, with the lights blazing from inside, it felt welcoming.

A row of stone steps ascended from the street and at the top, our landlady stood waiting for us, her arms folded and her face wearing a broad smile. She was a portly woman, possibly in her late fifties and she seemed deaf to the cacophony of musical notes that wafted onto the streets from the open door. Someone from above was torturing a piano, while, from a farther room, we could hear the muted blasts from a trumpet. Frida Sabo apologized as she took hold of a few of our bags.

"The musicians are allowed to practice between 4 and 6 during the week. After that, you will find us quiet as mice. Dinner is at eight," she instructed as she led us inside. "My cooking is plain, but nourishing. Don't be late, though. My regulars have good appetites. Breakfast, tomorrow, is at seven and for lunch, you are on your own. That was made clear, wasn't it, Mr. Borden?"

Alec nodded and confirmed that the dance company would be in rehearsals during the day. A hearty breakfast and dinner was all that was required. Next, he asked that we be shown our rooms, and our hostess pointed her plump finger toward a set of stairs that were covered with a threadbare carpet.

"The young ladies are in room 7. You and this blond young man will share room 8. I apologize for the crowded accommodations, Mr. Borden, but room 8 is very spacious. I think you will be comfortable. We're very busy this time of year. So many tours stop here. I'm sorry we couldn't accommodate all of your dancers. I hope you were able to find good rooms for them."

Alec told her he did, but that they were scattered throughout the city.

Frida Sabo nodded and went on.

"The bathrooms are at the end of each landing on every floor, including the basement. So, if one is occupied, find another. At the moment, counting the members of your troupe and my regulars, we number thirty-two; so one must show patience as well as ingenuity."

"I understand." Alec gave his hostess a tired smile. "We'll try not to make life difficult for your other guests. We're only here for three days and then we're off to Vienna."

"Vienna? A lovely city, I'm told, but then, Budapest is among the most beautiful in the world. I've never felt the need to travel." Our hostess laughed. "How could I afford to anyway, a widow with five children? Of course, they're grown now, my ducklings, so who knows? One day I may pay a visit."

Mrs. Sabo told us she'd see to our other luggage when it arrived and then she left us, but not before directing us to the drawing room where a special tea had been set. By the time we entered, most of our party had already gathered there. A cheer went up as we entered.

Returning the greeting, the four of us headed to the end of the room where a large table was laid with sandwiches, cakes and a huge urn of coffee. The space, too, was of a good size and though the overstuffed furniture was shabby, the cushions and arms were capacious enough to accommodate more than one person so that, together with the blaze that crackled in the fireplace, the room felt cozy.

With my plate piled high with sandwiches, I turned to look for a place to sit. I was happy to see that everyone had arrived safely and noticed that Anne Miller, a delicate woman in her early forties, had a spot on the arm of her chair where I could perch. She and her husband had retired from the Oregon Ballet Company the previous year, but had joined us for our tour -- Anne performing in the role of Siegfried's mother while Philip, her husband, played Von Rothbart, the evil sorcerer. I liked them both, though as a couple, they tended to bicker.

David and I wandered in her direction, in time to hear the end of the story she was telling about almost missing the train.

"I'd stuffed my ticket into my glove, you see, and then forgot. You can imagine how I drove myself crazy looking for it. I was about to fling myself on the mercy of the conductor -- even reached into my coat pocket for a hanky in case I needed to shed tears. That's when I felt my gloves and remembered. I was so relieved."

Her story was met with a wave of nervous laughter. A lost ticket was everyone's fear. Her husband of twenty-one years was less sympathetic.

"I told her to let me keep it. She always forgets where she puts things... but no, she had her own ideas. Serves you right, darling." He gave his wife a kiss on the top of her blonde head which did nothing to mollify her.

"As if you've never lost anything..."

"I'm not without my flaws," Philip conceded with a toss of his long brown hair. "And should I ever forget them, I have you to remind me... Still, we love each other, don't we?"

Anne gazed up at her husband, who was tall and handsome, and seemed inclined to forgive him. "I need a refill on my coffee," she said as she rose and offered her husband her hand. He bent his head to kiss it before leading her to the buffet as if she were a grand duchess.

"Well, well," David snickered once they were out of earshot. "There'll be no theatrics tonight. I guess they're tired. I could do with an early turn-in myself."

"What? You sound like an old duffer." Tom Donne, a dancer loaned to us from the Oakland Ballet Company in California, came forward and flopped into the spot Anne had vacated. He was performing the role of Benno, Prince Siegfried's friend, during our tour and was a strong, athletic dancer and one gifted enough to have challenged David for the lead role if he'd have been a permanent member of the company.

"Or maybe you aren't tired," he continued. "Just domesticated." He cast a sidelong glance at Susan who was still at the buffet table to underscore his meaning.

David blushed but seemed to take no offense. Tom, everyone knew, was a boyish twenty-six-year-old with red hair and freckles, who loved to tease. Women adored his attention and he gave it freely, being an accomplished flirt.

Ballet Noir

Alec, I knew, was impressed with his virtuosity as a dancer and if more money was forthcoming, I felt certain he'd offer Tom a permanent position. The luxury of growing his company hadn't crossed his mind until this recent grant. Normally, we survived on small donations from our fans and were always strapped for cash.

How we came to the attention of a wealthy backer remained a puzzle to us all. Alec had applied for many grants with the Seattle Art Council and had always been rebuffed. Naturally, he was dumbfounded when the Director of the Arts Council called him to say our company had been awarded a sizeable grant to tour the major European capitals. It was a dream come true, but as he couldn't recall submitting an application, Alec asked for more information. The Director answered there was none, but assured him the money was in hand and the Council would take its 10% administrative fees from the total before cutting him a check. That, in a nutshell, was how Tom Donne came to be in our midst.

After resting a couple of hours in the room I shared with Susan, I was ready for the dinner call. I thought I'd arrived in good time, but was surprised to find the majority of my colleagues already seated in the dining room, enjoying a hearty vegetable soup. This was followed by a salad course, then plates of paprika chicken and followed by a scrumptious apple strudel. A heavy meal and a day of travel left many with eyelids drooping and thoughts of an early night.

I would have liked to do the same, but seven of us had agreed to accompany Alec for a tour of the Opera Theatre, in preparation for our rehearsal the next day. He'd arranged to meet the stage manager at 9 o'clock that evening and, as the weather was marred by drizzle, he advised us to wrap up warmly.

A short while later, we gathered outside the boarding house, bundled up as instructed, and waiting for our transportation. We looked a motley crew: the Millers in their grey trench coats; Tom appearing deliciously wicked in a black pea-jacket, his leather cap pulled down over his forehead and David and Susan, off to one side, holding hands and wearing matching scarves. I was the only one cautious enough to carry an umbrella.

Late to join us, Alec hurried down the stone steps just as two cabs drew up to the curb. We piled into one vehicle or the other, all talking at the same time. As I'd grabbed a seat by the window, I strained for a glimpse of passing scenes but saw little, except for the glow of streetlamps reflecting off the damp pavement or an occasional lighted window that punctuated the night. Sometimes a figure was silhouetted in one of them, lonely perhaps, or seeking a moment of solitude.

Alec was the first to leap from his taxi when we arrived at the theater. He galloped up the steps of the main entrance, leaving the rest of us to jog behind until we caught up with him again at the glass doors of the foyer. A cheerful looking fellow waited to let us in, a man wide as he was tall, with a bald pate and a striking white moustache. I judged him to be somewhere in his mid to late sixties.

"Welcome, welcome," he cried as he threw the door open wide. My name is Lajos Voss, head custodian. Our stage manager sends his regrets. His first born child, a boy, arrived prematurely tonight. All is well, but he's at the hospital with his wife. I'm delegated to show you the premises."

Though his English was heavily accented, we understood him well enough and thanked him for his courtesy. He seemed to enjoy the responsibility, and as he led us up the wide, carpeted stairs of the Opera House, he pointed to the frescoes painted by Hungarian artists overhead.

It felt strange to enter a theater through the main entrance. As performers we were accustomed to the stage door and so we missed the glitz of the patron's experience. The opulence of this one spoke well of Hungary's respect for the arts.

We took our time examining the bowels of the theatre, particularly the dressing room where we would spend much of our time. Satisfied that we'd become familiar with our surroundings, Alec wandered off to examine the sound and lighting systems. Inevitably, we dancers wandered on to the stage and peered out over the many rows of seats and into the tiered balconies. Where I stood, I sent up a prayer that those empty spaces would be filled each and every night of our performance.

Anne murmured something to her husband about renovations performed since the two of them had last performed in the hall but her husband looked blank.

"Have there been many, darling? I don't recall."

"Yes. The carpeting is new. Anyone can see that. And the gilding is fresh. I remember it was terribly worn last time. Oh yes, there have been changes."

"Not surprising, is it? We were here when? Fifteen years ago?"

"You needn't make it sound as if it were the dark ages."

"In dancers' years, it is."

"We're not old, Philip. We could have continued as performers a few more years. Retiring early was your idea."

"*Both* our ideas," he corrected. "Alec asked us to take charge of the ballet school and we jumped at it."

"Yes, but we weren't desperate. Ulanova danced until she was fifty."

"True my darling, but Ulanova is the exception that proves the rule."

Anne blinked as if Phillip had struck her across the face. Her cheeks reddened and her lips trembled, though no words came forth. His remark seemed to strike her as insensitive, and so she turned on her heels, and with her back to him, she flounced off the stage. Aware of his blunder, Philip ran after her, his arms outstretched as if making a theatrical exit.

Tom was the one to state the obvious.

"They argue a lot, don't they?"

"Bicker," Susan corrected, being the romantic among us. "It's not serious. They always make up."

A wicked leer spread across Tom's face.

"Do they?" Well, maybe that's why they fight in the first place. I always say making up is the best part of a relationship. You agree, David?"

Susan answered for him.

"Don't be so cynical. Love is more than sex. If you've ever been in love, you'd know that."

Tom's grin faded, but only for a second. Then he slapped his hand over his heart, acting as though he'd been wounded.

"You do me an injustice, Madame. I assure you I've been in love before, lots and lots and lots of times."

"That's not love," Susan snorted. "That's an itch."

Her sweetheart laughed and threw an arm about her waist.

"Don't be hard on him, honey. He hasn't been lucky enough to find the right girl."

Taking the cue from his friend, Tom turned the corners of his mouth down, mimicking the face of tragedy.

"Yeah, honey. Why don't you show me some sympathy? I could use a little TLC."

Susan looked amused but put on a frown.

"Go on, laugh, Peter Pan. One day, some girl's going to put a ring through that pugnacious nose of yours and I hope I'm around to see it. As for me," she threw David a cat smile. "I'm already taken."

David returned that smile and the pair sauntered off the stage together.

"She's a cool one, isn't she?" Tom said as he watched her go. "Does Alec know what's going on between those two?"

"I'm not sure what you mean, but whatever it is, it's none of our business."

"I think she just made it our business, don't you? It sounded like an announcement to me." Tom looked down at me as he scratched his head.

"You aren't one to take a hint, are you? I *said* I don't think it's any of our business."

Surprised by my snappish tone, Tom raised his hands as if they were shields.

"Hey, bite off a guy's head like that, you'll never get a boyfriend."

"Did I say I wanted one? I'm not ready to make compromises. I haven't lived yet."

Tom pointed a finger at me.

"Now there I agree with you. Did you see how she dragged David off like that, as if he were her puppy? Or the way Philip chased after Anne? Those poor saps are on short leashes. I want a girl who dotes on me, not one who acts like my keeper."

"You mean *you* want the upper hand?"

"Touché, Ms. Bentley. Not all your brains are in your feet." That said, Tom strutted away with his hands in his pockets.

I watched him go, thinking of what he'd said about the politics of love. Mainly, I agreed with him. Love often seemed to be a tug of war. My parents had a good marriage, but without question, my father ruled in most matters. The same was true of his sister's marriage.

I knew I didn't want that kind of a life and at the moment, ties of any kind seemed unthinkable.

I wanted a career, and I doubted any man would be content to live in my shadow.

As I stood in thought, a cool breeze blew over me. Perhaps someone had opened a street door, but when I looked around, I saw nothing to explain it. Nonetheless, I buttoned my coat against the possibility of a second incursion.

As I was doing so, someone called out to me. The voice was barely audible yet I heard it clearly. I made a 360 degree turn on the stage to discover who had spoken but saw nothing. Had I imagined it? Or was Tom hiding in the shadows, attempting to spook me? I decided not to play his game and ignored him.

When the voice spoke again, I knew it was not Tom's. This time I scanned the balconies. Perhaps Alec wanted me for something, but again, I saw nothing but shadows. They hung in that unlighted hall like deep velvet curtains. Despite the report of my eyes, however, I felt a presence. The hairs at the back of my neck prickled and my body grew tense as I became aware of an unseen presence. This time, I squinted to better penetrate the darkness and suddenly, my view of the world changed. The empty seats seemed to come alive and take on the persona of an invisible audience, one that was holding its collective breath.

There it came again, that unmistakable whisper that could no longer be denied as imagination. "Tom? Is that you? Alec? If someone is playing a game, it's not funny."

I received no answer to my questions, but I next heard a gurgling, like someone being strangled. The experience was so frightening that without knowing if there was any real danger, I felt I had to get away and ran toward the wing, hoping to find someone who could explain my fear. Maybe a technician was testing with the sound system or merely clearing his throat. Any explanation was preferable to my uncertainty.

I ran, I confess, without paying attention to where I was going, and so it was not surprising that I should trip over a captain's chair I'd failed to notice earlier. How I'd missed it before, I didn't know but this time, it seemed to find me. As I tumbled over it, I fell and hit my head hard upon the ground. For a moment, I lay stunned, aware of a trickle of blood inching its way across my forehead. I must have done myself a greater injury than I imagined, for I could swear I saw the chair move, not only move but raise itself high into the air as if intending to come crashing down upon me. Instinctively, I rolled away and just in time to miss its fall. It made a dreadful noise and appeared to move again. This time I screamed, and loud enough to wake the bust of Beethoven that stood on its pedestal in the lobby.

Lajos Voss, the custodian, came running, his eyes round with the fear for what he might find.

"What is it? What's happened?" He was breathless as he knelt down beside me. "You've hurt yourself. There's blood smeared across your forehead."

He righted the chair and helped me to sit down. I was sobbing profusely by this time and could barely speak, but did manage a couple of strangled questions.

"Did you see someone? Hear anyone?"

"No. No one at all. But that cut of yours should be seen too. It's only a scratch but one never knows." He handed me his linen handkerchief so I could wipe away the blood. Then he stood over me watching with his arms folded. "I was coming to look for you when I heard you cry out. You sounded so terrified, I was afraid. What happened? Did you trip over this chair? I will remove it. It doesn't belong here anyway."

I told him I was sorry I'd made a fuss. I should have been looking where I was going. Under no circumstances was I going to tell him about a flying chair or voices. He'd question my sanity which was something I was already doing.

He shook his head, disinclined to accept my explanation.

"A person doesn't cry out like that over a stumble. Something else happened. Something you're afraid to admit, afraid of what I might think. But I won't frown, I promise you. I know what frightened you and you are not the first. Was it a ghost, perhaps?"

My jaw slackened in my surprise.

"You mean there is a ghost? A real one?"

The old man nodded.

"Oh yes. You're not the first to have seen it. It haunted the famous dancer, Yelena Natilova when she first performed here. We were on this very stage together. That was many years ago, of course, but it was the beginning of a legend."

"Madame Natilova? You knew her?"

"Of course. Who does not know of her? She was a girl when we first met, but she showed great promise." The custodian leaned forward as if intending to share a confidence. "We were chocolate lovers, she and I. If an admirer sent her bonbons, we'd finish them together. A lovely girl." Lajos Voss sighed as he stood, remembering. "I don't suppose you are old enough to have seen her dance."

"No," I answered as I wiped my eyes, my voice still weepy. "But she was my teacher. I thought she was a goddess."

The old man looked surprised.

"Your teacher? Well, isn't it a small world?" He clapped his hands together as he made this observation, his eyes crinkling with pleasure. It made me sad to think of her, but it was good to be with someone who knew her and I began to feel less afraid.

"I miss her very much. I wish I could have seen her dance, in person, I mean. I've seen films of her performances, of course. But what about this ghost? Did she really see one? Did you see it too?"

"No, I didn't see it; but she said she did and I believed her. It was the night before her first performance as Giselle. She was standing on the darkened stage." He pointed to where I had been terrorized minutes before. "And I was here, just where we are now, in the wings. She looked nervous as she peered into the hall. Her reviews in Prague hadn't been as glowing as the ones in Moscow. The Poles were taking their politics out on her. That's my opinion. We Hungarians are not so petty."

"But how do you know she saw a ghost? Did she say so?"

"Yes, a ghost; that's what she said when I joined her on the stage. I noticed she was acting a little strange. At first, I scoffed and said it was nerves; but I promised to scour the gallery for her to look for any traces. She watched me from the stage, standing with her arms folded as if she felt a chill."

"'It's your imagination, Yelena,' I shouted from the balcony, but she didn't believe me. So what could I do? I put her in a taxi back to her hotel and told her all she needed was a good night's rest. And I was right. That evening, she danced like an angel."

"Did the ghost ever appear again?"

"If it did, she wouldn't tell me. I asked her about it just before she returned to Moscow, but she pretended not to understand. She said I was making up the story to tease her. So, I let it go. But one or two dancers have had similar experiences, so I suspect there is a presence here. I don't think it means any harm. In fact, judging by Yelena's performance, I'd say its appearance was a good omen. Tomorrow, all Hungary will be at your feet."

• • •

Despite Lajos Voss' assurances, I slept fitfully. In my dreams I was chased by shadows that transformed themselves into bat-like creatures and dove at me from the theater's balconies. The more I tried to escape, the greater they grew in numbers until the air pulsated with web-like wings. If I cried aloud at any time, Susan never attempted to awake me and, contrary to my disturbed sleep, I awoke refreshed, cleansed of all anxiety.

Susan, unlike me, looked groggy when she awoke and for a time, she sat at the edge of her bed, staring down at her feet. In her condition, I had no difficulty beating her to the bathroom down the hall. In fact, I managed to beat everyone who was headed in that direction. The room I entered was large as a cavern, so I allowed several of my female colleagues to join me. The men, however, were obliged to stand outside, rapping good-naturedly on the locked door, their towels slung over their shoulders.

The women, especially, seemed in good spirits and we chatted amiably as we huddled around the sink or bent over the bathtub spigot. Ellen Gere, her voice pitched higher than the rest, made several failed attempts to garner our attention but finally did. She was a delicate blonde, lent to us by the Oregon Ballet Company, and as her father was of Hungarian extraction, she wanted to charter a bus to see some of the countryside.

"There's no time," everyone reminded her but she wasn't deterred.

"Couldn't we go shopping at least?"

Looking up from the basin where she'd been rinsing her face, Anne Miller looked amazed.

"Go shopping? Are you kidding? Remember how much we paid for a cup of coffee in Prague? Nine dollars. They wanted nine dollars for a lousy cup of coffee."

Ellen remembered but remained adamant.

"Okay, but it costs nothing to look. We can do that, can't we? Come on, you guys. This is Budapest, one of the most beautiful cities in the world. Shouldn't we have a little adventure?"

Susan was always the first to relent and, seeing Ellen's pleading expression, did so again.

"Oh, why not? We have the morning off tomorrow and Mr. Voss did tell me about a great place nearby where there are shops and places to buy pastries that won't cost an arm and a leg. Come on. Let's go. We don't get to Hungary every day."

To be honest, no one needed much coaxing and so we agreed: the next morning we would march on Budapest like free-spirited gypsies.

As we were having a good time, we forgot the men waiting outside. They didn't forget us, though. Soon they pounded on the door in earnest, and so, having finished our ablutions, we fluttered out the door like a cloud of butterflies, smiles plastered across our faces in answer to their catcalls.

At breakfast, everyone ate heartily, and I make no apology that each of us filled our plates to overflowing. This would be our last full meal until after the evening's performance.

Rehearsals went smoothly, though to the eyes of a novice, it might have appeared chaotic. Much of the time, we dancers stood in the wings to allow the lighting and sound specialists to occupy the stage. They shouted technical terms at one another and sometimes to their counterparts in the control room situated in the upper balcony. Lajos Voss was summoned on numerous occasions and asked about one piece of equipment or another.

During this interval, Alec kept his dancers busy by sending them on errands, the most important of which was to collect sandwiches for us from a nearby café. Susan and Anne were to make the run that day.

With all the wires and equipment lying around, no one should have been surprised when Susan tripped over something and let out a cry. Those of us on the stage rushed to hover round her while she assessed the damage. We had minimal backup to accommodate accidents. If the injury was serious enough, an experienced dancer from the corps would fill in or Alec might decide to cut her part. Either way, it meant we'd be rehearsing to adjust the performance until the curtain went up.

Fortunately, all Susan needed was a little rest and some applied ice. When the stage lights dimmed that evening marking the beginning of Swan Lake, the full company was ready to give the audience our best. The only other mishap occurred when David lost his grip on me during a turn, his hands being sweaty. I nearly stumbled, but righted myself so seamlessly that I doubted anyone in the audience noticed. Certainly, their applause was forgiving if they had. When we returned to the boarding house that evening, we were glad to have survived and were feeling hungry.

. . .

The next day was Saturday. Happily, I'd had a dreamless night and was ready for an outing when I joined Anne, Susan and Ellen in the hall after breakfast. Our landlady was waiting for us with instructions on how to catch the tram to V'aci Utca, a long pedestrian street that ended at an indoor bazaar called the Grand Market Hall. She informed us that the shops closed at 2 p.m. on Saturday, so we would be wise to get an early start. Then she gave us a brief lecture on the currency and sent us off into the brisk September air.

The early sun was veiled in mist as we hit the pavement, so we turned our collars up and hurried to our boarding point. Soon a yellow box, dotted with windows, appeared. Looking at it, I was reminded of San Francisco's streetcars that were also cheerful in appearance but noisy.

Perhaps our clothing or the tentative way we dropped coins into the conductor's hands revealed to our fellow passengers that we were foreigners. In any case, they smiled and nodded in a friendly fashion, following us with their eyes as we passed them looking for empty seats. Being a weekend, the car was sparsely populated, and so we easily managed window views. Along the way, a few of the residents pointed to statues or fountains for our approval and before long, the carriage took on a festive air, many of them behaving as if they were seeing their city for the first time.

One young man, who knew a little English, asked why we were in Budapest. His accent was thicker than goulash, but we managed to understand and told him we were dancers with the Seattle Ballet Company in the United States.

Delighted by what we'd told him, he rose from his seat and conveyed this information to the other passengers. The announcement was followed by a chorus of "ah-has and o-o-ohs" so that the four of us began to feel like Hollywood movie stars, especially when one elderly woman in a red-knitted cap rustled through her purse for pencil and paper so that we could provide her with our autographs.

We'd not passed many stops before the driver swiveled his head in our direction to indicate we'd reached our destination. As he did, the little tram fell quiet. This was to be our goodbye and everyone seemed saddened by it. The young man stood up again and, as if speaking for everyone, wished us a happy stay in Budapest. He looked so forlorn as he spoke that, for a minute, it seemed he might consider joining us. Then he shook his head as an invitation had been offered.

"No, I cannot attend you beautiful ladies.... Do not tempt me. Here we must part."

As we descended the steps of the carriage, the four of us blew him kisses and these he pretended to catch and tuck into the pocket of his worn jacket. Then the tram bell clanged, and the young man and all of our transitory friends disappeared down the track.

For a moment, we watched in silence as the train dew away. Then, as if a wizard had snapped his fingers, the sun broke through the mist and we awoke to the promise of a new adventure. The V'aci Utca, its shops already animated with strollers, unfurled before us. We four dancers linked arms and, full of expectation, advanced upon that magical place.

"Yikes!" Susan exclaimed as we stood in front of a large display window of women's fashions. "That cardigan costs nearly a week's wages. What's it made of, spun gold?"

Anne reminded us that we weren't buyers so cost didn't matter, but Susan pretended not to hear and wandered into the shop anyway. The rest of us followed and began fingering merchandise and pulling dresses from the racks. The price tags for outfits bore lofty numbers, so I drifted toward the window where a few Hermes scarves were on sale.

As I pawed through the pile, a shadow fell across the window. Glancing up, I saw a dark skinned woman, possibly in her thirties, peering at me. People flowed around her giving her gypsy attire disapproving looks, though I thought she looked wonderfully exotic.

She was still young, but already wrinkles scored her forehead and around her eyes. Her life might have been a hard one but her beauty hadn't faded -- especially those peridot-colored eyes.

Before long, a clerk spied the gypsy loitering at the window and hurried into the street to wave her away. She clapped her hands together as she went, as if she were shooing chickens. At first, the gypsy attempted to ignore her, but when a number of hostile faces gathered, her bravado faded and she disappeared into the crowd.

Anne came forward to discover what was happening.

"That was weird," she said, as she peered into the street through the window. "I could have sworn she wanted to speak to you."

I admitted I'd had the same feeling but as I'd never seen her before, I couldn't imagine why.

By now, the clerk who'd done all the shooing reentered the shop and offered a general apology to everyone present, first in Hungarian and then in English. Susan wasn't satisfied and took umbrage for the gypsy.

"What's your problem? Is there a law against standing in the street?"

The clerk flushed with immediate anger.

"You Americans know so little about other countries, especially about our gypsies. They aren't like us. They aren't really people."

"Not really people? Like the Jews, you mean?" Susan's grandparents had escaped from Holland days before Hitler's invasion, so her anger was palpable. "Come on," she said as the shop clerk squeezed her lips in a tight line. "Let's get out of here."

I tossed the Hermes scarf I held in my hand back on to the counter and followed my friend into the street. The others did likewise.

Ellen was a straggler but looked wide-eyed when she joined us.

"Wow that was surreal. I'm proud of you for speaking up, Susan. I would have said something, but to tell the truth, that gypsy was sort of creepy. Did you see how she looked at Tara? Like she was putting a hex on her."

"Maybe all she wanted was money for a cup of coffee," Anne countered.

Ellen tittered at Anne's suggestion but went on.

"No, I mean it. That woman wanted something. My dad used to tell me stories about gypsies all the time. A lot of them are charlatans, but once in a while, one had the gift, according to him."

Half-listening, Anne stood craning her neck, as if wanting something herself.

"I could use a cup of coffee, come to think of it. Where is that place Voss was talking about?"

"Down the street, I think," Susan answered. "But are you ready to cough up another $9?"

"Oh shut up," Anne snorted. "Right now I'd hock my husband for an espresso. Come on. Let's find that shop."

She struck out in the direction Susan had pointed and the rest of us followed like well-trained ducklings. We hadn't gone the length of a block when the gypsy woman appeared again, this time lurching from the shadows of an alley.

"The lady needs her fortune told, yes?" She reached out to catch my arm, hanging on to me with a viselike grip.

"What do you want?" I shouted, unable to break free. "Why are you following us?"

"Please, lady. Only a few forints. That's nothing to a rich American."

Anne came to my rescue and pulled her from me.

"What do you think you're doing? Leave us alone." She raised her purse above her head in a threatening manner and seeing it, the gypsy cowered.

"I have babies to feed. I need money," she whined. "Please, don't call the authorities."

Unnerved as I was, the tears trickling down the woman's face moved me.

"There's no harm done," I assured Anne who let her purse drop. Reaching into mine, I dropped a few coins into the gypsy's hand. She stared at them and seemed surprised. Then, having counted them, she closed her fingers over them with a firm grip, allowing her peridot eyes to scan my features.

"I wish I had good news, lady. But dark clouds are gathering. There is danger ahead. But a stranger... When he finds you, trust him. Otherwise, you will die."

Having delivered her message, the woman turned from me and disappeared into the throng, too quick for any of us to react. Anne was the first to speak as all four of us stared after her.

"What the heck was that all about? A scene from Dracula?"

Ellen shook her head and continued to stare in the direction of the path the gypsy had taken.

"I wouldn't mock her if I were you, Anne. Like dad said, some fortune tellers are fake, but not all. One of them predicted he would make a long journey and she was right. He came all the way to the United States."

Anne scoffed at Ellen's suggestion, being of a practical bent.

"Oh for Christ's sake, Ellen, if he'd ridden a mile from his village on a donkey, it would have amounted to the same thing." She placed an arm around my shoulder, a sign of affection she seldom displayed. "Pay no attention to Ellen's dad or that gypsy, Tara. It's all nonsense and you know it."

I wished I'd have told her that a month ago I would have agreed. Since then, my world had been turned on its head. I'd been haunted by dreams, mysterious wails and encounters with ghosts. As to the chair at the theater, I wasn't yet ready to accept it was more than a bump on the head. If I did, I'd have needed more than the piece of chewing gum Anne offered.

My friends regrouped around me and we continued on our quest for a coffee shop. By their mild banter, I could tell they were attempting to make light of what had just happened. As for me, I was still wrapped in the fog as we entered an establishment that was not only crowded, but noisy. The noise brought me to my senses as surely as if I'd been tossed into a pool.

Anne spied a young couple gathering up their coats and rushed forward to claim their spot. Others were in line ahead of us, but Anne pretended not to notice them, making a pretense of being foreigners who didn't understand the local customs. We endured several hard glances, but no one was impolite enough to object, so we sank down into the additional chairs we'd caged, grateful for a place to recoup.

As the pastry trolley rolled in our direction, I realized I was hungry. My companions must have felt the same because we ordered most of what we saw, including a confection called *soml'oi galuska* -- a sponge dumpling with chocolate and rum and whipped cream.

We ate hungrily and without much conversation except for a few groans to express our pleasure. Only when we were on our second round of coffee did Susan notice how solemn I looked and touched upon the subject of the gypsy again.

"You're not worried about what she said are you?" Her hand covered mine as she leaned in my direction. "Anne's right. It's all nonsense."

I nodded, but had to admit I wondered why I'd been singled out.

"Why not you, or Ellen or Anne?"

"Thanks a lot, Tara," Anne quipped. "That's all I need, a message of impending doom."

When she saw my face crumple, in no mood for sarcasm, she put her cup down and gave me a stern look.

"I'll tell you why she chose you. Because she read you for a pushover. And she was right. You gave her most of your money, didn't you?"

"Not all," I whined in my defense. "I've enough for the ride to the theater."

My friends couldn't help laughing, especially Susan.

"You're too tender-hearted," she teased. "That's why people come to you with their problems. You don't see them bothering Anne, even though she is older..."

"How kind of you to point that out," Anne glared at Susan from across the table.

"I-I didn't mean it the way it sounded," Susan apologized. "And of course everyone looks up to you."

"Like an elder statesman, you mean?"

In an ordinary world, Anne was still in her prime. But as a dancer, her career was coming to an end and no regrets or tears could erase that. Fearing a storm might be brewing, I pulled out of my funk in order to save the situation.

"Okay, everyone. I'm sorry for being a party-pooper. No more talk about gypsies. If we're going to see Budapest, let's do it."

. . .

Alec was waiting for us outside the stage door when we arrived at the theater. His strained features softened when he laid eyes on us and like an impatient proprietor, he waved us toward our dressing rooms as if we were escaped birds. By now, after an afternoon of sightseeing and with the excitement of the performance ahead, all thoughts of the gypsy had flown from my thoughts.

In full make-up and costume, I peered through the stage curtain's peek hole just before the lights went down. The house was full. Seeing me, Lajos Voss came over to confirm it. Reviews of the previous night's performance had spurred a rush of last-minute ticket sales. Not even his sainted mother could arrange to be seated this night, he assured me.

After he'd delivered his good news, he left me and Tom Donne took his place.

"A good crowd, isn't it? I hope nothing goes wrong."

Peering up into his green eyes, I asked what he meant. He answered with a shrug.

"I don't know. David seemed a little shaky last night. Maybe nobody saw it... Hey, where have you guys been all day? I spent the afternoon listening to Prince Siegfried go on and on about Susan and how wonderful she is."

"We went shopping. He knew that."

"All day?"

"Yes, all day."

"So, what did you buy me? A cable-knit sweater, I hope."

"I wanted to," I told him, sounding apologetic. "But I couldn't find one with a neck large enough to fit over your big head." I walked away to prepare for my cue while he stood with his hands on his hips, chuckling.

. . .

Contrary to Tom's foreboding, the performance went without a flaw that night. David, determined there'd be no mishaps, kept such a firm grip on me that a few feathers fell from my costume as if I were molting. But nothing untoward happened.

That night, when the ballet was over, the audience gave us a standing ovation. Alec, waiting in the wings, couldn't contain himself and made a sudden leap of joy, clicking his heels together as he did, before joining us on the stage.

By the time the final curtain rang down, everyone was elated. Even Tom reached out to give me a bone-crushing hug. Afraid he may have gone too far, he backed away and apologized.

"Sorry. I got carried away by my big head."

My laugh seemed to give him courage so he came closer again.

"Hey, tomorrow's Sunday. Let's have coffee before the matinee. There's a little bakery not far from the boarding house. I'd like to get to know you better."

"Coffee? Sure. I've nothing planned. How about ten?"

Tom grunted his agreement, then strode away as if he'd bagged an elk.

How like a man, I thought.

Lajos Voss appeared a second time when he saw Tom leave.

"A wonderful performance, Miss Bentley. Madame Natilova would have been proud of her pupil." He handed me a small box of bon-bons. "From me," he added shyly.

Having mentioned my former teacher by name, a breeze wafted across the stage, seeming to come from nowhere. The eyes of Lajos Voss caught fire when he felt it and his eyes twinkled.

"Is it the ghost, I wonder?" He pointed to a spot above our heads. "I thought I saw it this evening, there in the upper beams. Just a fleeting shadow, then it was gone. A good spirit, I think. But with spirits, one never knows."

Opening his gift, I offered him a bonbon and, for a time, we stood together, savoring the rich, dark chocolate.

"Do you believe in ghosts, Lajos Voss?" I asked, at last.

His expression sobered a moment. Then he shrugged.

"In this world, anything is possible. Maybe ghosts exist. Maybe they don't. What's important is what we believe."

CHAPTER III

Sunday morning, while Susan slept, I hurried down the stairs to meet Tom. He was waiting for me in the foyer, wearing his pea-jacket and sporting a pair of leather gloves. Frida Sabo stood beside him, her arms crossed over her clean white apron.

"So, you're going off, the pair of you. My cooking isn't good enough, eh?" By the glint in her eye, this mother of five seemed to imagine romance was in the air and approved. Tom offered a foolish grin and as I felt too awkward to respond, she drew her own conclusions. Giving us both a hug, she shooed us out the door.

Church bells were ringing wildly as we tumbled onto the pavement. A few stragglers hurried past but, generally, the street was empty. The pastry shop we sought was less than two blocks away and if we hadn't known where we were going, the scent of freshly-baked bread would have directed us there.

We entered to find a young man seated at the window, staring into the laptop perched on the table in front of him. He didn't bother to look up when the bell above the door clanged to announce our arrival. He was so deep in thought that even his coffee was neglected. I could see the congealed cream that was floating on the surface. He'd come for the Wi-Fi access, obviously, and not for something to drink.

One other sat slouched over his cup at a far corner of the room. Like the younger man, he didn't look up as we entered, but I sensed his interest in us, all the same. His features were hidden by a broad-brimmed hat and the collar was turned up around his ears. Despite these obstructions, an air of familiarity hung about him which I didn't connect with the man on the platform in Prague until sometime later. I only knew my eyes were drawn to him.

Tom claimed a vacant table and as I removed my jacket, he went to the counter to place our orders: two coffees and croissants. Outside, a light rain had begun to fall and, for a time, I watched as the wipers of the passing cars struggled against the water rivulets that cascaded down the glass. I wanted to blame the man in the hat for this change in the weather as he seemed like a black cloud himself.

Tom soon returned with a tray of coffee and pastries and these he placed on the table before leaving again to collect a sufficient quantity of napkins, spoons and sugar. Back and forth, back and forth, he went about his work like a busy bee while I watched with a growing impatience. When he finally sat down, his broad shoulders blocked my view of the man in the hat and I felt better.

Oblivious of my mood, Tom scooted his chair toward me, his face brightened with a smile.

"So, tell me something about yourself. Have you got a boyfriend?"

Surprised, I didn't know how to answer.

"Wow. You don't waste any time, do you? What about you? Have you someone in Oakland?"

Tom shook his head, but gave no further explanation.

"Sorry, I didn't mean to pry. It's hard to believe a girl like you doesn't have anyone, that's all."

"You know what our lives are like," I shrugged as I stirred the cream into my coffee. "When do any of us have time to meet someone?"

Tom nodded to indicate that he understood.

"Susan and David seem to be an item, though."

"We'll see if it lasts." I took a swallow of my drink while Tom leaned back in his chair, his head tilting to one side as he looked at me.

"When did you become a cynic, I wonder?"

Not caring to be called into account, my tone reflected my impatience.

"Look, I know Susan likes David and he seems to like her, but they come from different backgrounds. Susan's a Jew and David was raised as a born-again Christian in Iowa. A lot of issues have to be worked out. It's early days yet. If they do become an item, that would be great. I couldn't be happier."

"But they've known each other for a couple of years, haven't they? That's what someone told me."

"As dancers, yes. But the attraction seems to be recent."

"First friends and then lovers. Isn't that a line from a play?"

"I wouldn't know. I don't go to many of those either. I just hope whatever happens they can stay friends."

Tom took a sip of his coffee while he considered what I'd told him.

"I hope so, too."

I smiled, giving his arm a pat.

"Well, aren't you the romantic? I could have sworn yesterday you were the guy who said he hated entanglements."

Tom grinned not minding to be caught out.

"Hey, I'm a complex guy."

"Really? Tell me more. I can't believe you don't have a girlfriend, or do you prefer to play the field?"

Tom's green eyes softened when he heard my question.

"I did have, once. I mean, there was someone I cared for."

"Who? Is she a dancer?"

"No, play fair. I asked you first."

"But I've already said there isn't anyone. Not unless you count my crush on Alec when I was thirteen. That doesn't count. All his students get crushes on him, even some of the boys."

"Did Alec like you, do you think?"

"Don't be crazy. I was a kid. Besides, there's one thing you'd better understand about our Artistic Director. He adores his wife, Bridget. They've been happily married for many years. They met as dancers and even though he works with lots of pretty girls, he's never looked closely at one, if you know what I mean. Sure, he's a hustler. That's part of his job. He's always scrounging for money, but trust me, he and Bridget have a great marriage."

"If you say so."

"I do say so," I answered crossly. "If you've got something against Alec, spit it out."

Tom stared into his cup and looked guilty.

"I didn't mean anything by what I said. He's okay."

"Okay? I think he's..."

Tom's large hand touched mine as if to prevent a lecture.

"Look, I don't want to talk about Alec, Tara. It's you I'm interested in."

His earnest gaze, his wide eyes, his mouth a little open, took me by surprise. He appeared to be feeling vulnerable and I had no idea why or what I could say to him to make things better. I liked Tom. He was good-looking, funny and a very strong dancer, but I didn't want any intimacy between us. Guessing that's what he was after, I pretended to misunderstand.

"Okay, you don't want to talk about Alec, but I want to talk about you. You said you cared about someone once. Who was it and why didn't it work out?"

For an uncomfortable amount of time, Tom said nothing, just stared at his hands, as if he'd found dirt under his fingernails and couldn't figure out how it got there.

I decided to withdraw my question, but he shook his head when I told him, it didn't matter.

"No, I want to tell you. I'm having trouble finding the words, that's all. The girl I'm talking about was a few years older than I was, but to me, that made no difference. I'd have done anything for her. We were both students at the Oakland Ballet School. At first, I didn't think she knew I existed, but I kept hanging around and eventually, we became friends. She was gorgeous and a great dancer, but because of the difference in our age, she treated me like a kid brother so I never told her how I felt. Then she was made a principal dancer with the company which meant I didn't see as much of her."

"How old was she when she became a principal dancer?"

Trying to remember, Tom sucked in his cheeks and puffed them out again.

"I was about fourteen so that meant she was close to eighteen. God, when she entered a room conversations stopped. She was that beautiful."

Though I had no emotional ties to Tom, I confess his adoration of this girl made me jealous. I turned my head toward the window rather than let my resentment show. Outside, the rain continued to tap against the glass, a little fiercer than before.

Deep in his thoughts now, he took no notice of me but continued to share his memories.

"You'd have liked her. Everybody did. She was so shy that when she talked to people she had a habit of staring at the ground. Given her tremendous talent, I was surprised she wasn't spoiled by it."

"Doesn't sound like she and I have much in common."

Tom looked up, having caught the edge in my voice.

"What do you mean? You have a lot in common. You're a great dancer and beautiful." He fell back in his chair a second time to look at me. "Wait a minute. You're not jealous of her are you ... because of what I just said?"

"Of course not. I don't even know the girl's name."

"Sylvia. Sylvia Louise Huntington."

He spoke with such reverence as he mentioned her, he seemed to be uttering a prayer. I couldn't contain my sneer.

"If this Sylvia Louise Huntington is so wonderful, why don't you tell Alec about her? He's always scrambling for dancers when he can afford them."

I expected him to become annoyed for mocking him, but instead, he fell forward, placing his elbows on the table so that he could bury his face in his hands.

"What is it? What's the matter?" His behavior had changed in an instant, like a stoplight turning from red to green.

Shaking his head, he refused to look at me, so I let a silence fall between us, allowing him time to regain his composure. When he finally sat up again, he gazed out the window, using the same avoidance tactic I'd employed minutes before. Even so, I could see his eyes were bleary with unshed tears.

"There's a reason why I can't recommend her to Alec, Tara. She's dead. Shot through the heart years ago."

If I'd been kicked in the chest, I couldn't have been more surprised. A moment ago, I'd been filled with envy. Now what I felt was pity.

"Murdered? Why?"

Tom still refused to look at me yet I could see that his complexion had paled, as if someone had opened a vein to let all his blood flow out of him. He was in so much pain that I didn't know what to say or how to comfort him. I sat quietly and waited. When he spoke again, he seemed to be addressing himself rather than me.

"He wanted her to marry him and showered her with expensive gifts. But she didn't care about his money. She wanted to dance. You can understand that, can't you, Tara?"

I reached out to take hold of Tom's hand.

"Of course I can. If he loved her, he would have too. So what happened? Did they have an argument? Did he lose his temper?"

"No," Tom shook his head. "Nothing like that. He wasn't even there when it happened."

"Then how..."

"He hired someone, Tara. I told you, he had money. She wouldn't marry him, so he made sure no one else would."

"But he must have been arrested. He's as guilty as the person who pulled the trigger."

"They didn't arrest anyone. The police said it was a random shooting, probably gang-related and that Sylvia got in the way. That's their theory, at least. But I don't buy it. A single bullet through the heart? Does that sound like a gang war to you? She bled to death on the street with no one around while that bastard who arranged it sat sipping wine at his grandfather's villa in Tuscany."

"Tuscany?"

Tom's eyes hooked on to mine, suddenly alert.

"Yeah, why? What's Tuscany to you?"

"Nothing. It's just that Madame Lazaremko told me the man who's bankrolling our tour owns a winery in Tuscany. There couldn't be any connection, could there?"

"Did she say the guy's name? I'm talking about Antonio Moretti. If it's the same guy, I'd be happy to see justice is done."

"I hope you wouldn't do anything rash. You'd be ending your life, too. Anyway, it's not the same man. Madame was talking about a Russian, someone who'd be in his seventies by now. I got the feeling there was something between them at one time. You know what I mean. They were lovers or something. I think that's why she doesn't want to tell anyone his name."

Tom frowned as he took in my information.

"I don't get it. Why would a Russian with a winery be interested in us?"

"I don't know, but she did say he'd been a dancer with the Bolshoi and that he'd tried to kill himself. When he didn't succeed, he went to live in Tuscany where his family owned a winery.

"Why'd he want to kill himself? Tom frowned, looking puzzled.

"Because he was in love with someone and she left him. You'll never guess who it was. My teacher, Madame Natilova."

Tom sat up with a renewed interest in what I was saying.

"No kidding. Your teacher? Wow, that's a connection of some kind but I'm not certain what to make of it. Did Madame Larzaremko say anything else?"

"Only that she didn't like my teacher very much. They were at the Bolshoi together and I'm guessing she was jealous."

"Of your teacher's dancing? Or because they were interested in the same guy? Probably both," Tom snorted, drawing his own conclusion. "Ain't life a blast?"

We'd finished our croissants and exhausted the extent of our knowledge about the man behind the tour, so Tom and I stood up to put on our coats. By then, the young man with the laptop had disappeared, but the man at the far table continued to crouch like a spider at the center of his web.

CHAPTER IV

Our final performance in Budapest went well, but there was no time to celebrate. After the matinee, we hurried back to the boarding house to pack and say goodbye to Frida Sabo. She hugged us all as if we were headed for some war zone, almost making us late for the evening train to Vienna, a journey of about three hours. My parting with Lajos Voss had been equally sentimental. I'd presented him with a box of fudge which caused him to beam with pleasure. He gave me a peck on the cheek and I had to swallow back my tears because I realized I'd probably never see this dear, sweet man again.

The trip to Vienna was uneventful. No dark figures lurked on the platform, no shadows or strange whistles disturbed me. I'd actually enjoyed getting to know Tom and hoped my life might be returning to normal. Maybe what I'd suffered before was a viral infection or a surfeit of too much strudel. In any case, I boarded the train feeling hopeful.

Thoughts of strudel reminded me I was hungry. For the next three hours I thought of little else but food. By the time we reached Vienna, I could have eaten my leather purse.

As usual, Alec was in too much of a hurry to get everyone settled in their new accommodations to allow anyone to wander off, even for a cup of coffee. Once the youngest dancers were off to be billeted in the homes of local families, he attended to the corps members, leaving the principle dancers and crew to cool our heels.

We already knew where we'd be staying, at a small pension not far from the Vienna State Opera House where we were to perform beginning on Wednesday. Nonetheless, Alec insisted on seeing us off because he had an announcement to make. Once he'd quick marched us across the spacious station to a cluster of waiting taxis, he told us that a special dinner party had been arranged in our honor that evening and he gave us the address of an Italian restaurant where we were to meet at 8 p.m. The owners of the establishment were aficionados of ballet and were eager to meet us. After giving us our instructions, he left to attend to our stage equipment waiting to be loaded on to a truck.

Ballet Noir

8 p.m. seemed a long way off before dinner, so as our taxi pulled away from the curb, I cadged a candy bar from David. He always carries snacks on his person. But a candy bar wasn't enough. By the time we arrived at the restaurant later that evening, I'd have been willing to nibble on the legs of the tables.

Fortunately an act of such desperation wasn't required. Upon our arrival at the restaurant, we were welcomed with a delicious aroma and the promise of a hearty meal. The accommodations were cozy and could hold maybe fifty people, at most. That night, one long table had been arranged at the center of the room. Signor Forintino Brancaccio, the proprietor, greeted us with warm embraces and made us feel like old friends. He was an émigré from Bologna with a wide girth and a booming voice. He used his gravitas to overcome our chatter so that he could read snippets of our reviews from Prague and Budapest aloud. The critics had been kind and everyone was delighted, especially Alec. Having been neglected for so long at home, he no doubt felt vindicated.

As for our host, I took an instant liking to him. I judged him to be somewhere in his sixties. His hair and beard were already white, and if the latter had been long and not cut close to his chin, he'd have borne a strong resemblance to Santa Claus.

Hearing his declamations, his wife bustled in from the kitchen. Another waft of delicious aromas followed her through the swinging doors. If she was the cook in the family, no one would have guessed it by her size, which I imagined to be not more than a 2. She made up for her diminutive size, with an abundance of blue-black hair which she'd pinned in an unruly knot at the back of her neck. She was near her husband's age, I would guess, but her complexion was smooth like a fresh mango. She introduced herself as Anunciata, which her husband interrupted long enough to say was why he called her his *little nun.*

"Little nun?" she giggled giving him a gentle elbow. "I have eight children: five boys and three girls, and it wasn't by Immaculate Conception, I can tell you." Everyone joined in her laughter and if there was any stiffness of unfamiliarity left among us, it faded.

"Well now," said Forintino, who'd insisted we call him by his first name, "as our staff is off tonight, I must ask two of you to help me with the serving. In your honor, I'm happy to say my little nun has outdone herself tonight."

His wife blushed and attempted to deflect the compliment.

"I confess I had difficulties. Forintino kept sticking his spoon in the pots like an inspector general. If I hadn't stopped him, there'd be little left."

Her husband chortled and took no offense as he peered down at his large stomach.

"She knows me too well."

David and Tom stepped forward to volunteer for kitchen duty while the rest of us sat down at a table covered in red and white checkered cloths. Bottles of Chianti formed a line in front of us and seeing the size of the wine glasses, Susan gave me a nudge.

"David and I had a merlot before we came so don't let me drink too much. I'm already feeling a buzz."

"Eat lots of spaghetti. That'll soak it up."

Overeating wouldn't be hard to do. When the plates arrived, I realized Anunciata had planned for an army. First came an antipasto, marinated vegetables and olives and cheeses, soon followed by Chicken Cacciatore, Eggplant Parmigiano, quantities of Porcini Risotto and loaves of crusty bread. Everyone took second helpings and afterwards, we were served a lemon gelato to clear our palates. When our host rose to pour another endless round of Chianti, everyone groaned. He wouldn't take no for an answer, however and scurried round the table, filling our glasses on the pretext the wine would settle our stomachs.

Anne was the only one with the courage to resist. As he approached, she placed her hand over her glass.

"I'm sorry, Forintino, but if I put one more morsel into my mouth, you'll have to call an ambulance."

We sat back in our chairs, a little blurry-eyed, reviewing the carnage with satisfaction. Wine and tomato splotches bloodied the cloths and the piles of bread crumbs made it seem as if a cannon had been fired into a bakery.

Forintino and his wife too, viewed the devastation with pleasure. They had done their duty toward their guests. All that remained was to pour the coffee.

I was sipping the dark espresso when Signor Brancaccio announced that on Tuesday, we were invited to a ball. It was an annual event sponsored by the town's café owners and would be held at the Main Festival Hall at the Rathaus.

"It's a black-tie affair," he explained. "And everyone is encouraged to wear masks, the more fanciful the better."

A chorus of complaints went up among the women. "But we've nothing to wear!" To which Alec replied that he'd made arrangements for us at 11 o'clock the following morning at a local costume shop not far from the hotel.

Philip Miller frowned, still not satisfied and asked who was to pay for this expense. He and Anne were pinching pennies to build a home in Seattle and fretted over money, including a $9 cup of coffee.

Alec seemed to have anticipated the question.

"You all know how frugal I've been on this trip. So, if the ladies aren't too extravagant, there's money for costumes."

Anne's sigh was audible, a relief we all felt because few dancers have any money. Alec knew that better than anyone. Our little company had survived good and bad times precisely because he knew how to manage money.

With our meal ended, Tom, who'd been sitting beside me, rose and with several others, began carrying the empty dishes to the kitchen. The moment he left me, Anunciata slipped into his empty chair, her eyes bright as glass buttons.

"I've been wanting to talk to you all night," she said in a conspiratorial air. "I understand you trained under Yelena Natilova."

I nodded, surprised by her knowledge and said I'd begun my studies when I was six. My hostess looked pleased.

"She taught you well, obviously. I knew her, you know. Such a lovely dancer and so kind to me when I studied at the Bolshoi. My father supplied the company with most of their ballet slippers so it wasn't difficult for him to arrange for me to study there, with the recommendation of my teacher in Bologna, of course. I only lasted two years, but it was enough. I loved the experience, though Moscow is so cold in the winter and my Russian was atrocious. In a way, I was glad to come home. But I have wonderful memories which include those of your teacher."

"Thank you for telling me that. Most people have kind things to say about her. Only Natalya Lazaremko has said otherwise. You might have known her, too. She was probably a student around the same time."

Anunciata's black eyes flashed when she heard the name.

"Oh that one. Yes, I remember her as a horrid girl. Very competitive and always playing tricks. Only one student seemed to please her. A boy. Vladimir... Vladimir Reznikov. Yes, that was his name. He had great promise, that one."

"Madame Lazaremko said the same. I met her in Prague."

"Did you?" Signora Brancaccio placed a hand on my arm as if I needed comforting. "I haven't thought of her in years. I hope she's improved with age."

"I can't say she left a good impression," I answered truthfully.

"Yes, I imagine she came to see your performance and was jealous of your talent. So often that's the case with dancers."

"Actually, she came because she represents our tour's backer. She said if we do well, he may give us another grant."

Anunciata gasped in surprise.

"But how wonderful. Your future is assured. After Prague and Budapest, there can be no doubt of more money. And Vienna will embrace you, I'm sure. Who is this person our *dear* Natalya represents? Perhaps I know him."

"That's what's so strange. She keeps his identity a secret. Alec's poured on the charm, but she's like a clam and refuses to tell us his name."

"Pshaw! The woman wants to make herself important. No, she hasn't changed. She is the same self-centered person she's always been. I suspect she must have chortled when Yelena Natilova defected. That left the door open for her at the Bolshoi."

"She says not. In fact, she blames my teacher for what happened to this Vladimir Reznikov you mentioned. She told me he loved Yelena Natilova and nearly managed to kill himself when she left."

"She told you this?" The eyes of my companion narrowed. "Yes, I've no doubt she would. She'd use any excuse to bring Yelena down. But it's rubbish. Vladimir was a beautiful and promising dancer, but he was too melancholy. Today, a boy of his temperament would be on medications. They're all depressed, these Russians. Have you read their literature? They can make stones weep. No, whatever he did, Yelena cannot be held responsible."

"So you knew him?"

"Not well. He took little notice of me. Too much in love with himself. He did care for your teacher, I think. But being so young, perhaps he was more interested in the chase. It couldn't have lasted. Yelena's talents would have always overshadowed his. Naturally, I forgot about all these plots when I returned to Bologna."

"Why do you live in Vienna, now, may I ask?"

Anunciata Brancaccio shrugged and looked a little soulful. "What can I say? We Italians are a little crazy, too. I met and married Forintino. We raised our children in Bologna and when the European Union formed, we came here, thinking an Italian restaurant would be a novelty. And we've done well. When we retire and go back home, we'll have more than enough cash to build a fine home near our children."

"Any grandchildren?"

Anunciata blushed. "We are good Catholics. I have six already."

CHAPTER V

My first night in Vienna, I slept without incident. No shadows or frightening cries troubled my dreams. When I awoke, refreshed and happy, I was foolish enough to believe these hauntings were behind me. Alec kept us busy rehearsing most of that morning, except for the time he allotted to collect our ball costumes and grab a bit of lunch. This we did with enthusiasm, bleeding into the nearby cafes to enjoy the food and the passing scene.

What struck me about being abroad was how much people seemed to be alike. Passersby along the pavement seemed preoccupied, their shoulders brushing against others, but rarely acknowledging one another. Only the surrounding architecture was different. Instead of Seattle's glass towers, here the architecture was largely gothic or baroque.

Tom, David, Susan and I had fallen into the habit of becoming a foursome. On one particular day, a Tuesday I think, we lingered over our coffees engaged in a silly debate on how best to spend a million dollars. Tom said he'd buy a red Ferrari Enzo, but David thought a Bugatti Veyron with its 16 cylinders would be better. Bored by the subject, given her glazed expression, Susan suddenly blurted out, "I've never been to a masked ball. Have any of you?"

The two men paused to look at her as if she'd dropped into their midst out of the blue.

"I mean, do they play waltzes all night or can we get down and dirty?"

No one knew the answer to her question and David didn't seem to care. He suggested we ditch the ball and find some nightlife on our own.

"No way," Susan deflected. "I've already been fitted for my costume. I'm going as Cleopatra and Tara is Juliet. What are you guys wearing?"

"We're not telling," said David with a squared jaw. "We're supposed to keep our identities a secret. That's why we wear masks. Besides if we told you, it would be all over the company in minutes."

"You think I can't keep a secret?"

"I know you can't," David cracked.

Susan's cheeks reddened as she paused to consider her retort. That's when I decided to butt in.

"I'm not wearing a mask, really. It's a headdress, a filigree band with feathers low across my forehead. It's very pretty."

"Where's the mystery in that?" Tom shrugged. "I thought these balls were places of assignations. You know, a room full of horny lovers looking for their mates."

"What an elegant picture, Tom. It makes me go all shivery. I'm afraid I wasn't thinking about horny lovers when I chose my costume, which is elegant, by the way -- a floor-length white chiffon with a square neck and long sleeves."

"A horny lover might like that," Tom grinned and wiggled his eyebrows.

Susan was smiling again as she leaned toward David.

"I'm wearing an Egyptian gown with a deeply-plunging neckline. What would a horny lover think about that?"

"I'd say the night won't be wasted." Tom chimed in again, leering in a way that brought David to his senses.

"Quit drooling, will you. Susan's dance card is full."

Tom yawned with a catlike indifference.

"What does Alec say about you two mooning over each other? Or has he noticed yet?"

Susan looked serious again when she heard the question.

"He doesn't know yet and I hope you won't say anything Tom. Promise?"

"Why the big secret?" The redhead shrugged. "He's no fool. He's got eyes in the back of his head. He probably suspects already."

"To be honest, it isn't Alec we're worried about," Susan went on. "It's our parents. It's...it's complicated."

She didn't have to say anything more. Tom and I were aware of the differences in the couple's backgrounds. David had struggled hard enough just to become a dancer. If it hadn't been for a wealthy cousin who footed the bill for his schooling, David would be harvesting corn in Iowa. How would his parents react when they learned their eldest boy was in love with a Jewish girl? Susan was right. Alec's opinion was the least of their worries.

• • •

Bedlam prevailed among the dancers on the night of the masked ball. Anne couldn't find her earrings and asked to borrow a pair of Susan's. Susan found a ladder in her last pair of nylons and had to borrow a pair from Ellen and so the daisy chain of disasters went on. As for me, no matter how hard I tried, I couldn't fit my headdress properly over my chignon.

When Tom poked his head into my room in the midst of this chaos, he suggested I wear my hair down. I did and he was right. The moment I let it fall to my shoulders, the costume came together. My problem solved, I ran after him as he headed for the lobby, scared away by the chaos of primping women.

"Why are you wearing that Lone Ranger mask with a tuxedo?" I asked when I caught up him at the elevator. "That's not a costume, really."

"That's what the guys are wearing," he informed me. "You women can be the peacocks."

"The fancy plumage of peacocks belongs to the males," I reminded him. "But if you guys insist upon being boring, the women will make up for you. Wait till you see some of the costumes. Beside them, I look like a mud hen."

Tom gave me an appreciative appraisal.

"Oh, I don't know. You look pretty fine to me."

"Most women look fine to you."

Tom blushed a little when he heard me.

"Oh, come on, Tara. I'm not as bad as all that. Besides, I mean it. You look beautiful."

When the elevator doors opened at street level, the men of our party were gathered in a circle, all of them looking like stagecoach bandits, all that is, except for David. He was standing with the mask of a red devil tucked under one arm and whining.

"Okay, okay. You've had your little joke. I'm not wearing this thing, I promise you. Now, who stole my mask? Come on, who's got it?"

A loud guffaw went up among the group which went on until David threatened to boycott the ball if someone didn't come up with his right mask. Finally, Alec relented and told him to go back to his room and look under his bed.

David didn't have to be clued twice. He shot back upstairs and returned several minutes later, with the familiar black mask, and accompanied by the remaining female dancers, all in costume and wearing alluring masks that added mystery to their appearance. Seeing them, the men fell silent in their appreciation. Then they offered the women their arms and once the pairings were complete, the company slipped into the balmy night to await the taxis.

The Rathaus was ablaze with light when we arrived. Music poured through the doors and windows as we and dozens of others entered the Main Festival Hall.

The cavernous room looked as if it could accommodate three or four hundred couples, but that number seemed to be in attendance already with more coming.

To my right was a bank of windows facing Rathaus Park and, to my left stood a corresponding colonnade of pillared statues. Galleries ran off from these, which provided a feeling of airiness. Directly beneath the barreled-ceiling were tiers of loggia on three sides. From these heights, one could look down upon a polished parquet floor. The setting was ornate and perfect for a masked ball.

The costumes were lavish and, unlike the men of our party who eschewed any display of imagination, the headdresses I saw among the other guests bordered upon the phantasmagorical. Some were plumed or tinseled, others braided in gold, still others long and grimacing. The scene appeared to have been conjured from the Arabian Nights. In this setting, David might have experienced a twinge of nostalgia for the red devil mask he'd abandoned in his room. Certainly his Lone Ranger disguise was unable to hide the awe in his expression. This scene was so far removed from his farm boy experience, that overwhelmed by it, he swept Cleopatra into his arms and the pair waltzed into the center the of dance floor while the violins thrummed.

Alec turned in my direction, as if about to invite me to follow, when Forintino Brancaccio and his wife, a shepherd and shepherdess, appeared. They were wearing full masks but there was no mistaking the pair, not only because of the disparity in their sizes but also because the shepherd's booming voice was inimitable.

"Ah, you've come at last. Anunciata and I have been looking for you. We wanted you to see our costumes in case we could be of service this evening."

As he spoke, he pointed to a gallery not far from where we were standing. "Refreshments are on the left. The gentleman's and ladies' rooms are there also. You've already found the coatroom, so now you're free to enjoy yourselves. And Miss Bentley?" He gave a slight bow in my direction. "I hope to claim a dance or two this evening."

"I look forward to it, Signor."

Satisfied he'd done his duty, the restaurateur took hold of his wife's tiny waist and together they joined the dancers swirling in front of us, the pair of them displaying a lightness of step I wouldn't have imagined.

Alec and I followed them but had scarcely accomplished one turn about the room when Tom cut in. Stepping aside, our artistic director sniffed the air for anyone of importance, then hurried off to make whatever contacts he could. As I watched him go, I noticed that Anne and Philip, standing in one corner of the hall, seemed to be having a tiff.

After finishing one dance, Tom claimed several dances more until Forintino appeared and tapped him on the shoulder.

"May I?" He reached for my hand, not waiting for an answer, and swept me away, leaving Tom to stand alone, looking unhappy. I watched as he made his way to the sidelines and could feel his green eyes boring down on us until the music stopped. Then he was again at my side, ready to claim another dance. Graciously, Forintino conceded and went off in search of his wife.

Given Tom's attentiveness, I began to feel uncomfortable. I enjoyed his company. He made me laugh and his flirtatious manner amused me, but since he'd unburdened himself about Sylvia Huntington and her terrible tragedy, he'd seemed to grow dependent on me, as if by revealing his secret, he'd forged some bond between us.

Naturally, I empathized with his loss, but the incident was years old. Could he really be so moved by it? Or was he playing upon my sympathy? If the latter, what did he want from me? If he was looking for more than friendship, he would be disappointed. But how to tell him this without hurting him was a puzzle.

Needing a break, I told Tom I was thirsty, so he escorted me to an empty chair and went off for some punch. Those few moments alone to observe the dancers around me was heaven but all too brief. He soon returned with two glasses of something terribly sweet and sticky. Still, I drank it down, but slowly, hoping Alec or Forintino might rescue me. Neither of them did so I was obliged to take Tom's hand when he extended it.

Whether it was the effect of the punch or the press of so many people around me, I don't know, but after a few turns, I became dizzy. Though pirouettes were the tools of my art, I had the feeling that the ground beneath my feet was shifting. Worse, my vision clouded and I clung to Tom for fear I might faint. I could see his lips moving but what I heard was the sound of my pulse throbbing in my temples.

I was about to ask if we could sit down again when a stranger appeared at my side. He was taller than Tom's six feet and wore a Guy Fawkes mask so that his features were covered entirely. What troubled me most, was the broad-brimmed hat and his black attire. I had seen this man before and more than once. The moment I recognized him, at least his manner of dress, alarm bells went off in my head. He took hold of my waist and I attempted to pull away, but his grip was too firm and before I could raise the least objection, I was swept into the thick of the dancers swirling round and round until suddenly we spun off to the edges of the hall.

Despite my disoriented state, I was alert to a change in the atmosphere. By now, we had left the populated area of the central ballroom and were spiraling through one of the galleries. A couple stood leaning against one wall and, being locked in a passionate embrace, paid no attention to us as the music from the farther room first became distant, then fell into utter silence. The sensation was one of crossing into a foreign plane or a forbidden boundary for very soon, the ground beneath my feet fell away as did all of Rathaus. I was being propelled heavenward, a wind abrading my face as I stared at the stars in the firmament, dazzled by their bonfires and close enough for me to touch them.

I had every reason to doubt my senses and yet the world in which I found myself was as real as any I had experienced. The only way to account for my circumstance was to tell myself that I must have fainted earlier and was lost in a miasmic dream. Perhaps, even at this moment, concerned faces were peering down at me, wanting to help. My best course of action was to let go of my present illusion so that others could restore me to consciousness.

The moment I allowed myself to relax, I began to hear voices. They were calling my name. I wanted to answer but felt as if I were locked in a tomb. Then something at once terrible and wonderful happened. I recognized one of the voices as it rose above the rest. But how was it possible? Yelena Natilova had been dead for nine years. I couldn't be hearing her now, and yet I couldn't deny it either.

When the other calls fell silent, I saw her. She came drifting toward me, just as I remembered her, except she was no more than a silhouette, a line of white chalk drawn on to empty space. Her white hair was blown back and she stretched her arms toward me, extending herself, so it seemed, in a gigantic effort to reach me.

I did the same, my spirit filled with a bright light so that, for a time, we hovered like two puffs of smoke, never quite touching, but able to fix our eyes on one another so that we could speak with our hearts.

How long we hung suspended in that element, I don't know, but other voices, other figments joined us, their moans muted at first but becoming mournful wails and so loud that I was forced to press my hands to my ears to shut them out. Still, they took possession of me until, finally, their voices overmastered mine and I emitted such a doleful moan that when they heard it, these same spirits grew frightened, aware that what they'd heard was an echo of their collective sorrow. I felt as if the whole of human suffering was coursing through me like a colossal wave, so intense that neither phantoms nor mortals could endure it. I collapsed before that sullen multitude as the walls of the Rathaus reassembled themselves around me.

CHAPTER VI

A doctor, in attendance at the ball, examined me and suggested I was suffering from fatigue. His sole prescription was for a good night's rest, and so Alec escorted me back to the hotel looking worried the entire time. I didn't mind leaving the dance and was glad for an opportunity to sit quietly and think about what had happened. So many questions raced through my head. What had become of the mystery man that was among them?

All Alec could tell me in the taxi was that I'd been found alone and slumped in a chair in one of the upper halls. No one remembered seeing a man in a Guy Fawkes mask though we had waltzed among the dancers as boldly as if we'd been the guests of honor. Only Tom had seen the stranger but even he admitted he'd lost track of our movements.

Alone in my hotel room, my intention was to puzzle out the events of the evening, but the moment my head hit the pillow, I fell into a sound sleep. I don't recall waking once during the night nor do I remember any dreams. When I awoke the next morning, I felt refreshed and suffered no repercussions from the previous night. When Alec visited me the next morning, I was enjoying a hearty breakfast in bed.

I could tell from the set angle of his jaw he was about to tell me something I wouldn't like. Ellen Gere, he said, would take the lead for the evening performance and Susan would perform a solo in the castle scene. He was adamant when he added I was to spend the day in bed and that he'd send someone to check on me to make sure I did.

After he'd left me, Ellen popped in to add her words of condolence, though she could barely contain her excitement about replacing me. My thought was that if she couldn't hide her elation, she'd have done better not to visit. *Replace me? Over my dead body.*

A succession of other visitors followed Ellen. Everyone was curious to know what had happened, but I had little to tell and bombarded them with questions instead. No one remembered seeing a man in a Guy Fawkes mask and knew even less about his mysterious disappearance. I was left with their sympathy but nothing more.

Abandoned by everyone, I spent the morning attempting to piece together the events of the previous night. Uppermost in my mind was the memory of Madame Natilova. Our encounter had seemed so real, it was hard to believe it was an illusion; yet logically, what else could it have been?

My mind fell into a tangle. I needed someone to help me unravel it, someone who could think objectively. Susan was the obvious choice, except that she couldn't keep a secret. If Alec got wind of what I thought I'd experienced, he'd panic and send me back to Seattle. But if I couldn't confide in Susan, then who?

At noon, someone rapped at my door. I assumed the waiter had arrived with my lunch, but Tom appeared instead. In spite of the misgivings I'd felt about him the previous night, I was glad to see him. He entered the room almost reverentially, as if I were in intensive care.

"H-how do you feel?" He sat down in the spindle chair beside my bed, turning it around so he could straddle it while resting his arms along the back. "You gave everyone a scare, you know." He paused to examine me. "You look okay now, though. The rest has done you some good."

"Such a fuss over a little dizzy spell," I told him. "The punch was too sweet, that's all. It made me ill."

"And the room was hot," Tom added his encouragement.

"Anyway, I'm fine now."

"You sure?"

"Yes. I've been sitting here thinking about having it out with Alec. There's no reason why I shouldn't dance tonight. I don't even have a headache."

My comment met with Tom's enthusiasm and he sat up in the chair.

"Glad to hear it, because I gotta tell you, Tara, Alec's been tearing his hair out all morning. Ellen's a nice little dancer but she hasn't your fire. Her black swan could pass for a Sunday school teacher. Even David's a little frustrated, and you know how laid back he is?"

I listened to his complaints a minute longer then bounded out of bed. Energized by what he'd told me, I was determined to make use of the information and headed toward the bathroom to get dressed.

"Where are you going?" Tom called after me.

"I'm going to the theater to convince Alec I'm all right. I'll make him listen to me even if he doesn't want to."

"Don't worry. He won't argue with you. If you don't dance tonight, he's the one who'll have to take to his bed."

We were both laughing when the waiter appeared with my lunch -- cheese omelet, toast and a large pot of coffee. Trained in his duties, he didn't turn a hair to see me scantily clad with a man in my room and before leaving us, set down the tray on the bed, as I directed.

Once we were alone, Tom eyed my omelet so covetously that I shoved the tray in his direction.

"Here, you have it. You've drooled over it, already. I'm going to take a shower."

Tom dug into my meal without further coaxing. He was munching on toast as I turned on the tap but I could hear his conversation well enough as I'd left the bathroom door ajar.

"What I can't figure out is why the guy didn't go for help? Why leave you dumped in a chair? Did you have a fight or something?"

"No, of course not," I shouted above the roar of the water. "Maybe he did look for help but you found me first. Ever think of that?"

Tom seemed to consider my suggestion as a silence followed before he began again.

"Okay, but why didn't he stick around to see if you were okay? That's what any other normal person would have done. Naw, there was something strange about the guy. There's no excuse for a disappearing act."

"It doesn't matter. I'm fine and I'll never see him again."

I finished my shower and came out of the bathroom wearing my jeans and a tea shirt as I towel-dried my hair. By then, Tom had eaten my breakfast and was finishing the last drop of coffee.

"You're acting pretty blasé about the whole thing, Tara. It's not like you. It makes me think you're holding something back."

"You think you know me well enough to read my thoughts?"

Tom snorted as I tried to act cool.

"Oh come on, Tara, don't play games. It's not that I'm clever. It's that you're a poor liar. I trusted you about Sylvia, so you should know you can trust me. If there's a problem, maybe I can help."

He had a point. He had trusted me and it was also true that I could use some help. The question was, did I want to make Tom my confidante? How deeply should I allow him to become involved in my life?

On that clear morning, with the sun shining through the window and as Tom gazed up at me with an honest, open expression, I decided a moment of truth had arrived. I needed a friend and Tom struck me as about the best friend a person could have.

He proved to be a good listener from the start and didn't attempt to interrupt when I told him about everything that had been happening since the trip began -- about the cries in the night, the gypsy and even the ghost at the theater in Budapest. It was a relief to confess and once I started, I couldn't stop. I knew what I was telling him made me sound a little crazy, so I warned him when I'd finished that if he made a joke of what I'd said, I'd never reveal anything again.

To my surprise, making a joke was the last thing on his mind. He was annoyed that I hadn't told him what was happening sooner.

I sank down on the bed opposite him, feeling relieved.

"You mean you believe me? All of it?"

"Of course I do," Tom scowled. "You forget, I saw your mystery man. He's real, all right. And the gypsy, she was real because Anne and the others saw her. As for Voss's ghosts who can say? But at least we know you aren't the first to have experienced something." He tossed me a second stern look, like I needed some sense pounded into me. "There's nothing wrong with your head, Tara. Not being upset, that would be crazy."

Unable to contain my relief, I threw my arms around Tom's neck, and gave him a peck on the cheek.

When I released him, he pointed to the other one as he turned his head. "Come again? I didn't get that last part."

I threw a pillow at him instead.

"Worth a try," he shrugged. After that, he turned serious again.

"Do you suppose the guy drugged you somehow? I've been struggling to think how it could happen. I brought you the drink but maybe he dropped something into it while I was carrying it. The room was so crowded, it could have happened that way. Hundreds of people drank that punch last night but you're the only one who fainted. Or maybe he exposed you to something while you were dancing. Do your recall any peculiar odors or seeing smoke of some kind?"

I shook my head.

"No, nothing that I can remember."

"Yeah, but you don't remember much, do you? It could have happened one of those ways. I just wish we'd had a good look at the guy."

Tom and I hadn't known each other long and the first time we met, I took him for a charming rake. Now I was seeing another side of him -- a sweet and generous guy whom I could trust. I might have kissed him a second time but didn't. I wouldn't want him to think I meant anything but friendship. I went on.

"Could it be that someone in the company was playing a joke, like the one Alec played on David?"

My mysterious dance partner seemed the logical suspect, particularly as he'd disappeared. But I had a sense he was trying to protect me. No evidence could account for my feeling, but it was strong. Perhaps that's why I went so far as to suggest Ellen Gere might be the culprit. Tom snorted when he heard me. But when I pointed she was preparing to assume my role at that very moment, his cheeks reddened.

"Now that's crazy. She wasn't anywhere near you last night. She's a nice girl, Tara. Leave her out of this."

Feeling chastised, I was quick to defend myself.

"How do you know what she's like? She could have put someone up to it. She's the one who kept saying I should listen to the gypsy. Maybe this is all a set up."

Tom raised his voice to match mine.

"If you think Ellen's your competition, you're wrong, Tara. When this tour is over, she'll go back to her company, just like me. But you? My god, when we get home you'll have offers waiting from all over the country, maybe the world. You're becoming a star. Don't you realize that? Ellen's just a blip in your history. So lighten up."

Tom's words hit me like a shower of cold water. He was right about my future. If the reviews kept coming in as they had been, I did have a future and probably a big one. That he thought Ellen didn't compare also cheered me.

"Come on," I said as I grabbed my coat. "We can talk about this later. Right now, I want to get to the theater."

When we had reached the lobby and were half way out the door, I stopped in my tracks.

"I forgot my ball gown," I told Tom. "It has to be returned today." I left him to cool his heels while I headed back to the elevator.

"Hurry up," he shouted after me.

Back in my room, I discovered someone had taken the precaution of hanging my costume in the closet. The headdress was resting on the shelf above it. I grabbed them both and was rushing back to the lobby when my fingers felt something in one of the pockets. My ticket to the ball, I assumed. But I was wrong. What I found was a white business card upon which was printed, in an ornamented style, the words, *Orlando, Master of Magic*. Turning it over, I found an address. It was for a street somewhere in Vienna.

. . .

Alec looked relieved when he saw me enter the theater with Tom. Ellen saw us, too, and put on a brave face, but I could tell that's all it was. Her hug, when she greeted me, was limpid.

I could understand her reaction. Her parents, like mine, had made sacrifices to give their daughter the best dancing lessons money could buy. Her father was a mechanic and her mother cooked in a restaurant to make ends meet, so she was eager to justify their sacrifices. She thought that the evening performance would give her a chance to shine. Now I'd snatched that opportunity away from her. Unlike Tom, I knew she didn't have to worry about her future. She was a good dancer and her training was broader than mine.

She'd studied modern dance as well as classical ballet and I knew Alec was interested in choreographing for a combination of the two styles. If more money was forthcoming, I was sure he'd offer her a position with us. Otherwise, she was well-placed with the Oregon Ballet Company which was her home. Stepping aside for the evening wasn't the end of her world.

The afternoon rehearsal went well and Thursday night's performance justified my decision to dance. One or two mishaps occurred offstage -- Susan lost the tiara for her costume and one of the goslings wandered off so that the rest of the corps had to fill in her space. But despite these slight defects, the Viennese audience, accustomed to world-class performers, responded to us with unexpected warmth. We didn't receive a standing ovation, as we had in Budapest, but the curtain calls were numerous and the applause strong. By the time I returned to the hotel that evening, my room looked like a florist shop, conveying messages from well-wishers.

Changing into a skirt and sweater, I headed for the restaurant downstairs. Alec and the principal dancers were to meet the Brancaccios for a prearranged supper. Tom was seated with our hosts when I arrived. Alec had called to say he would be delayed at the theater. Likewise, Anne and Philip were off, performing their custodial duties. One of the young dancers had thrown up after the performance and they were escorting her back to her lodgings. Where Susan and David had gone to, nobody knew.

While the four of us waited, we shared a bottle of champagne, compliments of the house. The Brancaccios were already bubbly, spilling over with admiration for the evening's performance.

"An excellent entertainment," Forintino said, raising his second glass toward the ceiling. "To the Seattle Ballet, a little company with a big future."

"Here, here," Alec echoed as he hurried toward us and then sat down, eyeing the table for an empty glass. Anunciata handed him one and her husband filled it. Our director's eyes sparkled with pleasure through its amber light. After taking a sip, he answered Anunciata's question about the condition of the dancer who had been taken ill.

"Cramps is all. Anne put her to bed with a hot water-bottle. If she isn't better tomorrow, the corps will fill-in her space. Calamities like this happen all the time."

The restaurateur nodded like a Dutch uncle. "Yes. Yes. It's always difficult with girls."

"And where would you be without our 'difficulties,'" his wife sniffed, feigning umbrage. "You'd be without children or grandchildren. That's where you'd be!"

Forintino put an arm about his wife's shoulder and gave it a pat.

"I know. We men are indebted to you women for everything, including life. Here's to women." He raised his glass again as he'd done so often already that night. Anunciata ignored him and reached for her menu.

"It's time we ordered."

Forintino took the menu from her and tapped the side of his nose as if about to reveal a secret.

"I've arranged everything, my little nun." That said, he signaled the waiter and the flow of platters began: bowls of creamy mushroom soup and crusty bread, together with cold-cuts, cheeses and a fruit platter.

The fare was ample enough to satisfy everyone except Forintino who ordered three more baskets of bread, all of which he wolfed down almost single-handedly. His wife's frown had no effect on his gustatory habits, so she gave up and turned to address Alec.

"The night of our dinner party, Tara told me that you met with Natalya Lazaremko in Prague. I want to apologize if I sounded indiscrete in my remarks about her that night. I didn't mean to give offense, but I knew her, you know. We were students together at the Bolshoi years ago."

Alec wiped the soup from his chin with the cloth napkin and looked up in surprise.

"I didn't know you were a dancer, Anunciata. That couldn't have been so long ago."

She smiled at his flattery.

"After so many children, I can hardly pretend to accept your compliment. Anyway, I wasn't any good so nothing came of it."

"Maybe if you'd had the right artistic director," Alec winked. While he wasn't arrogant, he did make a habit of drawing attention to himself and his accomplishments. Anunciata didn't fully understand and blushed, thinking his was a flirtatious gesture.

"Never mind all that you wicked man. What I've been meaning to ask is if that was the first time you'd met her? I wasn't aware Ludmila had spent any time in the United States."

"I don't know that she has," Alec answered truthfully. "We met in Prague. She told me she represented the man who bankrolled our tour, though as to who he is or why we were chosen, she wouldn't say. The Seattle Arts Commission wasn't any help, either. Apparently, the award was as much a surprise to them as it was to me. What can you tell me about her?"

"Well," Anunciata sighed. "I don't remember her a being a truth-teller, so it's just as well that she didn't provide any answers. They'd have probably been half-truths, at best."

Alec wrinkled his forehead and looked his hostess straight in the eye.

"You don't think she's been misrepresenting her position, do you? Because she said we might receive another grant, depending on the tour's success. She wouldn't lie about that, would she? What reason would she have?"

Faced with his grilling, Anunciata hastened to correct her first impression.

"You must understand me. I only meant she might exaggerate the importance of her role. But you mustn't listen to me. I knew her as a girl. That was a long time before she was a prima ballerina. I doubt she'd stoop to false promises with you. No, the client is real and he intends to back a winner. I'm sure of that much."

"And you are a winner, Alec!" Forintino chimed in as if eager to add his reassurances to those of his wife's.

"Yes, but there are other companies, older and more established," Tom interjected. "Why pick one from the Pacific Northwest?"

Anunciata took his point and repeated his question again, as if it had stuck to her brain like a wad of gum. Her husband, unhappy with the direction of the conversation, grew agitated and attempted to smooth away these doubts like a man who abhorred wrinkled bed sheets.

"You both forget we have no idea where this generous man lives. It might be Alaska for all we know or the Gobi Desert. Let's not look a gift horse in the mouth. Good luck happens. Did I not meet and marry my little nun?"

His wife smiled at him benignly, as if remembering why she'd married him -- this man of a cheerful, indefatigable nature with whom she'd raised many children and prospered. Taking his hand which he had rested on her shoulder, she lifted it to her lips and kissed it. As a consequence, he thrust out his chest like a rooster at sunrise and announced the conversation had grown too serious. It was time for dessert.

At his signal, the waiter came forward with slices of coconut cream cake and for a time, we fell silent, savoring the rich confection. The evening seemed to be drawing to a satisfactory close when Anunciata dropped another clinker.

"She has a love child, you know. A girl, I think?"

Alec's fork stalled on its way from his cake to his mouth. Having lost the thread of conversation, Anunciata clarified her remark for him.

"Perhaps the news didn't reach the American newspapers, or maybe you were too young to remember Ludmila's temporary absence from the stage."

Aleck shook his head slowly.

"No, I don't recall anything about that."

"Oh yes. The story was in all the papers. The reporters couldn't get enough of her disappearance. The Bolshoi said she was taking a rest, but the rumors were rampant. A few suggested she'd been murdered and that the Kremlin was covering it up. But nine months later she was back again, poof, like the magician's assistant returned to the vanishing cabinet. Oh how the public loved that, and the rumors of an illegitimate child abounded. She was asked about her disappearance time and time again, but as you've observed, Alec, Ludmila can be very tight-lipped. She took up her career as before and people made happy by her return forgot about her misadventure. I will give the devil her due. She was a graceful dancer.

"But," Anunciata went on, tapping Alec on the arm as if she were about to impart a dark truth. "No secret can be kept forever. Years later, I came across an article in a wine magazine to which Forintino and I subscribe. It was about Vladimir Reznikov, the man you'll remember I thought Ludmila was in love with. Everyone nodded, including Tom who'd been in the restaurant kitchen at the time and hadn't heard her comment. "Well the story I read was about an award he was to receive for one of his labels. It mentioned that he wouldn't be at the ceremony but that his daughter would accept the prize for him. Cristina, I think her name was. As I knew Reznikov had never married, naturally, I put two and two together.

"Naturally," her husband teased.

"So who's Vladimir Reznikov, again?"

"A very wicked man, Tom."

•　•　•

Friday morning after breakfast, I went looking for my redheaded friend. I'd yet to mention the card I'd found in my costume. There'd been no time and I wasn't sure what to make of it. Maybe the card had been left on some other occasion, but I doubted it.

Wanting to check out the address but not wanting to go alone, I'd decided to take Tom with me. I called his room and his cellphone number but got no answer. Thinking he might be in the coffeeshop, I hurried downstairs. No one I knew was around, except Alec. He told me he'd seen Tom earlier but didn't know where he was now. Annoyed, I decided to go to Tom's room.

Several knocks on his door, each growing more insistent, raised no answer. I must have been standing outside the room long enough to arouse suspicion because a cleaning woman walked by with her cart and gave me a hard look. I decided to go back to my room and wait.

Half an hour later I was still waiting, peering out the window for any sign of him. When the room phone rang, finally, I almost leapt out of my skin. Unfortunately, Tom wasn't at the other end of the line; it was Alec. He told me he'd bumped into Anne and she'd said Tom had left early that morning with Ellen to do a little sightseeing. Alec advised me not to hang around but to do a little sightseeing on my own.

"No telling when Tom and Ellen will be back. Get out. Get some fresh air."

He hung up and left me standing with the dial tone still ringing in my ear. My next thought was to ask Susan to come with me. I didn't have to give her the full background. I'd tell a half-truth: that I'd found the card in my costume and was curious. She'd go for it, I knew.

She answered her cell phone on the second ring, but asked if we could check out the shop some other time. She was with David, trying to locate a hot night spot someone had told him about. I told her that would be okay then tried Tom's cell phone again. Still no answer, not even a request to leave a message. Maybe his battery had gone dead.

Disgusted, I threw my own cell on the bed and headed for the bathroom to throw some cold water on my face. I was upset, not only because I couldn't reach Tom, but also because he'd run off with Ellen without saying a word to me. He knew what was going on in my life. How could he run off like that?

The cooling water had no effect on my frayed nerves. I was furious with Tom and furious with myself. Why was I acting so helpless? I could check things out for myself. I wouldn't do anything foolish, just drive by to see what the place looked like. Alec said I should do a little sightseeing, so why not?

Ballet Noir

The taxi driver nodded when I showed him the address on the magician's card. His English was poor, but using sign language, we agreed on a fare and I climbed into the back of his car. I sat with my arms folded as he drove, still so annoyed with Tom that I didn't take in the view. I was thinking of all the things I'd say to make him feel guilty when I finally caught up with him.

The taxi came to a halt in the midst of my mental tirade. How long we'd been driving, I couldn't say. It might have been five minutes or forty.

Looking through the window, I could see the street was lined with ordinary row houses, each with stone steps leading to the front doors. On the pavement, a few preschoolers were playing while their mothers sat on the stoops, keeping an eye on them. The morning was a sunny day, but I did note a few cumulus clouds looming on the horizon. If they grew in number, it might rain.

The driver called out the address I was looking for to one of the mothers and she pointed to a basement apartment next to hers. A few of the children ran toward me as she did, curious about the stranger who'd just arrived. So far, the setting was normal and I didn't feel uncomfortable about getting out of the car.

As I closed the taxi door, the driver held out his hand, so I paid him but asked him to wait. Apparently, he didn't understand because the moment he had his money, he gunned his engine and drove away. I tried to attract his attention by shouting out and waving, but it did no good. I was left standing on the pavement, feeling abandoned like a traveler who'd just missed her train.

Unsure about what to do next, I decided to call Alec and tell him where I was. Maybe he could send a taxi for me. It seemed like a good plan until, after rummaging in my purse for a minute or two, I realized I'd left my cell phone on the hotel bed and had come away without it. For all practical purposes, I was stranded as I saw no visible means of transport either by taxi or by bus. I'd have to borrow a phone from one of the women on the stoop.

With the children still gathered around me, I approached the woman who had spoken to the taxi driver. She wore a blue and white bandana, looked to be in her late twenties and had a pleasant face.

She watched me approach and when I was near enough, held out her hand. I wasn't sure what she meant by it, but I took hold of it, rather than give offense. After that, she rose from the step and led me to the basement address she had pointed out earlier. A bell rang above her head as she opened the door of what appeared to be a tiny shop. She called out a name, then pushed me forward, smiled and then, without a word, left me.

The space in which I found myself was scarcely bigger than a generous walk-in closet. Facing me was a wooden counter and on the flanking walls were rows and rows of shelves containing glass jars, the contents of which appeared to be assortments of roots and twigs and multicolored powders. In plain language, it appeared to be an apothecary or herbal shop of some kind.

A pair of slippered feet made shuffling sounds as someone approached. Soon after, a withered hand pulled back the moth-eaten curtain that hung behind the counter to provide a glimpse of the darkened interior, living quarters presumably. Next a little man appeared wearing a nightgown and a pointed cap which gave him an elf-like appearance. He coughed several times before speaking to me and when he was near enough, I noticed an odor of camphor hung about him, and so strongly that I scarcely dared breathe.

"I'm sorry to bother you," I began, hoping he understood English. "I thought this might be a magician's shop. At least, this was the address I was given."

From his bent position, the apothecary, if that's what he was, peered up at me with a pair of murky grey eyes.

"Tara Bentley? Are you Tara Bentley?" His breath seemed to come in sips and it pained me to see how difficult it was for him to talk.

"Y-yes, I am. How did you know?"

"Are you alone?"

Turning around, I assured myself that the woman who'd brought me was gone. "As you can see, I am."

"No one is outside waiting for you?"

I shook my head to satisfy him and only then did he lean across the counter to deliver his message.

"He's waiting for you at Franz Schubert's grave, not far... in the Zentralfriedhoff."

"In the what?"

A crab-like finger pointed somewhere to my right. "Zentralfriedhoff. It's a cemetery. Ten minute walk from here, no more."

"Who's waiting for me? I'm not going to a cemetery to meet some stranger. Do I look crazy?"

Surprised by my sharp retort, the old man blinked, then fell into a coughing fit that was so severe I wondered if I should get help.

"Schubert's grave," he wheezed again, struggling to form the words. "He'll be waiting for you." Overcome with a new wave of convulsions, he waved me away and retreated from the room, dropping the blanket-curtain behind him.

By the time I returned to the street, no one was in sight. The children and their mothers had retreated into their homes, presumably for lunch as, by the location of the sun, I judged it was nearly noon. With no means of transport and no phone, I decided to walk in the direction I'd been given. My only hope was that I'd find a phone booth along the way.

Fortunately the day remained pleasant and I soon reached my destination as I'd seen no one to approach about a taxi or a bus line along the way. If I'd expected the cemetery to look like a scene from a Hollywood horror film, I was to be disappointed. A number of people were milling about at the entrance, many of them tourists with cameras and unfolded maps.

One young couple, who looked Japanese, stood at the edge of the crowd and were bent over their directions. They didn't speak English, but recognized Schubert's name when I mentioned it. They pointed to the map in front of them. From the layout, I determined that the site lay somewhere near the Church of Karl Lueger, a domed structure that was visible from where I stood. All I had to do was look for the sign that read *Musiker* and turn left. Schubert's grave could be identified by a tall white marker upon which three figures were carved, one of which was the likeness of the renowned musician.

I thanked the couple for the use of their map and entered the graveyard. Despite the clouds that continued to gather, the setting was bucolic and worthy of an 18th Century landscape. In the clear light, I had no difficulty finding the gravesite. A number of people had gathered there before me, clumping around the grave, their voices hushed with reverence for the great man who laid beneath their feet. If I harbored any misgivings about being there, I was hard-pressed to sustain them for the faces around me were those of ordinary vacationers, all smiles for one another and enjoying their holiday.

I'd not been at my post many minutes, when the atmosphere changed. The air felt damp and seeing the dark sky overhead, I considered leaving my post to take cover. As I stood, wondering what next to do, I felt a light tap on my shoulder.

Startled, I swung around and found myself looking into the eyes of a middle-aged couple who, by their round eyes seemed equally in a quandary. The plump man, somewhere in his late sixties, was standing beside a plump woman, whom I took to be his wife because they wore matching hats and scarves. The man tipped his and then spoke to me in what I assumed was German, though I understood not a word. When I said I was an American, they broke into a garbled English, simultaneously, which I managed to understand. They were looking for the section of the graveyard dedicated to famous writers. As I'd passed it along my way, I had no trouble directing them and they looked gratified. Encouraged by their friendly manner, I asked if I could borrow their cell phone to make a call. When they heard me, their expressions turned apologetic.

"No cell phone. Sorry. Most Sorry." The gentleman tipped his hat a second time and the pair waddled off like well-behaved penguins.

By now a chill wind had arisen in earnest, sending the bank of black clouds scudding across the sky. In another minute or two, I'd be standing in a torrential rain. Again, I thought of shelter and when I glanced around, I discovered I was alone in the graveyard, the other tourists having taken cover before me.

Drawing my coat collar up to my ears, I was about to head for a clump of trees several yards away when I detected a slight movement in the vicinity of Schubert's grave. Looking closer, I saw it was a man, just emerged from the shadows to lean irreverently against the headstone. He made no attempt to approach as if wishing to give me time to recognize who he was.

The moment I did, I backed away, my eyes reconnoitering for some avenue of escape if needed. He made no show to move, however, and so, not feeling threatened, I took the opportunity to get a good look at him.

From the distance between us, I judged him to be somewhere in his early thirties. His features were refined, his complexion olive and from beneath the wide brim of his hat, a pair of opal eyes gleamed with unfathomable intention. If I'd been required to draw the image of a dark angel, a face at once beautiful and haunted, this man could have served as my model.

"Why are you following me?" I asked once a comfortable distance existed between us. "I don't know you. What do you want? Do you speak English? Because you should know that if you persist in your behavior, I'll call the police."

"I do understand, Tara. And what you should know is that I'm here to help."

Jolted by his reply, I took another step backwards, my heart thumping against my ribs like a prisoner wanting to be set free. Again, I admit nothing in his demeanor was threatening. He continued to remain at a distance and made no sudden gestures. Yet, I knew he was treating me like a wild animal he wanted to tame and I didn't care to be treated as such.

"I don't need any help, thank you," I snapped. "If I have a problem, it's you. What did you do to me the other night? Don't pretend you don't know what I'm talking about. I want to know. Did you put something in my drink?

The stranger leaning against Schubert's grave looked up at the sky and, ignoring my question, suggested we take cover before the downpour. Not waiting for my answer, he turned and trotted off in the direction of the domed church without bothering to look back to see if I had followed.

At first I didn't and I remained where I was, feeling annoyed but pricked by my desire for answers to my questions. A cloudburst decided for me. Caught in a deluge, I sprinted past my stalker, reaching the sanctuary before him.

We entered the church, together, to discover a lovely interior painted a cerulean blue and gold. The walls were heavily-ornamented and the setting so inspiring, that it seemed a sacrilege to stand in its midst, shaking the rain from my garments.

As I slid into one of the back pews, my companion followed, removing his hat so that his dark hair, parted at the center, fell in silky strands to his jawbone. He was so beautiful, for that is the word I'd use instead of handsome, that I was reminded of the sculptured works of Gian Lorenzo Bernini.

"It's true," he confessed, beginning our conversation again. "I have been following you." He held up his hand when my lips parted to speak. "Hear me out. I am nothing but a simple man longing for a simple life."

"Then why stalk women?"

He looked pained by my retort but went on.

"I'm not stalking you. I've come to help." His gaze was so steady and penetrating that I was inclined to believe him but knew of no reason why I should.

"You keep saying you've come to help but I don't need any, unless you care to tell me what happened at Rathaus. Who are you, anyway?"

"You know who I am. My name was on the card. Orlando."

"Orlando what? Are you really a magician? Was the other night some kind of trick?"

"I'm known only as Orlando. And no, I'm not a magician in the way you're thinking. I don't pull rabbits from a hat."

"Then what do you do? I want the truth."

My companion glanced around the church before answering, as if to make certain our conversation was private. Except for a group of tourists who'd taken refuge near the altar, both of us could see we were alone.

He bent low to my ear to make sure only I could hear what he had to say.

"I don't know how to tell you this, but I believe you are in danger."

I reared back, my eyes full of reproach when I heard him.

"What? Are you another gypsy? Well, I'm sorry. I've already had my fortune told. You won't get a penny out of me. Now if you'll excuse me, I'm leaving."

I started to rise, but the magician or gypsy or whatever he was took hold of my arm and pulled me down beside him again. This time his patience seemed to have fled and he was the one to look angry.

"Last night was a test. I had to see if you were strong enough, if you could…"

"Let go of me," I snapped, pulling my arm away, my voice loud enough to turn the heads of the tourists at the front of the church in our direction.

Orlando lowered his voice aware of their concern.

"We can't talk here. Tomorrow, at midnight, I'll come to your room. 'Til then keep an open mind."

As he rose to settle his hat on his head, I looked up at him, dumbfounded. Where did this guy get his nerve?

"If you've got anything more to say, say it now," I snapped, "because I have a performance tomorrow. I won't be hanging around my room, waiting for you. Come near me again and I swear, I'll call the police."

"Then you'd better be able to tell them exactly who I am." He backed away, his eyes intent upon mine. "I'm Orlando, The Necromancer."

A moment later, he was gone.

CHAPTER VII

I didn't see Tom until just before the Friday night performance.

"Where were you all day?" I demanded, poking him in the shoulder with the intent of doing damage.

He turned to look at me, rubbing the spot where my fingers had dug in.

"Geez, I didn't know I was supposed to check-in. Why are you angry? Did I miss something?"

"I asked first. Where were you? Not with David and Susan. I know that."

His face turned red.

"Ellen asked me to take in some sites. You didn't say anything about meeting up so I figured, why not?"

"'Why not? After what I told you yesterday, did you think it was okay to trot off with someone else without letting me know? And yes, you did miss something. That guy from the ball showed up."

Tom's jaw dropped but he didn't have time to recover and say anything. The manager gave us our cue.

"Places everyone. The curtain is about to go up."

. . .

Friday's performance of *Swan Lake* went without a hitch. At the close, the patrons were on their feet, applauding and tossing flowers toward the stage. David gave me a kiss which Susan didn't seem to mind, and Alec was so chuffed that he made a point of hugging all the dancers.

I, too, was overjoyed, though yesterday's misadventure hung like a cloud over me. I had the feeling that Orlando, the Necromancer, was somewhere in the audience, keeping watch over me though his motives remained unclear.

At 11 that evening, I joined Alec and some of the other dancers in the coffee shop for a late night snack. Several bottles of wine had been left at our tables, tributes from hotel guests who'd attended the performance. With so many libations in hand, Alec was in full sail, tossing compliments to his crew as if his words were confetti. By the time supper arrived, I was feeling light-headed from drinking so many toasts.

Everyone looked happy. Anne and Philip couldn't stop smiling at each other, and Ellen, too, had stars in her eyes. Tom and I had continued our argument after the show so I refused to say anything more to him about my meeting with Orlando. He left me in a huff and now he was sitting beside Ellen, spending a good deal of time nibbling on her ear. Finally, I'd had enough, my mood being so out of sync with the others, that I tossed my napkin on the table. I knew I was feeling jealous and felt stupid about it as I marched toward the elevator.

Always sensitive to his dancer's moods, Alec left the others to catch up with me. His eyes held a question as they sought mine. I insisted I was fine and gave him a peck on the cheek, feeling grateful when the elevator arrived.

The clock on my night stand read 11: 50 as I entered my room. Everything was exactly as I'd left it. My skirt lay across the bed and the bathroom towels remained on the floor where I'd tossed them after my shower. The air of normalcy did nothing to relieve my tension. I peeked under the bed and in the closet to make certain no Necromancer was in hiding. The room was empty and when I was satisfied of this fact, I admit I felt a pang of disappointment.

From my open window, I had a clear view of the hotel entrance. The avenue was deserted. Not even an alley cat sauntered by, much less did I see the outline of a stranger in a broad brimmed hat. Orlando, the Necromancer, wasn't coming. Perhaps he'd been toying with me, or perhaps my threat about the police had scared him off.

From a distance, I could hear chimes ringing from a bell tower. Midnight had arrived and the world outside the hotel was as still as a picture postcard. Turning from the window, I sighed. The best I could look forward to was a good night's sleep.

My sigh became a gasp when, standing at the center of the room, I saw a dark apparition topped by a broad brimmed hat.

"I hope I didn't startle you. I presumed I was expected."

Presumed he was expected? If Orlando only knew how much.

"I thought I told you not to come."

The man opposite me shook his head. "I have no choice. Do you want the nightmares to continue?"

"Who told you about my nightmares? I've only spoken to Tom."

The Necromancer brushed aside my question. "She's reaching out to you, Tara. You saw her. You know she's real."

"The woman I saw is dead," I shouted. "This is some cruel game you're playing."

Orlando shook his head as he took hold of my wrists and pulled me to him.

"I wish we had more time, but we don't. You'll have to trust me."

The moment I felt his touch, a tingling sensation coursed through me. The feeling in my arms and legs grew numb. I should have been frightened but the sensation was like one of drifting off to sleep. The more comfortable I became, the more my will seemed to evaporate. I was so relaxed that when a vortex of clouds began to swirl around me, I felt no fear, but rather I had the sensation of joining an element larger than myself, like a tide pool receiving the incoming waves. I was about to disappear when Tom, like a wind swell, burst into the room. Sensing my danger, he leapt forward to free me from the Necromancer. I could feel his arms lock around my waist, but he hadn't the power to release me. Instead, the pair of us fell backwards into the black hole that had formed and in that dark place, we were buffeted like dandelion spores in a high wind.

I continued to feel Tom's arms about my waist, holding fast as we were pulled downward toward some unknown destination. I could sense the Necromancer's presence, too, not as a tactile experience, but more like an intuition. He was struggling to keep Tom and me together. If he failed, I knew, instinctively, the pair of us might be lost in the vortex forever.

His exertion must have been immense because once or twice his energy seemed to flicker and for one, terrifying moment, the life in me seemed to be drained by the surrounding energy. I recall letting out a cry, but in that doleful place the sound was absorbed by the wind's howl.

Whether Tom was experiencing similar fears, I couldn't tell. I knew only that he was with me and that our direction suddenly changed and we were being drawn upward toward a bright light. A dome of swirling color formed above us and we were headed for it at great speed. If I braced for the collision, I don't remember, but we broke through easily and found ourselves floating in a calm sea that can only be described as mindless consciousness. Our sensations were restored, but we could form no judgments.

Eventually, we came to rest before a wooden door. It hung suspended in the midst of a blue sky. Seeing it, Tom let go of me. He must have sensed, as I did, that I alone could enter there. No word passed between us, but I stared at my friend's face, trying to preserve his memory should I never return. Then I reached for the brass handle and stepped through the portal.

CHAPTER VIII

Was this a joke? Was I dreaming? Surely no breach between the living and the dead could be more narrow than the ordinariness of the room in which I found myself. Sunshine streamed through the window of what appeared to be a Tudor cottage, its light brushing the oak beams and hardwood floor with an amber glow. Comfortable chairs were set at intervals about the room, two of them overstuffed and with cabbage rose and periwinkle coverings. A fire burned in a hearth but seemed to give no warmth, though the white walls of the cottage flickered from the glow of the dancing flames.

In a far corner of the room, I spied a shadow. It appeared to be that of a woman. She was tall and straight but her silver hair let me know that she was old.

Aware that I had seen her, she stepped forward, shyly, like a girl about to take her first communion. As the details of her worn yet exquisite features became clearer to me, I noted that her blue eyes were brimming with animation.

"Madame Natilova?" I cried and reached out to embrace her. She stepped to one side, determined to avoid my embrace and pointed to one of the chintz chairs on either side of the fireplace.

The moment I sat down, I discovered that the padded cushion supporting me had no substance, as though I was sitting on air. Like the fire which gave no warmth, the entire room, seemed to be little more than illusion. Perhaps that's why Madame had eluded my embrace. She wanted to spare me the initial shock of my circumstances. I admit the feeling of insubstantiality that settled about me was disconcerting.

Taking the chair opposite mine, my teacher sat quietly and for a time, each of us sat taking in the other through our eyes. Death had not changed her. Her chiseled features, though weathered with age, remained beautiful. Her hair, no longer confined in its bun as I'd always seen it, fell in glossy strands about her shoulders.

"You are looking well, Tara Bentley," Madame said at last. The bell-like clarity of her voice was as I remembered it and I grew more comfortable.

"Thank you, Madame. You are looking well also."

"As well as can be expected," she smiled. "But, we haven't much time. I must tell you why I wanted to make contact and I hope you'll forgive me for being blunt. Someone is trying to harm you, my child. As yet, I don't know who, though I have my suspicion. These feelings of mine are too strong to ignore and I had to warn you. I've been reaching out to you for some days and once or twice I thought you heard me, but I couldn't break through. Finally, I turned to the Necromancer and he arranged this meeting."

"I have heard cries recently, Madame Natilova. And I felt a haunting at the Hungarian State Opera House. Was that you? I'm afraid I ran away because I was afraid."

My teacher shook her head to indicate she knew nothing of that.

"If there was a presence, it was Avdotia Istumine's ghost. She haunted me there when I was quite young. The theater was the scene of some of her greatest triumphs, so she thinks she owns the place. You may feel complimented. She reaches out only to the most talented, but she has no real powers of manifestation so I wouldn't think to reach you through her."

"You mean she lives at the Opera House?"

"Well, 'lives' isn't the right word, is it? But yes, she's chosen to remain there rather than move on. Some spirits do stay behind. The reasons vary, but usually it's because of some unfinished business. In Avdotia's case it's vanity. You needn't waste time worrying about her."

She returned to the topic of greatest importance to her, my safety. Of utmost importance was to listen to the Necromancer.

"Trust him, Tara. He's the only one with the power to save you."

I shook my head unable to comprehend what she meant.

"But how can he help if we don't know what the danger is? What if what threatens me is an illness? Wouldn't it be better to consult a doctor? How did you find this Necromancer, anyway? Does one put an ad in the paper?"

"Don't be impertinent, Tara. The situation doesn't call for a doctor. I know that much. But as to the Necromancer, I must be honest with you, I know little about the profession. He has a gift, that's all. Some people are remarkably sensitive which gives them the power to communicate with the dead. I think the one I found is quite handsome, don't you? Yes, I did rather well, if I do say so myself."

The sparkle in her eyes couldn't be ignored and it amused me to think that my teacher still had an eye for attractive men. It was so when she was alive, even in her sixties and they, I will admit, had an eye for her, even younger ones. I had to be honest, too, about the Necromancer. I told her he wasn't very communicative and that his manner of dressing in black was morbid.

"Slight defects," she said brushing my complaints aside. "What's important is his willingness to help. Not all of them will, you know, especially in a matter as serious as this."

"I know you're concerned, Madame, and I'm grateful for your warning, but have you any idea how crazy all of this sounds? I'm inclined to believe I've eaten a bad oyster and am having a nightmare."

"Try not to be obtuse, Tara. I tell you, you are in danger and you must put your faith in the Necromancer. He doesn't want anything and neither of us has anything to give. I'm lucky to have found him so don't be difficult."

Her arched expression rolled back the years and I felt again, as if I were a first-year student in my beginners' dance class.

"I'm sorry, Madame, but all of this is a bit surreal. I mean, look at this place. What is it? It looks real but it isn't. It's more like a reflection of what's real."

My teacher looked around and seemed to agree.

"I believe this is what's called an antechamber, probably drawn from one of the Necromancer's memories. Certainly, I've never been here before. Antechambers are created as a safe place where the living and the dead may speak to one another."

"How do you know? I mean who told you this?"

Yelena Natilova bit her lower lip as she thought about my question.

"I don't know for sure and you mustn't blame me for what's happened. The Necromancer would be here to answer your questions if you hadn't brought that young man with you. You should have come alone as you were supposed to. If you had, the Necromancer wouldn't be obliged to stay with this person. But as it is, he can't be left alone or he would go mad."

I'd forgotten about Tom until that moment. Glad that he was safe, at least, I tried to explain that I didn't bring him, but that he arrived of his own accord in an effort to save me.

"Save you? That's absurd. Why should he meddle anyway? You're no business of his, are you? Her eyes narrowed as she looked at me, growing suspicious that there might be some connection between Tom and me, after all. Knowing she was a romantic, I had to disappoint her.

"We're just friends, Madame. Nothing more."

Her sigh was unambiguous. She was disappointed.

"Well, I suppose it's for the best. Love poses so many difficulties if one intends to dedicate one's life to dance."

She glanced toward the windows with their fake patches of sunlight. For a moment, she seemed to be lost in her thoughts and when she spoke again, her voice was small, as though she'd forgotten I was in the room.

"A boy loved me once. Unfortunately, I didn't understand how much. How could I? He was so much younger than I. I imagined he was infatuated, nothing more. My crime was that I allowed myself to be flattered by his attention and did nothing to discourage it. Why should I? He was beautiful in face and form, a strong, athletic dancer with a promising career before him. Some speculated he might be the next Nijinsky. I never meant to harm him, but I misjudged the depth of his emotion. When I escaped to the west, I left him without a word of goodbye. I never dreamed he'd attempt to kill himself."

"Vladimir Reznikov, is that who you mean?"

Madame turned to look at me, her clear, blue eyes round with a question. I told her what Madame Lazaremko had told to me of the affair and when she heard my explanation, she rose from her chair and began pacing.

"Now there's an elephant dancer, if ever there was one. Of course she'd blame me. She was always mean-spirited. I know she was happy enough to take my place on the stage and in Vladimir's bed once I was gone. They had a bastard child, you know. Cristina. I don't suppose she told you that."

Madame's pale complexion seemed to color with annoyance as she thought of her old nemesis. Feeling guilty, I apologized for what I'd told her and hearing me, she turned from the window in surprise.

"Why should you apologize? It's Natalya who should be making amends. How in the world did you meet her, anyway? It must have been a sorry occasion."

In answer to her question I told her about the tour and that I suspected Vladimir Reznikov might be the person supplying the money. Madame nodded.

"He's rich enough. He could do so if he chose. But why? You don't suppose he's drawn a connection between you and me, do you? If that were true, it would explain everything, my forebodings, and your sudden good fortune. It's possible, he's planning to take his bitterness out on you. You must tell the Necromancer what you've told me. Vladimir isn't a man to be underestimated."

"But why harm me? I wasn't alive when you defected."

"Don't expect reason from the irrational, Tara. He might know you are the jewel in my crown, and if so, then his enmity must follow."

"But as you say, he's given me a great opportunity. Why pay for a tour of European capitals if what he wants to do is harm me?"

"Is it so difficult to see, Tara?" my teacher hissed. "He raises you up the better to see you fall. He destroyed his career because of me. Now he will destroy yours."

My teacher's body began to vibrate like a tuning fork. She threw back her head and uttered a heart-wrenching wail. What happened next, I'm not sure. She may have disappeared or I may have fallen unconscious.

. . .

I awoke at 9 the next morning to find Tom asleep in my bed. He was lying with his mouth hung open, snoring, and still dressed in his clothes from the previous night. I gave him a nudge and he shot up at once, looking stunned, as if someone had shot a gun beside his ear.

"What the..."

"Get up, Tom. It's late. I don't want someone to find you here."

"W-What do you mean? I was here all night? I don't remember anything. I came to apologize about Ellen. You probably guessed I was trying to make you jealous, but when I got to your room..."

He stopped speaking in mid-sentence and smacked his forehead with his large hand.

"My God, I must have been hung-over. You wouldn't believe the dream I had."

I rose from the bed and put on my terrycloth robe while continuing to look at him.

"I might. Tell me about it." I tried to sound nonchalant, but I was eager to compare his recollection with mine. I listened without interrupting and was gratified to learn our memories were the same, except for my visit with Yelena Natilova, which was to be expected.

I decided to come clean, telling him everything and assuring him what had happened hadn't been a dream. I don't think he blinked the whole time I was talking. I'd never seen him so quiet and I couldn't help wondering if he was waiting for me to stop so he could throw a net over my head and call for the men in white coats.

When I'd finished, he showed me he was still capable of surprises. Instead of arguing with me, or telling me I was delusional, he threw himself across the bed and looked under it. His behavior was so strange, I wondered if he might need the men in white coats more than I did.

"What are you doing?" I asked crossly. "If you're going to be sick, use the bathroom."

As he sat up, Tom scowled at me.

"What do you mean, what am I doing? I'm looking for the guy, the Necromancer. I'm here. You're here. Where's he?" As he sat in thought, the frown on his forehead deepened. "Hey, what is a Necromancer, anyway?"

I shrugged to say that I didn't know and inwardly wondered why I hadn't asked the same question long ago. Tom was taking the experience seriously and was already thinking ahead.

"We need to find this phantom," he went on. "He took us on a joy-ride and we need to know how. Until we find out, I'm sticking to you like glue, especially if there's any truth to your being in danger."

I had to admit, having Tom underfoot sounded like a good idea as my life was getting pretty weird. Still, to be fair, I had to give him a chance to back out.

"You don't have to get involved, Tom. It's really not your problem. Last night you were just a hitchhiker."

The look on his face when he heard me was that of a man who had bitten into a moldy apple with a worm in it.

"Listen, Tara, how I got into this doesn't matter. I'm in. You think I'd let you face this mess alone? What kind of a guy do you think I am?"

I had to admit, I thought he was a pretty great one and gave him a hug. I didn't deserve his loyalty and didn't understand why he gave it so freely. He was attracted to me, of course. But he was attracted to lots of women. Maybe Sylvia Huntington had something to do with it. Maybe he was giving me the support he would have liked to have given to her. In the end, his reason didn't matter. I was glad for his help.

When I released him from my grip, he sat grinning in an impish way that said he was ready to create some mischief of his own.

"So, what do we do next?"

The question was obvious, but as to the answer, I hadn't a clue, unless it was to wait for the axe to fall. Then I remembered the Apothecary shop and suggested we start there.

When he heard the suggestion, he took hold of my shoulders and forced me to look him.

"What Apothecary shop? What are you talking about?"

I remembered that Tom knew nothing about the business card and what followed, so I told him. Again he listened without interruption but exploded when I'd finished.

"My God, Tara, from now on, you have to tell me everything. No more secrets. Don't you realize what could have happened? Why didn't you call me? I'd have gone with you."

"I tried to call but you were with Ellen and wouldn't answer your phone."

Tom looked crestfallen and rubbed the back of his head with one hand.

"Yeah, I forgot to charge it. And yes, I should have checked with you before I went off with Ellen. Sorry. It won't happen again. Let's get some breakfast, then head for that shop. But first, let's find a dictionary. I want to know what a Necromancer is."

CHAPTER IX

"Here it is: *Necromancy.*" Tom and I had our heads together as we sat in the hotel coffee shop, waiting for our breakfasts to arrive. We were pouring over a dictionary the concierge had provided. "*The prediction of the future by the supposed communication with the dead...*" Tom's green eyes looked skeptical. "That's a crock. I don't know how that guy managed his illusions, but I don't believe this."

"You don't think what happened last night was real?"

"Course I don't. Do you?" When I didn't answer him, he continued to make his point. "Look, Tara, we were hypnotized somehow. I don't know how, but I aim to find out. Let's not give the guy more credit than he deserves."

"I wish you could have been with me in the antechamber, Tom." I didn't want to argue but I couldn't be dismissive either. "She was in the room. She was real. He couldn't have made her up because I know her mannerisms, the way she talks with her hands and arches her eyebrows to cut off an argument. It wasn't an illusion."

"Listen to yourself. The guy's got you believing in him already. Look," Tom waved his finger at me, "You may have been in that room, but the room was in your head. He used you and I'm going to prove it."

Tom closed the dictionary when breakfast arrived and dug into his plate of sausages and eggs. I didn't share his appetite. The best I could do was play with my oatmeal.

"But, what if he can talk to the dead?" I went on after I'd eaten all the raisins in my cereal. What then?"

My companion smirked as he looked up from his plate.

"Don't go crazy on me, Tara, please. Let's stick with a rational assumption. People can't talk to the dead."

"That's what you say, but what if you're wrong and Orlando's for real? What are we getting ourselves into?"

"Orlando?" Tom squinted over his sausage-loaded fork. "Is that the guy's first or last name?"

"That's what he calls himself, 'Orlando.'"

"Why? Can't he afford two names?" Tom chuckled.

Refusing to be pulled in by his joke, I continued to look serious.

"You were with him in the void. Did he say anything? Maybe we could find a clue there."

Before answering, Tom shoved the sausage into his mouth and chewed.

"He didn't say anything, as far as I can remember. Oh yeah. He did say one thing. I was to keep my mouth shut. After that, I woke up in your bed."

"What's this about Tara's bed?"

Tom and I glanced up to find David and Susan standing over us. Ellen was in tow, standing behind the pair. Seeing Tom and I together, her expression turned sour and she marched off to join Anne Miller and her husband at their table. Tom watched her go, his lips forming an apology which he was given no chance to deliver. Meanwhile, David pulled up two chairs from another table so that he and Susan could join us.

"Say again," David grinned as he sat down. "What were you doing in Tara's bed?"

Susan eased into the remaining chair, looking like a bird with a worm in its beak.

"Yes, tell us all. We're friends, aren't we?"

I decided to set them both straight.

"Don't get carried away, you two. Tom dropped by to say goodnight and passed out on my bed. That's all that happened."

Susan looked disappointed but David wasn't buying my story.

"Since when does Tom drop by to say good night? That's new isn't it?" He folded his arms and waited, which surprised me because prying into other people's business was something he normally didn't do. Susan was rubbing off on him. I didn't like being pressed to the wall and my answer reflected my impatience.

"Listen, David, if Tom and I had an announcement, we'd make it. We'll leave the keeping of secrets to Susan and you."

Susan reacted as though I'd slapped her.

"That's not fair, Tara. You know why we're keeping quiet. I thought you agreed."

Her chin wiggled with emotion. Any minute now, there'd be tears. I reached across the table and squeezed Susan's hand to stop them.

"I'm sorry. I'm being cranky. Tom was sprawled out on the bed, so I had to make do with a chair. I didn't get much sleep."

I'd counted on Susan's sympathy and got it, noticing as I did, that she had shadows under her eyes as well. I hoped the pair hadn't been quarreling.

"That's okay, Tara," she squeezed back. "I understand. Tom probably snored the whole time."

"Hey! I don't snore." Tom sat up in his chair, his eyes twinkling. "Spend the night with me and you'll find out."

Susan's cheeks burned a bright pink but David seemed amused by Tom's pass. Maybe he enjoyed seeing his girlfriend speechless. The ice broken, the four of us enjoyed our meal together, laughing and joking as we'd done many times before.

As the waiter cleared our empty plates, Tom broke away to make his peace with Ellen. I knew he had to apologize. He didn't like hurting people so I watched him go without pangs of jealousy.

Half an hour later, we rendezvoused in the lobby. Tom was waiting with a taxi, anxious to check out the Apothecary shop. We were headed for the sidewalk when Alec called out to us.

"Where are you both off to?" His eyes seemed to be appraising me as he approached. "Susan tells me you didn't get much sleep last night. Let me look at you. Are you sure you should be going out?"

Finding it hard to hide my exasperation, my hand drifted to one hip.

"I'm fine. I just wish you'd tell Susan she's not my mother. We're going out for some fresh air. Isn't that what you suggested earlier? I promise not to do anything strenuous, okay?"

Alec clucked a bit more but knew better than to keep too tight a reign on his dancers. We needed to have fun as well as dance.

"Just don't be late for the theater." He scowled a little as he shooed us off on our adventure. We didn't wait for him to have any more misgivings and hurried to our taxi.

The ride to the Apothecary shop seemed shorter than I remembered it, perhaps because I was already familiar with the way or because I was in a better frame of mind than before. When we arrived the scene was familiar except no children played on the pavement and only two women were sitting on a stoop, both of them smoking.

Tom didn't make my mistake when we stepped from the car. He told the driver, who spoke English, that he was to wait and would be paid when we were done with his services. The driver didn't argue and kept the meter running.

The Apothecary shop looked dark, almost abandoned as we approached. Tom knocked on the door, then cupped his hands at the window to peer inside. Seeing no movement, he knocked again, louder this time so that one of the women on the stoop called out to us in Hungarian.

Neither Tom nor I understood what she'd said, so the taxi driver came to our assistance. He explained that the shop's proprietor had been taken to the hospital. The woman who had spoken wasn't sure which one, but she said the man's name was Demeter Dobos. As far as she knew, he had no relatives in the city whom we could contact.

"How many hospitals are in the area?" Tom asked the cabbie.

"Public, private or community?"

Tom turned to me for instruction. When I shrugged, he sighed and looked hopeless.

"This could take all day, Tara, and we haven't got all day."

"Maybe we should go back to the hotel and make phone calls. That would be faster."

The moment I'd spoken, I regretted my words. On that beautiful fall morning, the last thing I wanted to do was spend it in my hotel room, making calls to hospitals. Tom seemed to agree and came up with an alternative suggestion.

"Tell you what, let's find a bookstore first. I want to find out more about Necromancy. The dictionary didn't tell us much. We can stop for coffee and a little sun before going back to the hotel. You know what they say about all work and no play?"

Hearing him, the driver volunteered that there was an excellent bookstore not far from where we were staying. We asked him to drive us there and he agreed. After thanking the Hungarian woman for her information, we climbed back into the cab and sped off.

By the time we got back into the center of town, the streets were alive with pedestrians. The faces of the strollers appeared relaxed on this Saturday morning, not pinched as they might have been during the week. Even their dogs ambled along beside them without straining at their leashes.

We paid the driver and were pleased that he'd dropped us off in front of a quaint-looking shop. Tables and chairs were scattered outside, all of them occupied by customers who sat reading over coffee and pastries. It was the perfect spot for a sojourn.

Our first duty was to find a book on Necromancy (one written in English of course) which we guessed might be tricky. Elbowing our way into the crowded entry, we hoped to find a knowledgeable clerk to help us. Inside, I paused to admire the wooden floors and beamed interior of the place. The walls were a rough plaster that bore the creamy patina of a long history, and dust was everywhere, as expected.

That so many books could be precariously-shelved from floor to ceiling was remarkable, if not a little dangerous, but the arrangement gave the business its character and made it seem as if we were visiting a private rather than commercial venture. To spend an hour or two browsing among the rows of reading material in this two-storied establishment would have been a delight, but Tom and I were on a mission.

The clerks behind the counter were being kept busy by a line of customers, so we decided to search through the stacks on our own. One elderly gentleman looked as if he might be a frequent visitor to the place. The book bag slung across his shoulder gave him the air of a scholar or possibly a professor. Tom decided to ask the man for his help and addressed him in English. The reply he received was muttered in words neither of us could understand, and then, looking cross, the stranger hurried away, as if he'd been set upon by fruit-flies.

Tom scratched his head as he watched him disappear.

"What's his problem, I wonder."

With no one to help us, I suggested we split up. Tom could check the upstairs while I continued to browse on the main floor. He agreed and hurried up the wooden steps, two at a time, leaving me to meander on my own.

As expected, most of the titles available were in a foreign language, but I stopped to admire them all the same. Many of them were old and beautifully-bound. Some of them had gilded edges and marbled papers and as I seemed to be in the section on folklore, I stopped to thumb through some of the illustrated pages. I was admiring the pictures in one volume I knew was a collection of Grimm's Fairytales when I thought I felt the ground beneath my feet move -- just for a second and so lightly that I could have imagined it. Looking about me, I saw no evidence that there'd been a tremor, so I returned to my book, giving the incident no further thought. As I stood examining the work of Arthur Rackham, I felt the tremor again. This time I knew something was amiss because the stack beside me teetered precariously. At any moment, the entire wall of manuscripts – large, small, thick and thin – could come tumbling down upon my head.

Behind me was an alcove, the entrance to a restroom. I leaped for it, taking shelter there just as an avalanche of books came crashing to the ground. The noise was ear-splitting and when I realized I'd had a near miss, my knees began to shake.

In the little time I had to regain myself, I heard footsteps rushing toward me. The first to appear was a man I judged to be somewhere in his mid-thirties, of average height, and elegantly dressed in a blue suit, his brown hair immaculately coifed. He looked stricken when he saw me.

"Are you all right? Are you injured?" He spoke in English though with an Italian accent. Perhaps he'd heard my cry for help when I'd first scrambled to safety.

Though I was still shaken, I assured him I'd suffered no harm and when he heard me, he looked relieved, admitting that when he'd come running he was afraid of what he might find.

"You sounded so terrified," he explained.

As he bent down to retrieve my purse, several clerks rounded the corner, looking non-plussed, as he had done. I assured them, as well, that I'd suffered no harm and they visibly relaxed, though I had to repeat myself several times before I could convince them I wasn't injured.

About this time, Tom appeared at the top of the stairs, his complexion the color of whey as he peered down at the chaos below. He didn't rush to my side as I might have expected but remained where he was, hovering above my head like a lost spirit. Finally, I waved him down and watched as he descended each stair as if it were a bog. By the time he reached us, the clerks had cleared away enough debris to make room for Tom and I and my new friend to stand facing one another. I was about to begin introductions when the man beside me raised his hand.

"Introductions aren't necessary, I assure you. I know who you are, dancers with the Seattle Ballet. Congratulations. You appear to have taken Europe by storm." The Italian looked around as he spoke as if looking for someone. "My grandfather was here a minute ago. He'd have loved to meet you but he seems to have disappeared. Perhaps the noise scared him off. I shall have to find him, so you must excuse me. Before I go, let me give you this." The man reached into his jacket pocket and withdrew his business card. "I'll be in Milan next week, in time to see you perform. So this isn't goodbye; only arrivederci."

That said, the stranger disappeared behind a row of books while I looked down to read the inscription written on the card: *Antonio Moretti, purveyor of fine wines.*

. . .

Once Antonio Moretti had gone, Tom exhaled as if for the first time in several minutes.

"Do you think he knew who I was? I've filled out since I was a kid, but I got the feeling he remembered me."

"Tom, do you realize I might have been killed just now? I know seeing him after all these years comes as a shock but what about me? Do you care if I'm all right?"

"Of course I do." Tom stared at me as if I had warts popping out all over my face. "You're not getting my drift. What happened just now wasn't an accident. You heard the clerks say it's never happened before. Moretti shows up and it does. That's no coincidence. The guy's a killer, remember."

"Are you crazy?" I shot back. "I've no connection to Sylvia Huntington. You do."

"That's right," Tom's ears were turning red as he made his point. "He could have seen us together and decided to settle an old score."

"That's a stretch isn't it? Especially when you're not even sure he recognized you?"

"Maybe," the redhead muttered. "But it's kind of funny. *'Of all the gin joints in all the towns in the world,'* this guy walks into ours."

He had a point, but I didn't want to dwell on it. I could only focus on one mysterious stranger at a time.

"Come on," I said, taking his hand. "The book can wait. You promised me coffee. After what's happened, I could use a shot of caffeine."

We exited the bookstore and stood a moment adjusting our eyes to the bright sunlight. Luckily, a couple vacated a table nearby, so Tom threw his pea-jacket over one of the chairs and went back inside for our drinks. I watched him knowing an old wound had been ripped open that morning, but I didn't know how to console him. Sitting in the sun with a cup of coffee was the best idea I could come up with on the spur of the moment.

Ages seemed to pass before he returned; so long in fact, that I wondered if some other pile of books had landed on him. Finally, I saw him coming toward me with two coffee mugs and a book clutched under one arm. The book he tossed on the table as he handed me my coffee. The title read: *Oracles, Magic and Necromancy -- The Ancient Arts of Divination.*

Tom sat down, explaining that after my accident, the clerks were only too happy to be of service. Happily, they'd managed to find a book written in English. He turned to the section on Necromancy and began reading aloud.

The Necromancer's art of divination is to use the dead as oracles, a method which poses great risk to the practitioner, as any rift in the natural order can open doorways to lands beyond the grave. Therefore, in summoning the dead, one must take precautions, as divination is best performed at a time of greatest disorder, midnight being the most suitable. For his protection, the summoner will draw a circle or pentacle on the floor inscribing it with holy words like God, God the Father, God the Son, and will also carry on his person a vial of holy water and a crucifix. After the summoning is ended, the body, if one is used, must be burned or it will retain a semblance of life which will wreak havoc and despair upon all whom it encounters.

When he had finished, he looked up from the pages and seemed puzzled.

"That doesn't sound like our guy. I didn't see a circle. Did you?"

"No, but he did come at midnight. Does the book say anything about drugs or Necromancy spells?"

Tom turned a few pages, then shook his head. Impatient, I took the book from him.

"Here, let me see." I scanned a few more pages but found nothing of any value. In fact, there didn't seem to be much on Necromancy. Most of the text was devoted to Alchemy. The list of hallucinogens in that section seemed both endless and surprising. Walnuts tossed into a fire, for example, could conjure images but they couldn't produce the sensation of flight which Tom and I had experienced.

"None of this helps," I said, allowing my voice to reflect my exasperation. If Orlando did something to us both, I don't see how. He didn't even know you were coming."

Tom nodded as he pushed back his chair and rose, grabbing his pea-jacket.

"Come on. It's nearly noon. We'll think better with food in our stomachs."

We'd barely vacated our seats when a young couple slipped in behind us. I didn't need the skill of divination to know they were besotted with each other. Happiness radiated from them like waves of sunlight. How glorious to be lovers on a bright Saturday morning in Vienna.

CHAPTER X

If Tom and I found no answers to our questions that afternoon, the evening performance of the ballet was a triumph. One could say the company had electrified the audience with enough juice to light up the sky. The Sunday matinee went equally well so that Alec began walking around with a perpetual smile on his face, like a miser anticipating his inheritance.

I wished I could have been happy about our success but the swelling wave of approval left me doubtful. I remembered Yelena Natilova's warning that our success might not be entirely of our making, but a rise to accentuate a fall. We'd worked hard, yes, but was it possible that the public's adulation was in some way the measure of Reznikov's power?

The notion struck me as fantastic, but a few days ago, I'd known nothing of Necromancy or antechambers. How much more didn't I know?

My fears had begun to gain a foothold on my outlook. By the time the company had packed and prepared to catch the night train to Milan, I had sunk into a dark mood. If Susan or David noted a change in my behavior, they said nothing when they joined Tom and me on the taxi ride to the station. Susan kept burbling about La Scala, and how it had been a childhood dream to perform there, while David was silent but smiled the whole time, no doubt pleased about the direction his career was taking. Only Tom, seated at the opposite window, seemed to reflect a mood similar to mine.

He and I had settled nothing in Vienna. We never discovered the hospital where the apothecary had been sent, nor did the Necromancer put in another appearance. Worse, Antonio Moretti had surfaced to cast a deeper pall over both of us.

"You haven't heard a word I've said, have you?" Susan's elbow jabbed at my ribs in an effort to force me to pay attention.

"What? No, I'm sorry. My mind was off somewhere."

She frowned and repeated her remark, speaking slowly as if to someone deaf.

"I said, I thought we should do something together in Milan. Go shopping, maybe or take a bus ride through the city. I'm bored with nightclubs."

Her eyes narrowed as she tossed a sidelong glance in David's direction. He didn't seem to notice as his own were glued on the train schedule.

I knew the atmosphere between them could be intense. Today, it seemed to blow hot and cold. I didn't know why as these days Susan and I hardly ever talked. At the start of our tour, when she spent so much time with David, I admit I'd felt abandoned. But with the recent events going on in my life, I'd become equally guilty. Her suggestion that we spend some time together was one I welcomed.

"How about visiting Leonardo de Vinci's *Last Supper?*" I suggested. "Tickets might be hard to come by, but we could give it a try."

Susan wrinkled her nose at the suggestion. Obviously, she had something different in mind. "Yeah. We could do that. Or we could go shopping. Milan's one of the fashion capitols of the world."

I agreed to her idea, though I thought it was a crazy one. Neither of us had any money.

At the station, we found Forintino and Anunciata Brancaccio waiting to see us off. As good restaurateurs, they'd come bearing food baskets and wine for our journey. We hugged them for their gifts and neither they nor we dancers could suppress our tears.

Finally, the train whistle's blast brought us to the dreaded moment of parting. My friends scurried to find our compartment, but I lingered, reluctant to say goodbye. Nonetheless, the moment arrived when delay was no longer an option. That's when Anunciata slipped an object into my coat pocket. My eyes met hers with a question.

"Don't open it until the train pulls from the station," she winked. "It belonged to my mother who lived ninety-seven years. May it give you an equally long life and a happy one."

She kissed me on the cheek then stepped away so her husband could indulge in one last hug as well.

"Goodbye. Goodbye, dear one," they waved as I boarded the train and opened a window so I could lean out to them. The engine began its slow, steady pull and so, eventually, our hands were forced to let go of one another. I remained at my post, nonetheless, until the Brancaccios looked to be the size of toy soldiers, their arms waving above their heads as I waved back.

When they had disappeared, I sat down, a lump forming in my throat. Missing them, I also thought of my parents. For the first time since the tour began, I wished I was home.

Susan in the seat next to mine, leaned toward me.

"What did she give you? I saw her slip something into your pocket."

In spite of my mood, I smiled.

"You don't miss much do you?"

"Not when it comes to presents."

She snuggled closer for a good view as I dug into my coat for the small package. Whatever it contained, it had been carefully wrapped with twine, paper and a thick covering of cotton. Inside, was a gold crucifix, about the size of my thumb.

"Oh, that's beautiful," Susan gasped, taking it from me and holding it up for a better view. Tom and David, seated opposite us, leaned forward.

"This is expensive." Tom drew his conclusion from the size of the diamond that served as Christ's halo. "Anunciata gave you this?"

I nodded.

Taking the pendant out of Susan's hands, he fastened the chain about my neck.

"I think you'd better wear it," he said.

He wasn't a religious person, I knew, but I understood what he meant.

• • •

Another clear morning greeted us when we reached the central station in Milan, a building of no particular architectural style, but beautiful in its decorations. If I'd been pressed, I'd have described it as a wedding cake, far too ornate for a transportation hub.

Alec alighted from the train almost before it stopped with Anne and Philip not far behind. The three of them began assigning the youngest in our tour to the host of new families already awaiting their charges. Knowing the routine, the rest of us headed for taxis to take us to our various hotels.

The ride took us past the Central Duomo with its gothic spires. La Scala was nearby where we were to perform on Thursday evening. I admit, the merest glimpse of the opera house filled me with awe, not only because of its history and its recent renovations, but also because in pure morning light, the plaza and the surrounding buildings looked like a painting by Constable.

Alec caught up with us not long after we'd checked into the hotel and were seated in the restaurant awaiting breakfast. As we'd had an uncomfortable night on the train, he suggested rest might be the first order of business, reminding us that we were invited to a reception that evening. He admitted he had no intention of following his own advice, however. After some eggs and sausages, he was headed for La Scala to meet with the manager and tour the facility. A few of the technicians were to accompany him. Anne and Philip, who'd performed at the theatre before the renovations, had asked to come, too. They wanted to see what changes had been wrought.

Susan thought Alec's suggestion a good one and, after her meal, headed for her room. David it seems, had other plans. He'd roped Tom into joining him to check out the locations of some nightspots he'd heard about. I wasn't invited he said because, like Susan, I needed my rest.

I didn't argue because I wasn't interested in accompanying them anyway, but I did wonder who made David my nanny.

With everyone off in their separate directions, I decided to go mine. As it was another fine autumn day, I stood outside the hotel, a little money jingling in my pocket, wondering which way to walk. The whole of Milan lay stretched out before me. I could attempt to see *The Last Supper* or failing that, I could consult the travel book my parents had given me. I knew I wasn't far from the Naviglio quarter with its plethora of cafés, shops and canals. At first, I considered going in that direction but with the Central Duomo in my line of vision, its impressive structure dominating the skyline, I headed for it.

If the structure's exterior spoke of grandeur, it failed to prepare me for what I would find inside. My impression, as I entered, was one of color and airiness. The light flowing from the stained glass windows threw patterns on the multicolored floors, providing me with the sensation of wandering through a vast flower-market. Because I had entered through the central nave, my eyes were drawn upward by rows of gothic columns, around which several statues were clustered.

Five additional naves and side apses were also within my line of sight, each heavily-ornamented, so that the sensation I had was one of peering through an ever-changing kaleidoscope, its ornate designs too dizzying to contemplate for long.

I decided to join several tourists who were headed toward an elevator that would take them to the rooftop. There, my guidebook promised, I would enjoy a 360-degree view of Milan with the Alps in the background.

The conveyance was crowded, but everyone was cheerful despite the injury done to a few toes that were stepped upon. Fortunately, the ride was short and, when the door of the elevator sprang open, we spilled out into the chilly air like so many billiard balls. One man, his hat caught by a playful breeze, performed several twists and turns before retrieving it, much to the amusement of those around him. After that, most of us turned our attention to other points of interest within the panorama of the beautiful city sprawled out before us.

Some visitors had already arrived, standing in clumps with their backs to the newcomers as they pointed cameras at the far horizon. A pang of loneliness overcame me as I saw so many happy faces. I would have liked to have had someone beside me, someone with whom to share this experience.

"It's a beautiful view, isn't it?"

The voice behind me was near enough so that I was forced to spin around, and there I saw the last person I expected to meet on that rooftop.

"You? Where have you been? Tom and I looked everywhere for you in Budapest."

"Why so cross? Aren't you happy to see me?"

I ignored Orlando's question and asked one of my own, unable to hide my irritation.

"Didn't you realize we'd be in a state of shock? Or don't you take any responsibility for your actions? How did you find me, anyway?"

Orlando continued to look taken aback. I suspect he'd anticipated a warm reception, not the scalding one he'd received.

"I'm sorry, Tara. I didn't think. You see, my friend was sick and..."

"Oh, please," I stamped my foot in protest. "You can be more original than that, can't you?"

"It's true," he insisted, his eyes wide with innocence. "You met Demeter. He was the apothecary who directed you to Zentralfriedhoff. You noticed he was very ill then, didn't you?"

I nodded that I did and he went on.

"Well, he was like a father to me and, knowing he feared death, I decided to walk with him part way. I think I helped because, as he was about to cross-over, he turned and waved, as if to say he knew he'd be all right."

Orlando's voice choked, unable to go on with his story, and for the first time since we'd met, I saw him as a person, like the rest of us, capable of raw emotion.

"I'm so sorry." I reached out to give him some assurance by touching his arm. "I should have guessed something important had happened. It's just that Tom and I needed some answers and we couldn't find you. I'm glad you could help your friend, truly. But you can see him again if you want to, can't you? I mean, you're a

Necromancer, after all."

A doleful smile broke across Orlando's lips. He must have found my ignorance amusing.

"It doesn't work that way, I'm afraid. I don't summon spirits. They summon me."

"What do you mean?"

He peered around and seeing the many people nearby, he suggested we go somewhere private where we could talk. He recommended a little restaurant he liked where we could have lunch.

"It's a little walk," he warned. "But we'll have worked up an appetite by the time we arrive."

I shook my head, not ready to go off with this man of whom I knew little and remained suspicious.

"First tell me how you found me. I didn't know I was coming here until I started walking."

Orlando smiled and said that part was easy. He'd followed me from my hotel. Having revealed his secret, he looked at me as if he expected to be exonerated, but I still had questions.

"How did you know where I was staying? There are lots of hotels in Milan."

His expression shifted from amusement to disappointment.

"You really should trust me, Tara. Didn't your teacher tell you that?"

I ignored the question. I was determined to get some answers and felt I deserved them.

"Tom thinks you drugged us that night in Vienna. What's your explanation if you didn't?"

"Look," he replied, his tone a little exasperated. "Let's suppose that somehow I did manage to drug you. How did I manage Tom? I didn't know he was coming. No magician's that good. And I'm not a magician."

As I'd used the same argument with Tom, I found it hard to refute his. Still, I wasn't ready to cave in.

"You keep answering my questions with a question. That's pretty annoying. What I want to know is how you knew where I'd be staying. Is that so hard?"

Orlando shook his head and, for the first time, seemed to take me seriously.

"No, that's not so hard. If you must know, Forintino told me."

Forintino Brancaccio? Y-You know him?"

"Of course. He's one of Vienna's finest restaurateurs. A Necromancer has to eat, like everyone else. I'm hungry by the way. Can we have lunch, please?"

Ballet Noir

• • •

The restaurant Orlando had chosen bordered one of Milan's canals. The day was becoming warm, so we chose to sit outside under a table shaded by an umbrella. From there, we enjoyed the passing scene: boats, pedestrians, and cooing pigeons. When the waiter arrived to recite the day's specials, Orlando offered to order for the both of us. I agreed but cautioned that I didn't like fish. I'd grown up in a city surrounded by water, but I'd never acquired a taste for anything with fins. My companion nodded his understanding and then spoke to the waiter in fluent Italian.

Afterwards, he told me he'd ordered lasagna with cheese, tomato and mushrooms to be accompanied with chunks of crusty bread and a carafe of red wine.

"I hope you don't mind that I kept the menu simple. The palate shouldn't be confused with too many flavors. Do you agree?"

"I don't think much about what I eat," I admitted. "At home, I'm always on the run between my classes at Seattle University and my dance schedule. I live on fast food, mostly; tacos, hamburgers, that sort of thing."

"But never fish and chips?"

I smiled as I shook my head.

"How about you? Any special likes or dislikes?"

Orlando thought a moment before answering.

"Asparagus. I know it's considered a delicacy, but I won't eat it."

"Me either," I smiled, glad to know we had something in common. "Actually, I'm not big on vegetables. Give me a hamburger and French fries any day."

"And yet you stay so slim. How do you manage it?"

"Dancing. Alec, he's our Artistic Director, says when I stop dancing I'll grow fat as a pig."

"It could happen."

"I know, but I'm not going to worry about that now. I want to enjoy myself."

"That's the luxury of being young, I suppose."

"Don't sound so superior. You're not that much older than I am. How old are you? Thirty-three? Thirty-four?

"About that."

"Which is it?"

He leaned forward as if to share a secret.

"Actually, I'm sixteen, but I've eaten so many tacos and hamburgers, I look older."

"Be serious." I threw my napkin at him not caring that it fell to the ground. He picked it up and handed it to me.

"There are twelve years between us," he said earnestly. "I'm thirty-three."

"That's not much," I told him, but he shook his head to disagree.

"Twelve years is a lot. In twelve years, you may be fat as a pig."

We went on talking in this light-hearted way while our meal was served, careful to skirt topics that were important but might spoil the good time we were having under the Italian sun. Eventually, however, the wine loosened my tongue and I couldn't contain my curiosity.

"How is it you do what you do? I mean does a person study to be a Necromancer?"

"Study?" Orlando squinted at me as if I confessed to being a car thief. "Lord no. It's a natural affliction. When I was young, I thought everyone talked to the dead. I didn't know I was different until I was about eight or nine. That's when my parents moved to Lichtenstein."

"Lichtenstein? So that's why you have that funny accent."

Orlando wrinkled his forehead.

"I don't understand."

"Not funny, 'ha ha.'" I mean your accent's hard to identify. But go on, tell me about Lichtenstein."

"Even with my funny accent?"

"Yes, even so."

"Once upon a time," Orlando began as if he were telling a bedtime story, "my parents moved to Lichtenstein. It was near the end of summer and I was lonely because I missed my former playmates. But one day, I met a boy who said he was my neighbor and as he was about my age, we got on very well, though there were times when he looked unhappy. One day, I asked him why and he told me his parents had moved away and left him. He missed them very much and wondered what he'd done wrong. Unfortunately, none of the neighbors would tell him where they'd gone. In fact they ignored him and he assumed it was meant to be a further punishment. I was the first person he'd talked to in a long time. He said his name was Derrick Lister and that in the fall, if I liked, we could walk to school together."

"I thought his parents must be very cruel and told my mother the story. She turned so pale when she heard me, I thought she might faint. There was no boy next door, she said, shaking her head vehemently. The family had moved away two years earlier and the house remained empty as no one would buy it. She insisted that I say nothing to anyone about what I'd told her."

"That night, I heard her talking to my father. She sounded frightened and my father didn't look happy, either. Soon after, we moved again, to a house on the other side of the village. They never spoke of the old house after that."

"When school started in the fall, I'd hoped to see Derrick Lister again, but he never appeared. I mentioned his name to a chum one day and he told me Derrick Lister was dead. He'd been murdered three years prior by an itinerant worker, a pedophile, who was hanged for his crime. After the verdict, the family moved away and no one in the village would buy the house, so it stood vacant and falling into disrepair."

"After hearing the story, I went back to my old house, one day, and found Derrick Lister alone in our former garden. I told him what had happened and that he he'd done nothing wrong. His parents hadn't abandoned him. They could no longer hear or see him. In a way, he had abandoned them. When he'd heard all that I had to say, he looked happy. He hadn't been bad after all. When he realized that, a door appeared in the sky and my friend went through it, turning once to wave goodbye. I never saw him again but from that time forward, I always knew I was different."

When Orlando had finished speaking, I didn't know how to reply. I was moved by his story and tears prickled my eyes as I tried to hold them back. All I could think about was the terrible burden he carried on his shoulders. I wondered if I could accept such a sad responsibility. To spend one's life living among the dead wasn't a pleasant prospect and I doubted I could do it. Suddenly, I understood how lonely he must feel, never being able to share his burden for fear of being thought mad. That he had shared his secret with me was touching, and I knew he was revealing himself in the hope I could learn to trust him. In a way, he'd succeeded for I had begun to pity him at least.

I suppose it was natural for me to ask if he saw ghosts among us, at the restaurant. He seemed to take my question seriously and swiveled his head from side to side, taking in the surroundings.

"No," he answered at last. "I don't see any ghosts. I guess that means the food here hasn't killed anyone."

He laughed heartily and I didn't mind because I was glad he could see some humor in his circumstances. I answered in kind.

"Maybe you've lost your touch, that's all." His reply was serious this time.

"I think that would be great."

I understood what he was saying but remembered what my teacher had told me, that not all Necromancers were eager to help. I asked him why he was.

"Why not?" he shrugged. "Most spirits find their way on their own, but some, like Derrick Lister, need a little help. I don't mind. Your teacher's summoning was a little different, though. She's the first to call me from the other side. I assume she had a powerful reason."

"Didn't she didn't tell you?"

"No. Maybe she wanted you to do that."

Orlando waited for my answer and with his eyes looking so intent, I didn't hesitate.

"She thinks I'm in danger, possibly from a former enemy of hers. She wasn't certain."

Orlando nodded, accepting the situation as normal.

"She must love you very much because in summoning me, she exerted a great will. We must take her warning seriously."

"Yes, but how can you help? The man she suspects is alive. That's not your area of expertise, is it?"

Orlando leaned across the table and took hold of my hand as if to provide reassurance.

"Apparently your teacher thinks it is. We both have to trust her and play the hand we've been dealt. I can't tell you anything more. This is all new to me, too."

"Okay, how do I know you won't disappear when I need you most, like in Vienna. You may be a Necromancer and can do all the things you say can, but when you keep appearing and disappearing, I don't know where I am."

He let go of my hand and probed into the folds of his voluminous coat to pull out one of his cards. Next, he wrote something on the back and handed it to me.

"I'll always know if you're in trouble, but if it makes you feel better, I've given you my cell phone number."

CHAPTER XI

After lunch, Orlando walked me back to the hotel. Tom was standing on the pavement outside. When he saw the Necromancer, he winced as though someone had stepped on his toe.

"So, what happened in Vienna?" he asked when we are near enough to hear him. "Tara and I looked everywhere for you. Do you know that?"

"It's all right, Tom," I said, placing myself between the two men. "He had his reason. I'll explain later."

My words fell on deaf ears. Tom continued to glare at the Necromancer.

"So when did you blow into town?"

Orlando turned toward me ignoring Tom as Tom had ignored me.

"I enjoyed the morning. Let's do it again, sometime." Orlando bent down to give my cheek a peck, then he strolled away, probably aware that Tom's gaze was boring into the back of his head.

. . .

The four-star hotel where the reception and dinner were to be held was near the public gardens with a small courtyard of its own. The three-storied exterior looked old, but the lobby suggested a recent remodeling. The walls were white and the furnishings, a muted brown and beige. A few guests were ensconced in the leather chairs, reading the paper or glancing at their watches as if waiting for someone.

Fresh from our taxis, Alec and the rest of us were directed to a room that was also a clinical white, but decorated with classical prints to give the place some color. Most of the guests had arrived before us and were holding glasses of champagne. Our hostess, Madame Natalya Lazaremko, hurried forward as we entered. As on the previous occasion, she had dressed to be the center of attention. Her gown was a long-sleeved jersey sheath, obviously by Pucci; its purple background ornamented with multi-colored flowers in gaudy hues. Her black hair, which was piled high upon her head, appeared to be held in place by a single peacock feather. Despite my conservative taste, I had to admit I was dazzled by her.

Alec tried to explain our tardiness, but Madame was in no mood to hear it.

"What matters is that you've arrived, at last. Now come with me. I have someone I want you to meet."

She took hold of Alec's arm to lead him away, giving him barely enough time to shrug out of his coat. Tom and I followed, a little behind, because we weren't sure we'd been included in her remarks. Ahead, three men stood talking to one another in a jocular fashion, as if someone had just told a good joke. Madame Lazaremko, with Alec in tow, sallied into their midst and made no apology for her interruption. Tom and I halted on the outside of the circle, our gaze fixed on the face of Antonio Moretti.

Allow me to introduce our prima ballerina, Tara Bentley, and Tom Dunne, who dances the role of Benno in our production," Alec said, waving us forward, after his own introduction.

Moretti extended his hand to me, his dark eyes flashing with the pleasure of having surprised me. "I must confess, Mr. Borden, that this young lady and I are already acquainted. We met in Vienna."

Alec snapped to attention and gave me a *why didn't you tell me?* look. When it came to any important connections, he didn't like being kept in the dark.

Moretti went on to explain.

"She didn't know who I was and the time wasn't right for a full explanation of who I was. She'd had an unpleasant experience in the bookstore when we met. A load of books nearly fell on her and I came to see if she needed assistance. Fortunately, no harm was done." Moretti paused to address me directly. "Did you find the book you were looking for, after all that?"

"The one on Necromancy? Yes. Thank you."

"Necromancy?" Alec blinked as if he were seeing spots before his eyes. "Since when did you take an interest in Necromancy, Tara? That's not stuff to be filling your head with."

"More to the point," Madame Lazaremko cut in. "What were you doing in Vienna, Antonio?"

Her possessive tone didn't seem to faze the man.

"Have you forgotten, Ludmila? Grandfather and I were attending the wine conference. Why should that concern you in any case?"

A touch of frost was in the air after this last exchange and the two men who'd been present before we arrived mumbled something about needing to refill their glasses. They disappeared quickly after that and I would have liked to join them.

Madame took no note of their departure, but fixed her gaze upon me as if I were guilty of having set a trap for Moretti. I stared back in all innocence and so she dropped her gaze, admitting to those of us who remained that she'd forgotten about her godson's trip to Vienna.

"Godson?" Alec's tone was unctuous as he struggled to return the atmosphere to one of conviviality. "Surely not. You're far too young, Ludmila. You barely qualify to be Moretti's sister."

Egregious as his compliment was, it brought a spot of joy into the older woman's cheeks, even as she protested his was flattery. Nonetheless his words bought him enough good will so that he ventured to ask if Antonio Moretti might be our mysterious benefactor. The man addressed looked confused.

"I'm sorry," he said, frowning a little. "I assumed you knew. The man behind your tour isn't me, but my grandfather."

Madame Lazaremko chimed in at once, as if to correct her godson.

"I don't think you should scatter his involvement about willy-nilly, Antonio. You know how he covets his privacy."

"In this case, I think we can make an exception," Moretti countered. "After all, if we're to do business together..."

"Business together?" Alec looked so surprised, he almost stood on tiptoes. "You mean the question of another grant has been settled?"

"That conclusion would be premature," Madame Lazaremko replied coldly. "After all, the tour isn't over."

"But Ludmila, the reviews have been wonderful," her godson objected. He looked as if he was about to say more but our hostess cut him off.

"Don't interfere, Antonio. You know nothing of this matter, let alone have attended a single performance."

Not wanting to be the cause of tension, Alec withdrew his question. "Of course, you're right, Ludmila. We have to earn our stripe. At least now you can tell us who the fellow is?"

Having no reason to decline, Madame Lazaremkov spit out the name.

"Reznikov. Vladimir Reznikov."

Tom and I stood frozen in place when we heard her, our worst fears confirmed. If he was feeling as I was, he would have liked to run away, deep into the night, screaming. Fortunately for us, Alec saw nothing of our reaction. He was too busy staring at the ceiling, as if, like a cobweb, he might find a memory there.

"We're not talking about a former dancer, are we? The guy who tried to kill himself... Wasn't that the story?"

"Vladimir did dance with the Bolshoi at one time," Madame answered, her voice constrained. "He'll be flattered to know you remember, it being so long ago."

"He must be in his seventies by now, isn't he?"

"Seventy-five, to be precise," Moretti volunteered. "But he continues to take an interest in ballet."

Tom suddenly found his voice and it wasn't friendly.

"Yeah, but why us? Why a company in Seattle? Was that you're doing?"

Alec looked like he wanted to throttle his dancer who, by his manner, threatened to gum up the works.

"Have you two met before?"

"Yeah. I was with Tara at that bookstore. By now, Tom's complexion approached that of a ripe tomato.

For his part, the Italian looked puzzled. Aware of the animosity directed at him, he stood for a moment, as if scanning his memory for some connection between them. Apparently, he could find none because eventually he shrugged, mothballing his concern as if it were a winter garment and addressed the question put to him.

"I had no part in my grandfather's decision, I can assure you. But either Mr. Borden or Miss Bentley can raise the question when they meet him in Tuscany. My reason for being here is to extend his invitation for them to stay at the villa a few days to talk about mutual opportunities."

When he heard what Moretti had said, Alec rubbed his hands together like a man about to sit down to a steak dinner. He opened his mouth to accept when Tom stepped in again, sounding like a barking dog.

"What's he want with Tara? Alec makes the decisions, not her."

Alec gaped at his dancer, not knowing what to make of his bizarre behavior. As the skin above his shirt collar began to turn red, I knew I had to step in.

"Tuscany sounds wonderful, but I'm afraid I can't accept. My term at university starts soon. I have to get home the minute the tour is over. Sorry."

"I'm afraid the invitation isn't a request, Tara. Think of it as a command performance. If you fail to appear, I'm afraid Vladimir will be too disappointed to think of anything else." Madame Lazaremko almost looked happy as she delivered her information.

Alec turned to look at me, his complexion having changed chameleon-like from rosy to pale.

"Come on, Tara. There's such a thing as late registration. Your dad's a professor. He can pull a few strings. Of course Mr. Reznikov wants to meet you,

you're our swan. You can't let everyone down."

When I failed to respond to his guilt ploy, he tried another.

"Look, you don't have to decide this instant. Talk to Susan. Maybe she'd like to come to Tuscany with us." His eyes met those of Moretti, who seemed to be more malleable than Madame Lazaremko. "That would be all right, wouldn't it? If one of our other dancers came too?"

The grandson nodded, much to Alec's relief.

"There, you see. Susan can come with us."

"I don't want Susan," I replied petulantly. "I want Tom."

I'd spoken in haste, without stopping to realize how my remark would be taken, but Alec was not one to let the grass grow under his feet.

"Okay. Tom can come." He glanced at Moretti, hoping to receive approval despite the tension he'd seen between the two men earlier.

The grandson wasn't happy with the suggestion. He scowled as if he'd been invited to have lunch in a sewer, but eventually, he demurred.

"If it would make Miss Bentley more comfortable, then of course. It won't solve her school problem, however." Turning to me, he explained he understood my concern as he'd been a student for a term in San Francisco. "That's where I earned my Master of Wine credential. I still have a few friends from there."

"And some you don't," Tom muttered.

Everyone stopped to ponder the significance of that last remark, but not for long. Always one to avoid an uncomfortable situation, Alec took hold of Madame Larzarmeko's arm so they could circulate among the guests. Once we were alone with Moretti, Tom wasted no time in picking a fight with the Italian.

"What's your game? You could have told us who you were at the bookstore. Had you been following us?"

"Don't be absurd. Why should I follow you? You're not of the least importance to me. It's you who seem to have some business with me. Why don't you spit it out and be done with it?"

"You want to know what's between us. Okay, I'll tell you. Sylvia Louise Huntington. She's between us. Does that ring any bells?"

Moretti looked as if he'd been hit between the eyes with a blunt instrument.

"Of course it rings bells. She was the woman I was going to marry."

"Liar." Tom's complexion was firebox red again. "She'd never have married you. I know because I was her friend. She turned you down and because you couldn't have her, you had her killed."

"Killed?" Moretti reached to steady himself with the back of a nearby chair.

Even so, his eyes looked glazed and out of focus. "You're insane. I wouldn't harm a hair on her precious head. Who are you to make such an accusation? I've never seen you in my life."

Tom stood with his hands clenched and his knees slightly bent, as if ready to spring. Placing my hand on his shoulder, I tried to calm him, but he brushed it off, not looking at me but glaring at Moretti.

"A man like you thinks money can buy anything, but not Sylvia. You couldn't buy her and that's why she's dead. After all these years, it's time you came clean."

Moretti let go of the chair and took a step toward Tom with his nostrils flaring.

"Listen to me, you demented fool, I was in Tuscany when she died. The police said it was an accident. She was in the wrong place at the wrong time, that's all. You think I don't feel guilty because I wasn't there to protect her? Of course I do. When I think of her lying alone in the streets as the blood ran out of her..."

Moretti couldn't go on. His hands clamped over his eyes as if he hoped darkness would expunge an image that tormented him. Bent over as he was, he looked broken, his ribs gasping for air. Then, as if his misery could no longer be contained, he made a sudden leap at Tom's throat.

The fight was on. Tables and chairs flew as if they had wings only to fall back down again, thunderous as cannonballs. "Stop it. Stop it," I screamed. But I might as well have been alone in a cave. Everyone's eyes were riveted on the fight. After a few more chairs took flight, Alec and Philip came running from across the room. Now four men were enjoined in the struggle, two trying to kill each and the other two trying to keep the combatants apart. After much grunting and swearing, the two with good intentions prevailed. Phillip grabbed Tom by his collar and pushed him out of the room and into the street where he was probably shoved into a taxi. Alec, in the meantime, helped Moretti to his feet, then began to right the overturned furniture. His host looked embarrassed.

"Either the man can't hold his liquor or he's a damned fool," he grumbled, loud enough for everyone in the room to hear. Next he adjusted his tie and combed back his hair to make himself presentable, like a man planning to leave. But before he did, he addressed himself to me.

"I'm not a violent man, Miss Bentley, I assure you. Perhaps one day soon, I hope you'll give me a chance to explain." That said, he strode toward the gawkers who parted before him.

I watched him go, not knowing what to think about Sylvia Huntington's murder. I did know she'd been loved by two passionate men.

Alec pulled up a chair and asked me to sit down. He wore a grim expression. Madame Lazaremko had stormed out behind Moretti and he knew the hope of a new grant was in jeopardy. He wanted to know why. What had Tom and Moretti been arguing about? I wasn't going to give him details as I feared it would lead to more unwanted questions. I told him a half-truth that they'd once been in love with the same girl and hadn't gotten over it.

Alec let out a puff of air. I suppose, for him, the story was as old as human life. But that didn't change the passions.

"Well, here's a pretty mess," he exclaimed when he'd heard me out. "Not much I can do about the past, but now that I know the reason for the bad blood between those two, maybe I can salvage something. One thing's for certain, if the invitation to Tuscany holds, Tom isn't going with us."

I rose to my feet, intending to make myself clear by looking Alec in the eye.

"I'll promise you one thing: if he doesn't go, I don't go either."

CHAPTER XII

During Tuesday's rehearsal, Tom kept his distance from everyone, including me. I knew he was embarrassed, so I let him have his space. Alec said he'd talk to him that morning to see if he could clear the air. I suspected he might bring Tom around, being his boss, but he'd face stiff winds with Moretti. At least I hoped so. Their irreconcilable differences gave me an easy out for a trip I never intended to take.

At noon, sandwiches were delivered to the theater. Alec refused to let us wander off as he was dissatisfied with the way rehearsal was going. The weather was pleasant so Susan suggested we eat outside in the plaza. She wanted to invite Tom but I said it wasn't a good idea because Alec wanted to speak to him. Unfortunately, my remark gave her the opportunity to ask me about the previous night.

"You were there, Tara. What happened? People are whispering all sorts of things."

David, who was standing beside her, suggested she leave the subject alone, but he'd have done better to waste his advice on a goldfish. Besides being a gossip, Susan took an interest in people. She liked Tom, especially, because he flirted with her and made her laugh. Naturally, she scowled at David's suggestion.

"Tom's our friend. If he's in trouble, we should help."

Not having an argument to that, David wandered toward the orchestra pit to pick up our sandwiches. While he was gone, Susan pressed me for details.

"Come on, Tara. You were standing right there. What were they arguing about? I won't believe you if you say you don't know."

As I had for Alec, I mumbled something about a quarrel over a girl and hoped that would satisfy, but I should have known better. My explanation was like pouring gasoline onto a fire.

"A girl? Who was it? Do I know her? Mr. Moretti lives in Italy. Tom's never been to Italy before. How could they like the same girl? Was she an exchange student, or something? More to the point, which guy does she like best?"

The questions came so fast, like water from a spigot, that for a while, I wasn't obliged to say anything. Then Susan caught on.

"Well? What gives?"

David returned with our sandwiches at that moment, his face creased with worry.

"Alec is talking to Tom right now. He's got his arms folded across his chest and he doesn't look happy. In fact, both of them looked pissed." He spoke in a whisper as he handed us our lunches, though being far from the wings, the precaution was unnecessary.

"Pissed? Why should Alec be pissed? It's got nothing to do with him. Tom should tell him to mind his own business." As she spoke, Susan rummaged through her sack to make sure she'd received the tuna fish sandwich she'd ordered.

David slapped his forehead with his hand and looked incredulous.

"None of Alec's business? Are you kidding? Tom decks the guy paying for this tour, and it's none of his business?"

Susan rewrapped her sandwich to carry it outside, looking a little smug as she did.

"But he's not the guy footing the bill. He's the grandson."

"Same difference."

"Not really."

Not wanting to hear any more bickering, I rose from my seat and headed up the aisle toward the exit.

"Come on you two. If we don't move, the benches will be taken by the time we get there." Twenty minutes later, Tom found us in the open air, soaking up the sun. His manner was cocky as he squeezed in between Susan and me, behaving as if we'd been keeping the bench warm for him. Perhaps Alec had decided not to give him a dressing down and chose to play the diplomat, instead. If so, would he be as successful with the Italian, I wondered.

Tom pulled a pastrami sandwich from his sack and began eating. David saw it and his eyes grew to the size of bicycle wheels.

"Hey, I ordered pastrami, but I couldn't find it. Maybe that's mine." He took a swipe at the one Tom held in his hand, but the redhead was too quick for him. All David got was a handful of air.

"Too bad," Tom munched happily. "It's mine now."

"You're a cheat. You know that?"

Susan didn't care whose sandwich it was. She was after more juicy stuff.

"Is everything okay, honey?" She put an arm around his shoulder and looked at him with a sympathetic expression. "Because you can tell us if it isn't."

Tom stopped chewing and knowing what she was after, gave her a mischievous grin.

"Thanks honey, but I've got my pastrami sandwich. I couldn't be happier."

After our break, all of us feeling better, we sauntered back toward La Scala. I brought up the rear because I wanted time to myself. I didn't want to think about Tuscany or Moretti or Reznikov. I wanted to experience the world as it was before my dark adventures had begun. This day was a momentous one, despite all that had happened. Soon I'd be performing on one of the great stages of Europe and possibly the center of western culture. My parents had made this possible. They'd sacrificed so much of their own comfort to give me this opportunity. Now that their dream and mine was about to come true, I wanted them with me. I wanted to see pride shining on their faces. Or maybe what I really wanted was to be a child again, with nothing more pressing to do than to finish my homework and practice standing on points.

Tears watered my eyes when I realized how disdainful I'd been of my innocence, always wanting to grow up, always wanting to be independent. Now that I had, a part of me wanted to go back.

Tom noticed I'd fallen behind and joined me.

"Hey, it's going to be okay. Don't worry. All I have to do is apologize and I'm willing to do that. What happens to you is more important than my pride. I'll be with you in Tuscany, that is, if you still want me."

He'd assumed my tears were for him and maybe they should have been rather than for me. Tom was proving to be a brave friend.

"Of course I want you with me, you idiot. But I never said I was going to Tuscany. That's what everybody assumes."

Tom grinned back at me, his smart-alecky self-restored.

"Hey, Tara, don't make me waste a good apology. Anyway, I think we should talk to that Necromancer guy, first. See what he thinks."

Squinting at him, I refused to believe my ears.

"I thought you didn't trust Orlando. What's made you change your mind?"

"I don't trust him. I trust you and me, but I've given what's happened a lot of thought. I don't understand what he did to us in Vienna, but I also don't see what the guy has to gain if it was a con. Let's go along with him for a while. He may have an idea or two. The problem is, we don't know how to find him."

I dried my eyes, feeling less helpless than I had minutes before.

"Have you forgotten? He gave me his cell number."

. . .

At 5 o'clock, we met Orlando at a wine bar some distance from the hotel. We didn't want to risk questions that might arise if someone we knew saw us.

He was waiting in a dark corner of the room, nursing a glass of red wine. Tom ordered two more glasses when we sat down. After a grueling day of rehearsal, I took a couple of sips and began to feel sleepy. I must have dropped off because when I awoke, the two men were squabbling about some soccer match that had taken place the previous day. They sounded like scrapping children so I interrupted to remind them we were meeting to discuss important business.

Once I had their attention, I told Orlando about the invitation to Tuscany. Tom pitched in that he thought we should accept. I argued the opposite. The two of us batted the pros and cons back and forth for a time, while the Necromancer listened. Finally, we ran out of arguments and stopped for breath, hoping to learn what Orlando thought. His opinion was what we'd come for. As usual, he answered my question about whether I should go or not with a question.

"What if you don't go? What if you run back to Seattle? What happens next? Tom heads back to Oakland, and I'm left talking to ghosts in Vienna or somewhere else on the continent. You'll be alone. Are you prepared for that? Or do you imagine Reznikov will get bored and give up his game?"

Tom took a slight offense at the suggestion that he'd leave me on my own, but we both realized Orlando's questions were fair. If Alec didn't get a new infusion of money, there'd be no hope of Tom staying with the company. He'd be forced to return to Oakland.

On the other hand, what could any of us do, even Orlando, if Reznikov was as dangerous as we feared? Tom wasn't shy about asking that question. He wanted to know if the Necromancer was all smoke and mirrors or if his powers were for real?

Orlando pressed his lips together to form a sign of his impatience.

"Look, I'm sorry you don't trust me, but you're the ones who made the phone call."

Tom raised his hand to placate him.

"I know. I know. But if I knew what happened in Vienna, I'd feel better."

"I wish I could satisfy you." The Necromancer sighed as he leaned back in his chair. "I'd feel better, too, but I can't. Lots of things happen in life that are mysteries. That doesn't make them unreal. What about Stonehenge or black holes? We don't know much about them, but they aren't imaginary."

"That's not the same as what happened in Vienna."

"Necromancy isn't science. I'll admit that, if that's what's bothering you."

"Yeah, it's more like hocus-pocus."

Orlando offered a thin smile as he swirled the wine in his glass, watching it make crimson waves.

"I have a great respect for science, but it has its limitations. I can't explain what happened in Vienna in scientific terms. Maybe there is one but until we find it, you'll have to keep an open mind. That's how we learn, isn't it?"

Tom shrugged and appeared to be listening.

"You doubt what happened in Vienna is real. I don't because I've had similar experiences too many times to write them off as a brain tumor or mental illness. All I can say is that some experiences can't be measured or stamped or catalogued."

"So you want me to believe that you whisked Tara and me out of that hotel and off somewhere into space?"

"Whisked may not be the right word. I don't think we went anywhere."

"What do you mean? Something happened – I felt like I was flying."

"I don't doubt that you did, but if a fourth person had entered the room that night, I think that someone would have seen the three of us clinging to each other. That's all."

"Listen, Orlando, my stomach doesn't churn like that when I hug a girl like Tara. I know the difference. Something did happen."

"Okay, let me put it this way. I think our minds shifted to another state while our bodies stayed where they were."

"You mean like, 'Toto, I don't think we're in Kansas anymore?'"

"Yeah, that's right, Tara, sort of a dreamlike state."

Tom's face soured.

"That was no dream we all shared."

"Look, think of a three-way floor lamp," Orlando hurried on. "It can shine at 50 watts, 100 watts or 150 watts. Each turn of the switch, we see the energy jump from one level to the next, but the lamp stays where it is, doesn't it? I think that is what happens in an altered state."

"People aren't light bulbs. I don't see how that can work."

Orlando drew his chair closer to Tom's. If he hadn't convinced the redhead, at least he had his attention.

"Think of it this way. Our bodies are pure energy, just as Einstein wrote in his equation, $E=MC^2$. Our brains are nothing but neurons that communicate with one another through ions. Ions are governed by the laws of quantum physics –

which means they can do a lot of weird things that classical physics never contemplated. In the real world, altered states occur all the time. Waves become particles. Particles become waves..."

"So you're saying our brains shifted energy levels, making it possible for Tara to talk to her teacher?"

"Yes!" Orlando exploded, slapping his hand on the table to indicate his satisfaction. "Yelena sent out a beam that affected our minds, making the shift possible. That's my guess, anyway."

Tom considered the explanation but came up with an objection. If she can alter our state of mind, why does she need you?"

"She tried, Tom," I reminded him. "All those strange cries I heard, those shifting shadows. They were hers, but she couldn't break through. All she accomplished was to leave me thinking I needed a psychiatrist."

"That's the difference between Necromancers and ordinary people," Orlando smiled. "We're not afraid to be a little crazy."

"You're like a conduit or something? You boost the frequency so the dead can break in?"

"Something like that."

Once he understood the concept, Tom's reaction to Orlando was the same as mine.

"Jesus, bro! How do you live with dead people yammering at you? If it happened to me, I wouldn't listen."

Orlando looked up from his wine glass with a melancholy gaze. "Tell me how."

Tom couldn't begin to answer that question and Orlando, seeing the red head turn contrite, took pity on him.

"Look, don't waste your time feeling sorry for me. I meet some interesting people in my line of work. Problem is, they can't write letters of recommendation."

Tom snickered, glad for the relief the joke afforded. But as he leaned back in his chair, his hands jammed in his pant pockets, the earnestness of the gaze he afforded the man seated across the table led me to believe he viewed Orlando with a greater degree of trust than before.

"So what do we do now?" Tom asked after a period of silence. "Maybe we should contact Tara's teacher again. She might have some new information."

Orlando seemed pleased with Tom's enthusiasm. Nonetheless, he was dead set against it. "I know how to receive communications," he explained. "But I've no clue about how to send them. At least, I've never tried."

Tom digested the information before coming back with another question. "So how do these dead people get in touch with you, then? Do they moan? Rattle chains? Ring you up on the telephone?"

Orlando laughed, though he answered Tom in earnest. "They introduce themselves like you and I would at a first meeting. Mostly, they come at midnight, but not always. Anyway, that's not the point. I've never attempted to open an antechamber on my own, not without assistance from a spirit on the other side. Even with the help of Tara's teacher on the night of the ball, I couldn't control the forces. Too many spirits got through."

"What if we tried some hour other than midnight? Would that help?"

Orlando considered my suggestion, then shook his head.

"No, midnight's best. If we're going to initiate contact, it should be at the highest energy point."

Taking Orlando at his word, Tom slapped his large hand on the table. "Great. When do we go?"

CHAPTER XIII

Wednesday's rehearsal might have seemed mundane compared to our plans to make contact with the dead, but, unwittingly, Alec made it a challenge, too. He'd become paranoid about the thought of a negative review. If we were going to have one, he seemed to assume La Scala would be the place. As a consequence, he behaved like someone with a compulsive disorder. David and I were required to rehearse Tchaikovsky's third act *Pas de Deux* so many times, we could have performed it in a coma. Every move, every step, every gesture had to be "just so."

His anxiety lay like sack-cloth and ashes over the entire corps, and we began to doubt our worthiness as performers. By the time we broke for lunch, everyone felt emotionally battered as did our feet.

Given the stress of our performance, I suggested to Tom that we cancel our meeting with Orlando that evening. He agreed and left a message on the Necromancer's cell phone when he failed to get an answer.

Unfortunately, the afternoon rehearsal, when we performed with the orchestra, seemed to go worse than the morning's. The conductor was an intimidating man who looked as if he could upend the universe simply by raising an eyebrow. Alec behaved like a novitiate having an audience with the Holy Father in his presence. He listened to the maestro's comments with his hands pressed together as if in prayer and scarcely dared to look into eyes of the figure who towered over him. As a consequence, Alec's demands on us grew more insistent and beyond human capability. By the time he called his dancers together at 3 o'clock that afternoon, most of us, men and women, were on the verge of exhaustion.

We expected an upbraiding as we gathered around him but were stunned when he decided to shower us with praise instead. We were going to knock La Scala on its ass he said, as he released us to enjoy what was left of the afternoon.

No one needed any prodding to leave the theater. We spewed from its doors like a volcanic eruption, scattering our joyful noise along the main street in our search for food and relaxation.

Susan steered David, Tom and me toward a pastry shop she'd reconnoitered earlier. Today, she was threatening to eat two cream puffs and her weight be damned. I was glad to see her behaving so spiritedly because for most of the morning she'd seemed withdrawn.

Tom and I lagged behind the other two a little to check our cell phones. Sadly, neither of us had received a message from Orlando. Tom looked disgruntled as he shoved his phone into the pocket of his pea-jacket and then hurried to catch up with David and Susan. I remained behind, slowed down by the thought that Alec might need a little relaxation, too. He'd been working as hard as the rest of us. I thought I should ask him to join us. Shouting my intention to Tom, he shouted back that he'd save chairs for Alec and me.

By the time I reached the theater, the atmosphere inside had changed dramatically from the chaos that had existed there fifteen minutes earlier. Alec and the conductor seemed to be alone, talking together on center stage. They were standing, with their arms folded and looking relaxed. All trace of reverence in Alec's demeanor had disappeared. He was speaking to the maestro as much a master of his realm as the musician was in his. I could see his pride shining through his eyes. This was his moment of validation. I decided not to spoil it. I left the theater saying nothing, leaving my Artistic Director to enjoy the full measure of respect he deserved.

I found my cohorts outside the bakery, slumped at a table under the shop's yellow awning. They looked so wasted, I was surprised no one had called for an ambulance.

Susan dropped her feet from the chair next to her so I could sit down and handed me a menu. They'd already ordered and I regretted my choice of a Neapolitan when their berry-tarts arrived, slathered in whipped cream. Tom wasn't friendly when I took a bite of his, howling as if I'd drawn blood.

For a time we sat saying little, just relaxing and enjoying our pastries. The only interruption came when an attractive young woman walked by, inducing our male companions to poke and prod one another like a pair of schoolboys. Happily, the tables were turned when a gaggle of schoolgirls wandered by, all smiles and giggles for the two men.

David took their admiration in stride but Tom, unable to control his blush, made himself the object of more giggles.

"I can't remember being that young," he growled as he turned away to stare into the bakery window.

How long we might have sat in the blissful peace, I can't say, but I suddenly remembered an envelope I'd been given that morning from the hotel desk. In a hurry, I'd stuck it in my pocket and forgotten about it until that moment when I shot up in my chair.

Susan peered over my shoulder to read the signature on the envelope.

"Antonio Moretti? I hope there's no problem about the money. Alec said the quarrel had been patched. You did apologize didn't you, Tom? "

"It's nothing to do with Tom or the money," I assured her. "It's an invitation to dinner this evening."

Susan displayed a broad cat smile.

"Lucky, lucky girl. I bet he takes you someplace special. He must have pots of money. Did anyone notice the gold cufflinks he wore other night? Solid gold, I bet."

"You're not going, of course. Not tonight."

Susan frowned at Tom before taking my side.

"Why shouldn't she go? She's a free agent. I think he's sort of dreamy. I like the way his lock of hair falls over his forehead, makes him look rakish."

"Makes him look like he should buy a comb," David muttered with his arms folded.

Tom wasn't listening to the banter. His eyes were on me.

"Tara, you can't. You just can't."

I understood what he was trying to convey without the use of words and a part of me agreed. Still, I was curious and inclined to accept.

"I don't see how I can avoid it. We can't afford to alienate him."

"Yeah, you've already done that for us, Tom."

"You don't know what you're talking about, Susan, so butt out."

"Hey bro," David chimed in. "Tara's our friend, too. Why should you care about who she dates? You're just friends, aren't you?"

Tom was growing red in the face again so I came to his defense.

"Tom has his reasons for saying what he did. We'd made other plans, but they don't have to wait." I turned my eyes toward Tom's. It's not a big deal, really. I promise, I'll be back before midnight."

"Yeah, before the carriage turns into a pumpkin," David snickered and seemed his old self again. Tom, however, wasn't placated.

"I still don't like it."

. . .

I found Antonio Moretti waiting for me as I stepped from the elevator that evening. Despite his Armani suit, a soft grey, and his gold cufflinks which gave him a polished appearance, he looked nervous. I wasn't comfortable either. Standing near him, I felt dowdy. I was wearing the same black jersey dress I'd worn to the cocktail party when we'd first met. The only item new to my attire was the gold cross Anunciata Brancaccio had given me.

"You look beautiful – beautiful!" He seemed about to kiss my hand so I locked them behind me as I peered down at my dress.

"I'm afraid you've seen this outfit before. One can't travel with much wardrobe on the road."

Moretti's eyes followed mine.

"And yet, you've managed to look different. Perhaps it's the crucifix. That's new, isn't it?" My hand reached up to touch the cross in a self- conscious gesture.

"Yes. It's a gift from someone I met in Vienna."

"He must be very rich." My companion eyed me curiously. "The cross is old, I think, and exquisitely crafted." When I failed to satisfy his curiosity, he went on. "Are you Catholic?"

"My parents are Unitarians but I'm not anything, really."

"You believe in God, of course."

"I guess so. Why? Does it matter?"

Moretti laughed, put off-guard by my frank reply, apparently.

"Forgive me, but it's natural to wonder about a young woman who possesses both talent and beauty."

"I like your tie," I deflected.

He looked down as if he'd forgotten what he was wearing.

"I'm not certain about the shade, whether it's pink or raspberry. I wore it to impress you with my feminine side. I understand that's important to a woman these days, no?"

He looked boyish as he spoke and I smiled in spite of myself. When I asked where we were dining, he looked even more pleased with himself.

"*Il Teatro.* One of the finest restaurants in all Milan."

The ride to the restaurant was short and when we arrived, the maitre d' seemed to be waiting for us. He rushed forward as we entered and addressed my companion in the manner of an old friend. They exchanged a few pleasantries after which the restaurateur escorted us through the main dining area and on to a small patio which held no one but ourselves, an arrangement I gathered my host had arranged.

Moretti pulled out a chair and I sat down, my eyes admiring the white linen and the sparkling glasses that were as yet to be filled.

"I've already chosen the menu," he informed me as he took the chair opposite mine. "But you needn't worry. No fish. I consulted with Alec before asking you to dinner. You don't mind my little inquiry, I hope?"

In fact, I did mind, and didn't much care to have Alec serving as matchmaker either for my good or the good of the company. I let the feeling pass, however. It would be years, if ever, before I'd dine in so elegant a setting again and I was going to enjoy myself.

The sommelier came forward and poured a butter-colored liquid into Moretti's glass for his approval and then filled mine. For a while, we chatted amiably over trivial matters -- the weather, of course, and how mild it had been, and the travails of living out of a suitcase. Before long, the waiter appeared again with our appetizer, grilled vegetables with an eggplant mousse. It was delicious, but I was obliged to pace myself as I'd been warned several courses were to follow.

The evening wore on smoothly enough. Moretti was easy to talk to and by the time the main course arrived, crispy chicken with rosemary potatoes, I'd told him about my favorite movies, books, and even my favorite fashion designers. His curiosity seemed endless and I endured it hoping to gain the same latitude.

To my surprise, he answered my questions with candor. He even volunteered that his godmother wasn't really his godmother but his grandmother. She hid the fact because Moretti's mother, Madame Lazaremko's daughter, was born out of wedlock, a source of shame to his relative.

"Are you shocked?" he asked after he'd revealed the family history.

"Of course not. This is the twenty-first century, not the dark ages. I suppose in your grandmother's youth, attitudes were different. But my knowing does pose a problem. What if Madame finds out I know her secret?"

"She won't unless you tell," Moretti answered. "But either way, it doesn't matter. I wish she'd be more open. Perhaps, then, she'd be willing to talk more about my mother. I never knew her, you see. She died giving birth to me. And that's part of the problem: Grandmother thinks her daughter's death was a punishment for her indiscretion. The fact that I, too, am illegitimate compounds her guilt."

"But women die in childbirth all the time, married or not," I protested. "And what about your father? Shouldn't he come in for a little blame?"

Antonio sat for a moment before answering.

"In a way, it could be said that he was punished. He was killed in a barroom brawl a few months before I was born. I don't know the details of that either as neither of my grandparents will talk about it."

He looked uncomfortable discussing the death of his parents and my heart went out to him a little. Certainly, here was a very different picture of a man than the one Tom had painted. His Armani suits and gold cufflinks notwithstanding, I doubted Antonio Moretti was an over-indulged human being. Rather, he struck me as lonely. Having been robbed of both parents and left in the care of eccentric grandparents would explain it.

"And what about Vladimir Reznikov, your grandfather? Does he suffer from guilt, too?

My date emitted a light chuckle.

"Him? No, I assure you, the idea of guilt would never occur to him."

"Did he never offer to marry your grandmother?"

Again, he paused and looked thoughtful.

"I think she would have liked to sanctify their relationship, but he never proposed and she was never one to beg. Sometimes, I think all he cares about are his books."

Antonio stabbed at a slice of chicken on his plate but made no attempt to eat it, his gesture seeming to be one of protest rather than of hunger. When I suggested he might feel resentment toward his grandfather, however, he denied it.

"No, no. There are no hard feelings between him and me. I enjoy his absolute trust. That's why he's turned the workings of the winery over to me. But, I do wish he'd be kinder to Ludmila. They argue so much. It makes me unhappy."

"Are they together a lot?"

"Oh yes. She lives at the vineyard, unless she and grandfather have one of their seismic eruptions. Then she storms off for a few days. But she always comes back."

"I suppose she loves him in her own way."

Moretti looked up from his plate to clarify.

"She loves him to distraction, I'm afraid. The imbalance is destructive because he doesn't reciprocate her feelings, at least not to the same degree. I think she reminds him too much of his past. He could have become a very great dancer they say, but an automobile accident put an end to that."

"An accident? Is that what you were told?"

"Yes. An unfortunate accident." Antonio laid down his knife and fork to look at me, earnestness shining from his eyes. "But that's all in the past. I want to know more about you."

"I think I've told you everything there is to know about me, but you haven't told me about your father. Was he a vintner too?"

"A vintner? No, not unless you think of our field hands as vintners. My mother fell in love with a man beneath her station, which was part of the problem. I'm named after my father and there's a story behind that too."

"I'd like to hear it."

Moretti cocked his head a little as he looked at me.

"You're not bored by all this talk about myself?"

"Not at all. Please, go on with the story."

"Well, I have my father's name because of Ludmila. It was her daughter's dying wish and she honored it, even if it meant sneaking behind my grandfather's back to make sure Antonio Moretti appeared on my birth certificate. Grandfather had presumed my surname would be his, so he was furious when he found out what grandmother had done. I can only imagine how high that argument registered on the Richter scale. In any case, he refused to accept the one I'd been given and that's why he refers to me as Isaac."

"Isaac? Is that a family name?"

Another chuckle.

"No. It's his tribute to Newton. You see, not only did Newton make contributions to science, but he was also a great Alchemist. Many people don't know that. In any case, Alchemy is my grandfather's passion, hence Isaac is the name he would have chosen for me."

"Alchemy? I thought Alchemy was as dead as Latin or the carrier pigeon."

Moretti wagged a finger at me.

"Never let my grandfather hear you say that or you'll find yourself in for a lecture."

We'd finished our cherry flambé by this time and as the waiter carried the empty dishes away, my host became serious. Putting his hand forward, he asked if he could hold my crucifix. Without understanding why, I did as he asked and released the clasp about my neck.

He took the pendant from me and cupped it in his palm before closing his fingers over it.

"The other night, your friend raised an outrageous accusation against me which wasn't true. As I do believe in God, I swear to you upon this holy crucifix, that I have never contemplated harming anyone in my life and especially not Sylvia Huntington. She was dearer to me than the air I breathed. I am innocent of the charge, Tara. I hope you can believe me."

The mere mention of Sylvia's name seemed to dredge up enormous pain. Antonio's lips trembled and if the eyes are windows to the soul, I could find no guilt in his.

CHAPTER XIV

The clock in the hotel lobby read 11:45 when I parted from Antonio Moretti. I barely had time to kiss him goodnight before I made a dash for the elevator. Other guests, returning from dinner, crowded in behind me so that we made a stop at every floor. By the time we reached mine, I was so anxious that I elbowed my way to the front, indifferent to the clucking noises of those I'd inconvenienced.

After fumbling with my keys, I discovered the room I'd entered was empty. The clock on the nightstand read five minutes to midnight. Where was everyone? It occurred to me then that perhaps we were to meet in Tom's room. I made another dash for the elevator. The needle above the door indicated the vehicle was on its way down. My heart sank. Tom's room was on the one above mine so I decided not to wait but headed for the emergency stairs. My hand was on the handle when the door was flung open. Tom and Orlando stood blinking at me.

"Where have you been? It's almost midnight," I screeched.

Tom's reply was snide.

"We've been in the bar, waiting for you. I saw you kiss lover boy. Must have been an expensive dinner."

The argument that was about to follow was avoided when Orlando took hold of both of our arms and shoved the pair of us in the direction of my room. After fumbling with my keys a second time, I managed to gain entrance a minute before the clock was about to read midnight. I had just enough time to note that Orlando was dressed in his usual manner, appropriate for the occasion, but that Tom, for some reason, had donned a plaid shirt of red and green wool.

"You look like a traffic sign," I hissed for want of something nasty to say.

"And you're going to freeze in that flimsy dress," came his retort.

"Shut up, the pair of you. I need to get centered or God knows what will happen to us." Orlando's threat sobered us both.

"S-should Tara and I be doing something?"

"Yeah. Shut up."

Tom pressed his lips together, not as a gesture of annoyance but as one of silent obedience. His relationship with Orlando had changed visibly. I wondered when his skepticism had turned to this unquestioning faith in the Necromancer. Was it a guy thing? Had they bonded over wine and sports talk? I didn't know, but somehow I felt like an outsider.

"I need you two to concentrate on the last time we shifted levels. Your thoughts have to be aligned with mine. Got it?"

"Got it. When do we start?"

Orlando threw his arms around Tom and me as a bell in a distant tower began to strike.

"Now, Tom!"

The room went black.

. . .

One of us couldn't have been concentrating because our second journey was nothing like the first. Stronger currents than before threatened to pull us apart and send us each hurtling through space in different directions. Orlando was clutching Tom and me so hard I could feel the muscles of his arms tremble. What's more, the medium swirling around us wasn't air, but a sticky, placenta-like fluid in which we could breathe or, in my case, hyperventilate.

The tattoo of a gigantic heart was thrumming in my ears, as well. I wanted to put my hands on either side of my head to drown it out, but losing contact with Orlando, I knew, would be fatal. Instead, I clung to him with greater energy just as he was doing with me.

Shutting my eyes, as I did, was a foolish reflex because cutting off one of my senses only heightened the rest. I started to scream, my throat in full throttle, but against the drumming, my voice was a sparrow's chirp in the midst of a storm.

I feared I would go deaf, that I would never hear a human voice again, much less the music of Tchaikovsky and then, as suddenly as it had begun, the drumming stopped. My eyes remained shut but I sensed I was floating on a gentle air current. If Tom and Orlando remained with me, I was unaware of it. I simply gave myself to the immediate sensation and grew more and more calm as I did.

What a fool I was to surrender myself so completely in this wild, unpredictable place. Without warning, the floating ceased and, like Alice, I was dropped down a long, long rabbit-hole. The sensation was of falling, the opposite of floating. I screamed again and this time, my eyes popped open. To my surprise, I found I'd been delivered to the antechamber -- that familiar room of overstuffed chairs where a pale light filtered through the windows. Tom and Orlando stood on either side of me, their dazed expressions no doubt mirroring mine.

Yelena Natilova hovered at a far corner of the room, looking equally bewildered. When she clapped eyes upon Orlando, she came forward.

"Have I summoned you? I don't recall. How extraordinary. I *must* be getting old." She laughed at her little joke before noticing me, but became perturbed when she did.

"Why is Tara here? And this stranger?" She examined Tom with narrowed eyes as she spoke. "Have you brought me an offering? I feel very much in need of one."

"A-An offering?" Tom glanced at Orlando for guidance as did Madame Natilova.

"Why is this man here?" she scowled in her imperious manner, the same look she once used to quell a room full of noisy dancers. "I didn't summon him. I've never seen him before."

The Necromancer cleared his throat, a nervous gesture before answering. Then he told her that *she* hadn't done the summoning. *He* had. The information wasn't received graciously.

"You summoned me? *ME*? Now I shall definitely require an offering." She returned her gaze to Tom, as if he were responsible for the offense, causing him to look pale so that freckles appeared to pop out on the bridge of his nose.

"Y-You don't mean b-blood do you?"

"Don't I?" My teacher squinted at him a moment longer before relenting. "What have you brought? You weren't foolish enough to come empty-handed, were you?"

Tom fished into the pocket of his jeans, desperate to placate her. What he found was a packet of Life Savers and these he held out in his open palm.

Yelena Natilova sniffed at them and looked offended, but she snatched the candy, anyway.

"I prefer chocolate," she complained as she tore at the wrapper. "I used to eat it by the pound. Never made me fat."

The three of us watched as she rolled one of the white lozenges around with her tongue.

"Ah, sugar! I feel better already." Next, she dropped the remaining five or six disks down her throat. "No use savoring them," she explained. "I don't know how long I'll be here."

Knowing she was playing with us, I laughed and Tom looked relieved when the ghost did as well.

"May we sit down?" The Necromancer remained serious and explained we'd come in this unprecedented way on a matter of grave importance.

My teacher waved us toward the overstuffed chairs and perched herself on the arm of the one Tom sat in. Either she enjoyed making him nervous or she was indulging in a mild flirtation. I decided it was the latter when her transparent hand brushed his cheek. That he didn't flinch seemed to please her.

"All right," she began, her tone serious once more. "You summoned me. How can I help?"

The Necromancer served as our spokesman. He told her about all that had happened since my last visit, repeating some of what she knew about my haunting in Budapest but this time drawing a connection between it and my misadventure at the bookstore where I encountered Reznikov's grandson. After that, he got to the heart of the matter and informed her about the proposed visit to Tuscany.

Madame Natilova made no attempt to interrupt while Orlando spoke. The more she listened, however, the more alarmed she appeared to be, her hand sometimes drifting to her cheek or her heart. When he had finished, she repeated the essential points. Tom and I sat bobbing our heads for encouragement, and when she was certain she'd understood everything, she began to form her own opinions.

"That Vladimir has become a student of Alchemy could be significant. Unlike magic, which is sleight of hand, Alchemy is a true discipline. With his brilliant mind, if he chose to make a study of it, I'll venture he's become its master and capable of enormous evil."

"You must have sensed something dark, otherwise you wouldn't have reached out to Tara. What was it Madame Natilova?"

"I can't be definite about that, Tom," said my teacher as she looked down at the young man beside her. "Let's just say I knew something out of the ordinary was about to happen, something unnatural and that Tara was in danger. If Vladimir is behind it -- and the evidence suggests that he is because any other interpretation would require too much coincidence -- then what it is remains a mystery to me."

"What about the other ghosts?" Tom prodded. "Did they sense that anything is out of the ordinary?"

A pensive expression drifted across Madame's face, as if she were spying Tom from behind layers of fog.

"I wish I could answer that question, dear boy. But you see, when I enter the antechamber, all memories of that other place fade. The powers that be, I suppose, don't want the living to learn much about the world beyond the grave. But as this matter pertains to Vladimir, believe me when I say, I'm certain whatever he's discovered will be put to no good."

Madame rose and paced a little in thought, speaking quietly as if to herself.

"But why Alchemy? That's the question. If he wished to avenge himself against me, a bullet through Tara's heart would do, or poison. No, there's more to this than meets the eye. I know little of Alchemy except that it concerns the transfiguration of matter."

"Turning lead into gold? That's all bunk, isn't it?"

Orlando didn't seem to agree with Tom's assessment. His eyes narrowed and for the first time since we'd begun our discussion, he ventured an opinion.

"Turning lead into gold is of no consequence, but the power to transfigure matter is."

Yelena Natilova nodded her head vigorously, as if she'd been thinking along the same lines.

"With it, he could breathe life into the inanimate universe or cause the dead to rise and walk among the living."

Tom snickered, his response to an idea that was too much to take in. When he saw the sober expressions of the rest of us, however, he sat back in his chair.

"Go on then. Tell me. What's the worst that could happen?"

"Don't you see, Tom?" Madame Natilova's voice strained with impatience. "If he could control the living and the dead, he'd be a god and not a benign one, I fear."

"That's a bit of an overkill isn't it? If he wants to harm Tara, as you said, a bullet would be easier."

The Necromancer seemed to agree.

"Maybe we are wandering down the wrong path, Yelena."

"No, we are not wrong." My teacher stamped her foot but made no sound. "None of you know how Vladimir thinks. I do. And yes, he wants to harm Tara but she is not his real target. I am."

Tom looked mystified, his green eyes blinking.

"'No disrespect, Madame Natilova, but how could you be in any danger? You're already dead."

"Can't you see what he intends? Must I spell it out for you? He plans to use Tara as a beacon to summon me, just as the Necromancer has done tonight. If he finds me and he has the power of transfiguration, he can either destroy my soul or make me his slave."

A light dawned in all of us, but Tom was the one who spoke out.

"My gosh. I didn't realize. You're right. That would be unthinkable. We can't let that happen."

"My teacher let out a sigh as if she'd endured hours of labor that had finally come to an end.

"Thank you, Tom. I'm glad you agree, at last. Whatever happens to Tara also happens to me. Our destinies are entwined."

My mouth opened but Madame would brook no interrupting. She waved me to silence with her hand.

"The facts are as they are, Tara. You will have to be brave for the both of us. Fortunately, you have the Necromancer to assist you, though I suspect this is new ground for him, too."

"Don't forget me. I'm ready to help." Tom stood up as if to remind my teacher he was in the room.

"Yes, she has you, too." She gave him a wistful smile as she reached up to brush his cheek with her hand a second time. Then she turned her attention to the Necromancer.

"You will stay with her, won't you? You can't possibly abandon her knowing what's at stake."

"With Tom on duty, I'm not sure my help is needed, Yelena." He offered her a thin smile as he spoke.

Hearing him, Tom threw his arm over the Necromancer's shoulder, the humor of the remark having escaped him.

"'Course I need you, buddy. We've got two villains at work here, remember? The grandson's killed once, already."

"You don't know that," I objected. "You weren't there when Sylvia died. You're blaming Antonio because you're jealous."

Tom jutted his chin out when he heard me.

"So it's 'Antonio' now, is it?"

"Antonio? Sylvia? What's all this about?"

Tom gave my teacher a summary of the young dancer's death and when he had finished, asked if she possibly knew who killed her. From her pained expression, I could see that Madame Natilova had taken a liking to Tom and sympathized with his loss, but in life she'd always been honest so it had to be the same in death.

"I don't know anything about this Sylvia Huntington, I'm afraid. At least I don't think I do? Was she a good dancer?"

"The best."

"Well, if it will help, I could make inquiries. Maybe someone on the other side is aware of her. Do you want me to try?"

"I wish you would. Somebody around here needs to get her head straightened out." A pair of green eyes flashed a belligerent glance in my direction.

Madame's response was to hold out her hand expectantly.

"In that case, I shall require another Life Saver."

Looking flustered, Tom fished in his jeans a second time. He came up with a lozenge covered in blue lint.

"You don't want this, I suppose."

My teacher snatched it from him before he had time to blink.

"Of course, I do. You don't suppose I worry about germs, do you?"

She popped the treat into her mouth and as her outline began to fade, the Necromancer threw his arms around Tom and me. After that the antechamber went black.

• • •

That next morning I overslept. At five past noon, I hurried to the elevator still buttoning the coat I'd thrown over my tee-shirt and jeans. Antonio and I had arranged to meet at a little coffeeshop three blocks away. No good could come of our being seen together. Tom would be hostile and Susan's imagination would run wild.

Being late, I was already feeling flustered when a man in a chauffeur's uniform came up to me. He pointed to a limousine a short distance away and asked me to follow him. Antonio stepped from the car and waved so that I could see him.

He was casually dressed in a pair of jeans, and a pale blue pullover. A gold crucifix hung about his neck, smaller than mine, but it glinted in the sunlight. I wondered if he'd worn it to remind me he was a man of honor.

"It's a beautiful day," he said when I was near enough to hear him. "There's a little restaurant on the outskirts of the city, famous for its home-cooking. I want to take you there. You needn't worry about the drive. I'll have you back in plenty of time for your performance."

Not waiting for my reaction, he bundled me into the vehicle and the driver soon pulled away from the curb, speeding us toward some unknown destination. Tom, I knew, would be furious if he learned that I had gone off somewhere with Antonio without telling him, but I hadn't anticipated these plans and didn't know what I could do about it.

Seeing that I was deep in thought, my companion assumed I was worried about the evening performance.

"Don't worry. You'll be wonderful. Everyone's been singing your praises. Even grandfather."

I looked at the man beside me in surprise.

"Your grandfather? He's never seen me dance, has he?"

"No, but he can read the reviews."

I decided to pursue this opening in the conversation.

"I'm curious. Why has your grandfather thrown so much money at our little company? How did he hear of us? We're so far away?"

Antonio gazed at me, his expression innocent.

"I admit, I have no idea what brought your group to his attention. It isn't as if we don't have dance companies in Italy. I'm afraid you'll have to ask him that when you meet. Though in this case, I'm glad he did what he did."

He gazed at me with an admiration that felt sticky. I hoped he wasn't allowing his imagination to run ahead where he and I were concerned.

"I'm always happy to make a new friend," I answered gingerly. "But Seattle is a long way from Italy and I'm at the beginning my career, as you know."

"Of course. I understand. But there's no harm in a man being happy, is there?"

I smiled and turned my head toward the window not knowing what more to say.

A half hour later, the limousine stopped in front of a little cottage somewhere on the rural outskirts of the city. The exterior was white stucco and the roof shingled. Inside, the dining area was of good size with most of the tables occupied by customers who were talking and laughing while they attacked the generous portions on their plates.

When she saw us, the hostess hurried forward, her face brightened with a smile. She was a testament to the restaurant's largesse as she was as round as she was tall, a woman of middle-age with iron grey hair that she had drawn into a bun. Her eyes twinkled as she led us to our table. Perhaps she thought Antonio and I were a couple and smelled romance in the air. Certainly the window view from our table was romantic, a slate of green fields and trees dressed in the motley colors of fall.

Antonio perused the menu and proposed to order for us. I offered no objection as I was unable to read Italian, anyway. He chose wisely for we were soon sharing a delicious meal of Risotto Milanese and something called Osso Buco, Veal shank with Porcini mushrooms.

As for the wine, it was delicious but I restricted myself to a single glass, mindful of my evening performance.

"Tell me about your grandfather," I said out of the blue, interrupting my companion's endless talk about the wine business. "I'm anxious to impress him. You said before he studied Alchemy. "

"Yes, that's how we happened to be in the bookstore where you and I met. He's always looking for rare books on the subject." Antonio put down his knife and fork to look at me. "I thought we'd exhausted this line of conversation when we had dinner together."

I ignored his objection.

"So that's why you were at the bookstore. I remember that you lost track of him while you were there and had to go looking for him. I presume you found him?"

"Yes. He'd gone back to the hotel for a nap."

"Without telling you? That's a little odd, isn't it?"

Antonio wiped his mouth with his napkin looking a little impatient.

"My dear girl, he's an old man. He has his moods. I accept that. I only wish you found me as interesting as you seem to find him."

"Doesn't my desire to understand him for your sake please you?"

My remark earned me a grudging half smile, so I went on.

"I still don't see the point of studying Alchemy. Like I said, it's a dead subject. Why pursue it?"

"If you say that to him, you'll never make a good impression, I assure you. If you want my advice, stay away from the subject."

"Why? Are you afraid I'll make a fool of myself? That I won't understand?"

My companion laid down his knife and fork a second time, as if determined to put this conversation to rest.

"My darling girl, why do you bother your head about an arcane subject? Let Grandfather's obsession be his own. At your time of life, you should take an interest in other things. Like me, for example. I certainly take an interest in you."

He picked up his wine glass to offer a toast.

"To La Scala and your triumph this evening."

I refused to drink which surprised him until I explained that a toast of that nature before a performance was considered bad luck. He looked stricken and set down his glass.

"I apologize. I didn't know." He returned to his veal and was quiet.

After a suitable period of silence had passed, I brought up the study of

Alchemy again.

"Aren't you afraid your grandfather may blow up the place one day with his experiments? Wasn't it Alchemists who invented gunpowder?"

My companion sighed, resigned to the idea that my curiosity about Alchemy was unrelenting.

"Grandfather is a brilliant man. I do not fear his experiments, and yes, the Alchemists did invent gunpowder. You see, the great prize in Alchemy is to master transfiguration, the power to transform matter, including oneself. They believed this power resided in the brain and if they could discover where it exists, then men could become gods."

"Haven't we done enough damage to the planet as mere mortals?" I scoffed. "Imagine the damage we could do as gods. I'm not religious, but I think the idea is blasphemous."

Antonio looked amused and pointed his fork at me from across the table.

"Mock me if you will, but a God Module has been discovered in the brain. What neuroscientists are debating today is *why* it exists. Has our search for the meaning of life shaped our brains? Or are our brains designed to reveal our higher power? Alchemists believed it was the latter. The quest presupposes spirituality."

"But they failed miserably, didn't they?"

"Oh, I don't know about that. Carl Jung incorporated precepts of Alchemy into his study of modern psychology."

"Did he? I'm surprised. Pursuing knowledge via Alchemy in the modern age seems like driving a horse and buggy when there are automobiles."

Antonio shrugged and went on with his meal, but not before observing that some terrains were more hospitable to buggies than cars, even in the modern age. He looked pleased with his remark, as if he imagined it was clever enough to end the conversation.

"I don't think what I said was funny," I sniffed. "Do you think having a serious conversation with me is a waste of time? I suppose you think that all I want to hear is flattery. Well, I don't. Rather than being put on a pedestal, I'd prefer to be taken seriously."

Antonio looked up at me, his face looking pale.

"My dear girl, I didn't mean to offend you. I do apologize."

"I'm not your 'dear girl' by the way. I'm not a girl. I'm in college where I get good grades."

The moment I spoke out, I realized I sounded more like a petulant child than an adult and wanted to eat my words. But the eyes staring back at me were round with desolation. Till that moment, I hadn't realized I had the power to hurt him. His expensive clothes and his gold cufflinks notwithstanding, he seemed desperate for my approval. Seeing the damage I'd done, I was quick to apologize.

When I did, he leaned forward and took both of my hands in his.

"My dear Tara, I promise I take you very, very seriously. You're the best thing that's happened to me in a long time. I'm not very good at relationships, but I too got good grades in school. If you'll teach me, I promise to do better. Please, give me a chance."

. . .

As we left the restaurant, a light rain began to fall. By the time we reached my hotel, it had become a downpour. Antonio instructed the driver to pull up at the front door. After that, he got out of the car, and used his umbrella to shield me, as he walked me to the revolving door. He didn't enter the lobby with me but gave me a kiss on the cheek before I left him.

Tom saw us together and glowered as I entered the hotel. He'd been waiting for me. I'd forgotten we'd agreed to share a taxi to the theater. He rose as I approached.

"I thought we agreed…"

I shook my head to prevent his lecture.

"No, *you* and Orlando agreed. I never did."

"What are you playing at, Tara? You know what's at stake. You know the danger and still you go wandering off on your own. I bet you didn't tell anyone where you were going. Alec wouldn't have a clue if you went missing, am I right?"

He *was* right but I wasn't going to admit it.

"I didn't go missing, as you can see. Stop worrying. Give me a minute to get my gear from the room or go on to the theater without me. It's your choice."

I headed for the elevator knowing Tom's gaze was boring into my back.

He called after me.

"Of course I'll wait. I know my duty even if you don't know yours."

Ten minutes later I found him, true to his word, seated in the same chair as before. His hands were jammed into his hips, a sign our argument wasn't over. He'd probably used the time to think up more objections.

Fortunately, David and Susan appeared and they suggested the four of us share a taxi. I was happy with her suggestion. At that moment, I'd have agreed to a ride with the Mafia rather than face the scene that was brewing.

As we headed for the theater, everyone in the cab was quiet. I knew why Tom and I weren't speaking, but I had no idea what was going on between David and Susan. Both of them looked out of sorts. Whatever was troubling them, I hoped it wouldn't affect the performance.

Alec was outside and looked relieved when he saw us. We'd been the last to arrive, apparently, and he didn't spare the sarcasm.

"Glad you could make our little soiree tonight. Hope you weren't inconvenienced by it."

Tom pushed past him as he opened the car door, his face sullen.

"We're not late. What's the big deal?"

Alec watched his disgruntled dancer disappear but didn't make a reply. He probably assumed we were all suffering from nerves. Tonight was going to be a make or break event for us.

Susan and David took their sweet time heading for the dressing rooms, but I raced past them to catch up with Tom. The ride in the cab had cleared my head. I wanted to apologize and to tell him he was the best friend I could wish for. When I was close enough to take hold of his arm, I promised him that in future, I wouldn't take any chances.

He grunted when he heard me and tried to pretend I was making a fuss over nothing, but I could tell he was relieved.

. . .

By the fourth curtain call after the end of the performance, the audience was still on its feet, applauding and whistling. As Antonio had predicted, we appeared to have conquered La Scala. Alec was so happy, he looked liverish. He was still shivering with joy when I hugged him after the final curtain.

Despite the audience's enthusiasm, the evening had not gone smoothly. Susan lost her headgear a second time and Ellen, overcome with nervousness, vomited in the wings right after the castle scene. As for me, I considered my performance to be lackluster. Given all that was going on in my personal life, I'd decided to take no risks and danced by the book rather than allow inspiration to consume me. No one seemed to notice, or perhaps La Scala's audience preferred precision over passion.

What I do know is that each time the audience sent up cheers, my mind was clouded by doubt. Was Reznikov behind their enthusiasm? Was Alchemy the reason for my success? My aching muscles and throbbing feet said otherwise, but I couldn't shake my fears.

To a rational mind, these suspicions would have sounded absurd, but I had been subjected to too many anomalies of late to discount the idea entirely. Consequently, the more those around me were jubilant, the more I felt cut off from them.

Unlike me, Tom saw no reason not to celebrate. I watched as he gave every girl within the range of his long arms a firm embrace. It occurred to me then that if he didn't stop soon, he'd suffer from tennis elbow. The scene was one where I could have either laughed or cried. I might have done both if someone had not whispered in my ear.

"I warn you, Ludmila is seething with jealousy."

I spun around to see Antonio's brown eyes shining at me like wet bark.

"You were magnificent tonight. There's no other word for it. Even grandmother has had to concede. She wants you to have dinner with us tonight to finalize the arrangements for Tuscany. We won't have to stay with her long. She'll tell us her plans and then you and I can run off for a nightcap."

His was a simple invitation but it plunged me deep into despair. How ironic, I thought, that each artistic success was drawing me closer to a tragedy similar to Odette's.

I managed to decline his offer of dinner, as I'd rather eat sand than spend the evening with Madame Lazaremko. Besides, my excuse was an honest one as I had made other arrangements.

Antonio looked disappointed but rebounded with an alternative: that he and I have brunch together the next day. Having neither the wit nor the courage to refuse a second time, I agreed.

• • •

Tom and I had agreed to grab a bite at a nearby bistro that evening to consider our next move against Reznikov, if we had one. Slipping away proved to be difficult, however. Not only had members of the audience decided to flood the stage, but Alec seemed determined to introduce me to every one of them. To complicate matters, Ellen had recovered from her vomiting episode and had a grip on Tom's arm tight enough to require a crowbar to remove her. David was with Tom, too, probably trying to drag him off for a little nightlife. Susan wasn't far away, close enough for me to see the smudges under her eyes. I doubted she was up to another pub-crawl, but I also knew she'd never allow her handsome beau to be out on his own.

Almost an hour passed before I arrived at the bistro and found Tom seated in a booth. He'd already ordered a chicken sandwich with fries. I slid into the banquette opposite him and when the waitress returned with his order, I asked for a bowl of chili. We sat in silence while Tom poured catsup over his fries and savored a few.

"God, I'm hungry. I never danced so hard in my life. You were great, by the way. A little restrained, but flawless. Actually, I don't know how David kept his hold on you. Sometimes you literally seemed to fly."

I thanked him for his compliment, but mostly I appreciated his honesty. I had been restrained, if not dull, and he was willing to say it.

After taking a bite from his sandwich, he leaned forward to speak in confidence.

"I left Orlando a message. Don't know if he'll come, but I told him where we'd be." He paused as if assessing my mood, then decided to take a crack at Antonio, anyway.

"I saw you with lover boy in the wings. What did he have to say?"

As we hadn't spoken properly the whole day, I decided the present was a good time to tell him what I'd learned at lunch concerning Reznikov's interest in transfiguration.

Tom couldn't react as the waitress had brought my chili. He had to wait until she was gone, but when she was, he let off steam like a boiling tea kettle.

"Your teacher was right on the money, wasn't she? She knew what he was after. I still can't believe it. The idea is so fantastic."

"You can say that after all we've been through?" I opened a packet of crackers and crushed them over my bowl. Tom looked around to see if anyone nearby might be listening. The bistro was sparsely populated. We would have been safe with megaphones. Nevertheless, Tom kept his voice low.

"Orlando should hear what you've told me. He could probably advise us what to do next. I wish the heck he were here."

"Someone mention my name?"

Tom and I looked up, surprised to find the Necromancer peering down at us. He was dressed in his usual black attire so we should have seen him against the background of the red and white diner, but we hadn't.

"Spooky," Tom admitted as he slid to his left to make room for the new arrival. "How do you do that?"

"It's a trade secret." Orlando grinned and snatched a handful of Tom's fries as he joined us. "So what's up?"

I repeated my story from lunch while Tom hovered to pipe in if I left anything out. Naturally, I told Orlando about Reznikov's interest in transfiguration, but when I said I was pretty sure Antonio knew nothing of his grandfather's intentions, Tom rolled his eyes back into his head as if they were a row of cherries in a slot machine.

"Come on, Tara. He must know something. He lives with the old guy. Am I right or am I wrong?" He turned to Orlando for support, but when he got no support, only silence, his expression became one of incredulity.

"What? Am I the only person not born in a cabbage patch? I can see why Tara might defend the guy. He's good looking and has money, but you should be able to see right through him, Orlando."

"Except we don't have any hard evidence. Draw the wrong conclusion and the mistake could be fatal."

Tom slammed his shoulders against the fake leather behind him when he heard that.

"Fine. I'll get more information. I'll keep my eye on this guy like he's my twin brother. I'm going to prove to the pair of you that I'm right."

Orlando nodded his agreement.

"That's what needs to happen. We don't know much about this man except that he once fell in love with a dancer. Maybe his grandfather is using that history in some way."

"How? I don't get the connection."

Orlando's eyes wandered covetously over Tom's unfinished sandwich. He looked hungry. Tom shoved his plate and the bottle of catsup in his friend's direction.

"Go on. You can talk with your mouth full, can't you?"

Needing no coaxing, Orlando dug in. For a while Tom and I sat watching him chew. I noticed then that his eyes had darkened into hollows, like Susan's and he looked thinner, almost gaunt. Where had he been since we'd last seen him and why was he behaving as if he hadn't eaten in days? I knew better than to ask, though. Orlando was an "as needs to know" kind of guy.

"We have to consider every possibility," he said when he'd finished the sandwich and was taking a swig of Tom's cold coffee. "As I said, it's vital that we learn the grandson's role in all this. Maybe Tara's right. Maybe he's just a pawn, like she is."

Tom shook his head, almost imperceptibly, as if he wanted to avoid an argument but was holding on to his firm opinion.

"I might buy that if Moretti's hands were clean, but they aren't. You know what I'm saying, don't you?" He looked at Orlando expectantly, though I was the one to chime in.

"If you're asking him to agree with you about Sylvia Huntington's death, don't. He wouldn't be such a fool. I keep telling you, you haven't got any proof."

Tom stuck his chin out when he heard me.

"I don't need any proof. I just know."

"How? How could you possibly know? You weren't there."

Rather than allow a storm to build, Orlando cut in, addressing his remark to me.

"What Tom's saying about Moretti could be true. You don't have any proof either. You need to keep an open mind."

Tom crimped his face at me so that I wanted smack it, but Orlando was right. I didn't have any proof either. Defeated, I threw myself back against my seat and stared at my chipped fingernail polish. I wasn't in a blue funk for long, though. A minute later, Orlando turned to give Tom something to chew on.

"Tara's right about one thing. We have to give this guy a little more play. She brought back some good information today. Maybe she should see Moretti again. Let's see what more she can wriggle out of him."

"You can't be serious." Tom looked stunned, as if a scorpion had scuttled across the table. "We can't leave her alone with this guy. No way."

"I've been alone with him, *twice* and nothing's happened."

"You got lucky, that's all. Nope. It's too risky."

On impulse, I reached out to grab Tom by his sweater. One way or another, he was going to listen to me.

"Will you stop being so stubborn? Orlando's right. That's why I'm having brunch with Moretti tomorrow at eleven. And, by the way, you're not the boss of me."

Tom's complexion roiled from red to white and red again after I let go of him.

"So you want me out of it. Is that what you're saying?"

"No, of course not. I want you to keep an eye on me. Just give me a little room to breathe."

The pair of us sat staring at one another, and for a moment, I was afraid Tom and I were on the brink of losing each other. I was breathing hard when Orlando rose and settled his hat on his head.

"Where are you going?" we asked in unison.

"We're done here," he answered, looking down at us. "You two can go on arguing if you want, but I heard an agreement. We give Moretti a little more rope and Tom stays on the alert."

"Yeah, but Tara won't..."

The Necromancer was gone before Tom could finish his sentence.

CHAPTER XV

At 11 o'clock the next morning, Antonio and his limousine were waiting for me outside the hotel. Tom was nowhere in sight which puzzled me a little. Maybe he was sightseeing with Ellen or in his room pouting as he'd never really come around to Orlando's and my position. *Never mind*, I thought. *I can't let him interfere with what I needed to do.*

The day was warm, a nice opportunity for a walk, but Antonio told me we were driving to a park within the city, near the Arch of Peace. I'd read about the Arch in my tour book; the little tome that was proving to come in handy. According to its description, the structure was designed to replicate the Arc de Triomphe in Paris and stood at the edge of Parco Sempiore, a lovely forested area in the center of the city.

On the way, Antonio announced that, as the weather was fine, he'd planned a picnic. When we stopped, the driver retrieved a large hamper from the trunk and followed us as Antonio led the way through the trees until he came to a spot beneath a large birch tree. After that, the driver set about his work, at once, emptying the contents of the hamper onto a large linen tablecloth.

As we were to sit on the grass, I wondered that my host had dressed so elegantly, in grey flannel trousers and a blue blazer thrown over his polo shirt. I, for once, felt dressed for the occasion. I'd chosen to wear my denim skirt with a white tee under a black sweater. Nonetheless, when I saw the completed setting: the china, linen napkins, and gold-rim goblets, I felt as if I was at another formal event.

Antonio gave the driver instructions to return an hour later and then we both sat gingerly upon the grass which, happily, was dry.

"I hope you don't mind eating al fresco," Antonio said as he poured wine into my goblet. "But as you can see, my hotel provides a sumptuous basket and a picnic struck me as a good idea."

"A jug of wine, a loaf of bread -- and thou beside me singing in the wilderness?"

Antonio smiled as he offered me a piece of chicken.

"You are an admirer of *The Rubaiyat?* Then we have something else in common besides dance."

As he spoke, he cut off a slice of Gouda cheese for himself and savored it.

"I hope everything's to your liking." His eyes settled upon me appreciatively. "I've tried to think of everything. That little box with the gold-wrapping is for you." He pointed to a small package in front of me. "And before you ask, yes, Alec told me you fancied chocolates."

I gave him a quick smile in response which was polite but not entirely sincere.

"I suppose you know my blood type by now."

He took a few grapes from the bowl of fruit and popped them into his mouth before answering.

"I confess, I have made a study of you and of your beautiful Seattle. As we've had so little time together, I've been forced to get to know you by other means."

"That seems a lot of work when you know I'll be going home soon."

"I know. But it pleases me, all the same. By the way, I've put my knowledge to good use. I have a surprise for you later this afternoon, one I'm certain you'll enjoy."

"A surprise? What is it?"

"If I told you, it wouldn't be a surprise, would it?"

"Alec doesn't know everything about me," I told him, feeling a little annoyed, as anyone would be who was being investigated. "For all you know your surprise might backfire."

Antonio tapped the side of his nose and winked.

"I have other sources."

"Who? I'm beginning to feel like you're spying on me."

"Not spying," my companion objected. "Taking an interest, that's all. But if you must know, your friend Susan was my informant this time. I like her very much, by the way. We had coffee together the other day when you were out. A good sense of humor, that one."

"Susan? She didn't say anything about having coffee with you."

"I asked her not to. It would spoil the surprise."

Antonio dug into the chicken while I made a mental note to discourage my chatty friend from playing matchmaker in the future. And Alec too. They might think romance was in the air, but in their innocence, they could reveal information that would put me in danger.

Alone with Antonio, I began to feel uneasy. Perhaps I'd been wrong to treat Tom's reservations so lightly. Suddenly, I missed him and wished he were with me.

"You know so much about me," I said, intending to change the subject, "tell me about your life in Tuscany. When you were a boy, did you play sports?

Apparently pleased by my interest, my companion was forthcoming. He told me he'd enjoyed tennis when he was younger and had won a few tournaments, but eventually, the business of the winery took up too much of his time and he gave up his hobby.

"I suppose you could say the vineyard is my sport, my lover, and my life nowadays."

"That sounds lonely."

Antonio shook his head.

"Not at all. I travel and meet lots of people in the trade. I have a talent as a vintner, I suppose and grandfather was all too happy to step aside so he could spend more time with his musty books."

"But when you were younger, didn't you miss the companionship of people your own age?"

My companion shrugged. "I suppose it may look that way from the outside. But knowing no other life, I never thought about it much."

"So you're happy with your lot?"

"Contented might be a better word. Sylvia made me happy. Oh yes, with her I was a different man. But when that world collapsed, I rededicated myself to the winery, a life I knew and could trust. And there I've stayed. I hope to have a family, one day, of course. In fact, I long for one, but I haven't met the right woman... at least not until now."

Antonio's eyes sought mine and there I saw a longing that forced me to look away, not knowing how to receive it, not even sure I wasn't offended by it. I drew my cardigan tight around me as if it could protect myself from his adoration and stared out into the middle distance, noticing that the trunks of the motley-colored birches had dropped shadows like thin bars against the grass.

I had not escaped into my thoughts for long when something caught my eye. The movement of a leaf or a squirrel perhaps? No. Upon closer inspection, I could see the outline of a man crouched behind a tree. I knew who it was at once and gasped. Hearing me, Antonio's gaze followed mine. When he saw who the man was, his face colored, but only for a moment. Good breeding required him to treat the intruder with courtesy.

"Tom... over here. We're having a picnic. Come join us."

Once discovered, the redhead stood up and having no graceful means of escape, ambled toward us with his chin pressed to his chest. He was embarrassed, obviously and I was embarrassed for him. Perhaps he imagined I'd be angry. If so, he was wrong. My impulse was to hug him, feeling nothing but gratitude. He'd had been keeping an eye on me, all along. What a wonderful, dear friend.

Regardless of his smile, Antonio made no effort to control the sarcasm in his voice upon further greeting.

"Out for a stroll were you? There's a park tour at two, if you're interested in flora and fauna."

I moved my skirt to one side to make a place for the new arrival.

"Come on," I patted the ground to my left. "Have some wine. It's delicious."

"By all means," Antonio chirped. "And we've plenty of chicken. Plates are in the hamper. Feel free to dig in."

Antonio filled a fresh glass and handed it to Tom.

"By the way, Tom, thank you for your note. You and I got off on a wrong footing the other night. I, too, would like to make a fresh start. After all, we have at least one interest in common: Tara."

Tom said nothing but took the plate I handed him and piled it high with most of what he saw. I'd never known him to be without an appetite and this afternoon was no exception.

While he chewed, I struggled to find a common thread of conversation between the two men but received little encouragement from either of them. Tom couldn't talk wine and Antonio wasn't interested in sports, and while both men did their best to please me, the result was that Antonio sat with a smile plastered across his face and Tom avoided all eye contact as he bent over his plate. The seconds of the remaining hour crawled by like little barges needing to be pulled by a rope. I was ready to ditch the pair of them and run away with the chauffeur when he appeared, at last.

Seeing him, too, Antonio rose to his feet and helped me to mine as he addressed himself to Tom.

"I'm afraid Tara and I will have to leave you now. I'd have made other arrangements if I'd have known you'd be joining us, but as it is..."

He paused to reach into his pants pocket, pulling out two tickets to view Leonardo de Vinci's, *Last Supper.* When I saw them, I forgot myself and threw my arms about Antonio's neck. He hugged me back with an energy which forced me to become aware of my mistake. I stepped away, not daring to look at Tom who I was certain was scowling at me.

"I'd better shove off," he grumbled as he stood up and shoved his fists into the pockets of his jeans, looking as if he was afraid of what he might do with them, otherwise. "Thanks for lunch."

"My pleasure, I assure you. Can we give you a lift anywhere?"

Tom answered no, which gave Antonio leave to take a proprietary hold of my arm to lead me to the limousine. I walked away feeling terrible and twice looked back to give Tom a wave. He didn't see me, apparently. His eyes were too busy throwing daggers at the back of Antonio's head.

• • •

Anyone who's seen the *Last Supper* will share the excitement I felt upon seeing it for the first time. The colors were so vibrant, I found it hard to believe it was completed in 1498. As the allotted viewing time was fifteen minutes, I stood as close to the painting as I could, attempting to breathe in every detail.

Not everyone was as engaged with the viewing as I was. Antonio hardly looked at the work. I could feel him watching me the entire time. The intensity of his gaze, as if he wished to commit to memory every aspect of my being, was unnerving, especially from a man who, as yet, I hadn't completely decided was a friend or foe.

What did I know about him, after all? Only scraps of information that left me feeling ambivalent. I was touched by his candor, his boyish aura and the loneliness he exuded even though he refused to admit this emptiness to himself. But I hated his possessiveness and sometimes wondered if his generosity wasn't a gambit to create an obligation rather than joy. If so, he would fail with me. I, too, was an only child and used to being doted upon. I never felt obliged because of it.

When he touched my arm to signify that our viewing time was over, I had so convinced myself that I was being manipulated by him, that I shook him off and in a pique, walked away intending to put some distance between us.

He kept pace, as might be expected. The faster I walked the faster he walked, as well. Soon, we were almost at a run. A feeling of panic washed over me, much as it had at the Hungarian Opera House. The walls seemed to close in and to escape, I broke into a run, needing air, needing sunlight, needing to be free of Antonio.

I hit the pavement outside at a fast clip, hurtling past the waiting limousine. In the street, traffic was moving at a hectic pace in both directions. I plunged into it, as if escaping from a fire. Horns blared from all sides as I dodged bumper after bumper with no higher purpose than to reach the other side. That I could be injured and end my career never occurred to me. My single thought was escape.

The noise became deafening as more drivers saw me. Still I ran, thinking as I did, that I must be caught in a lucid dream. I could see myself behaving irrationally in a world so bizarre that it couldn't be real. I was convinced I'd open my eyes at any moment and realize I'd been dreaming, but the nightmare persisted. A driver, changing lanes, had failed to see me until he was almost upon me. I saw his stricken expression through the windshield as he slammed on his brakes, coming to a halt inches from me. By that time, I had fallen to my knees, a foolish gesture that would have left me more vulnerable, but an instinctive one. Perhaps I was expressing an unconscious desire to die rather than be maimed. I didn't know. But when the driver stepped out of the car, spewing vindictive curses at me, I knew I would live.

By now, Antonio had reached me. He and the driver helped me to my feet and together they steered me back toward the limousine. The entire time, I was covered in shame and kept apologizing. Once in the car, however, away from the public view, I became silent, feeling as if all language was drained from me.

Antonio sat beside me and so quietly, I could hear my heart beat. He didn't ask for an explanation and I was grateful because I hadn't any. What I'd done was a mystery to myself. Again, that niggling dread that I might be going mad, came to me like a whiff of foul air.

How long I sat in that wallowing silence, I don't know, but eventually, Antonio took hold of my hand and spoke softly to me.

"You mustn't feel ashamed, Tara. When Sylvia died, I suffered panic attacks for two years until I sought counseling. I don't know what happened to you today, but this tour must be exhausting for you. And I'm a little to blame. I've been so dazzled by you that I've not given you time to rest. I hope you can forgive me. I'd planned another surprise for this afternoon, but it can wait. Let me buy you a brandy before taking you back to your hotel. I've found a little of the hard stuff can be a restorative."

I nodded to say that a little brandy would be nice and Antonio instructed the driver to take us to the Galleria Vitorio Emanuele II, another upscale arcade of shops and mini-boutiques. The day was warm as we got out of the car and faced the shoppers who were out in force. These women with their dark glasses and beautiful head-scarves were as oblivious of my earlier fiasco as they were to the sparrows flying among the rafters above their heads. I was allowed to pass among them without inviting their curiosity and that was a comfort.

Antonio and I walked to a quiet bar where I could fortify my nerves with a snifter of brandy. The lights were low as we entered, as was the jazz quartet whose music poured from the radio behind the bar. Antonio sipped a glass of white wine and pretended to take in the scene around us, but I knew he was keeping an eye on me. This time I didn't mind his attention. I knew he was concerned.

The brandy went down warmly and my body relaxed as though I'd been soaking in a hot tub for several hours. Neither of us spoke much, but when my lids began to droop, Antonio suggested that we go for a walk. I agreed. A splash of fresh air was just what I needed.

We hadn't gone far when we stopped before the window of a small boutique. Without saying why, Antonio went inside and beckoned me to follow. A woman in her mid-fifties greeted us and suggested we take a seat in the pair of Queen Anne chairs nearby. Still a little sleepy, I was happy to sit down and to accept the coffee she offered. Once we were settled she left us but returned in good time with a tall, blonde model in tow. This new woman was wearing an elegant, crème colored satin tuxedo with flared pants. The outfit was lovely and I perked up immediately, like a child being given a beautifully-wrapped present. Antonio looked pleased. This was my second surprise of the day, he told me. The ensemble was mine and he'd brought me to the shop for a fitting.

• • •

The Friday and Saturday night performances of *Swan Lake* went well. No mishaps occurred either on or off stage. Each night, Antonio appeared after the final curtain with an armload of flowers. I didn't quibble. Having accepted his dinner outfit, rejecting his flowers would have seemed hypocritical. There was the unforeseen dividend that came with making him happy. He raised no objections when Alec spoke to him about Tom coming with us to Tuscany.

I gave Tom the good news when we met at a wine bar after Saturday performance. He looked relieved and as we sat talking, our first opportunity since our brunch in the park, I asked how he'd managed to find me that day.

"It was easy," he grinned. "I knew when you were meeting, so I sat in a taxi and waited. Pretty simple, really."

"No, it was clever of you and I appreciate it."

"Not so clever. I got ditched, remember? When I told Orlando, I thought he'd never stop laughing."

"You talked to Orlando? When?"

"I called him after you and Moretti drove off. I wanted to know if he thought I should follow since he knew where you were headed. He picked up on the first ring. He was about to call me, he said, because he was leaving Milan that day."

"What? Leaving? Why?"

"He didn't say. He just wanted me to keep my eye on you."

"When's he coming back?"

"He didn't tell me that."

"Didn't you ask?"

"You know Orlando. You can't get anything out of him if he doesn't want you to know. He didn't offer, so I didn't ask."

"That's great. So we're on our own. What happens if we run into trouble? I knew he'd do this. I just knew it."

A few patrons turned their heads in our direction, probably thinking Tom and I were having an argument. Tom lowered his voice as if to encourage me to do the same.

"He said not to worry. Nothing's going to happen for awhile. He'll catch up with us in Venice."

"How can he be sure nothing's going to happen? He's not clairvoyant. He talks to the dead, that's all."

Tom's face broke into a timid smile.

"Yeah. That's all."

"It's not funny. You can't imagine how I feel. I don't know who to trust. Sometimes, I don't even trust myself." As he knew nothing about my nearly being hit by a car, Tom looked puzzled. Still, he could see I was agitated and so he took both of my hands in his.

"What are you going on about, Tara? You can trust me and you can trust Orlando."

"You used to think he was a fraud. What's changed?"

His ears turned pink before he answered. What I'd said was true and it appeared that he couldn't explain the change to himself. He just knew he trusted Orlando and that I should too.

"He's the real deal, Tara. Count on it."

I wasn't satisfied and suggested we give Orlando a call.

"If he'd wanted us to know where he was going, he'd have told us. You know that. Look, don't worry. I'm here, too, for you. Just don't go running off with Moretti without telling me. Okay?"

I agreed to keep Tom informed and tried to draw comfort from what he'd told me. Orlando did have a knack for knowing when trouble was brewing. If he said nothing was going to happen for a while, then I should be satisfied with that. It wasn't great news but it was some. Still, a girl needs a shoulder to cry on once in a while. I hoped Tom's would be big enough.

. . .

With the Sunday matinee concluded, a jubilant Seattle Ballet Company boarded the train for Venice in the early evening. Two and a half-hours later, we'd arrived at the Venezia Santa Lucia station. From there we were to take water-taxis, known as vaporettos, to the various hotels and surrounding villas where we would be staying. Anne and Philip had agreed to stay at one of the more spacious palazzos with our youngest dancers. Their decision seemed to have been made more from a desire to be alone together than from any obligation due to their charges. The pair had stopped bickering and that they were affectionate to one another was plain to everyone. Apparently, the tour had revived happy memories and a second honeymoon was underway.

In contrast, Susan and David's relationship seemed to have deteriorated. On the train to Venice, the couple barely spoke. Susan stared out the window and David occupied himself with his smartphone. When Tom and I attempted to spark a conversation, the monosyllabic replies we received were discouraging, so we retreated into our private thoughts.

I'd had a good snack before boarding the train to Venice but when we arrived, I was hungry again. Alec, always in a hurry, wouldn't allow any delays, of course, and hustled us out of the station toward the waiting vaporettos. Within minutes, we were speeding along the Grand Canal and being exposed to jaw-dropping views of Venice at twilight.

Leaning over a rail at the bow of our boat, I was alone, watching the water churn beneath me, when Tom appeared. He looked nervous and kept thrusting his hands in and out of his pockets like a man who had something to say but couldn't get comfortable.

"It's a beautiful city," he muttered at last, as if answering my silence. "Too much gothic architecture, though. I keep expecting to see dead bodies floating in the water. I wish we'd hear from Orlando."

I turned from the railing to get a better look at him.

"I feel the same way. Something's not right. Maybe we should call."

"Already did. No answer. I wish the guy would show us more of his hand. He never tells us much, does he?"

"What do you talk about when you're alone with him? It can't all be about Reznikov."

We shoot the breeze about cars or sports, sometimes. Or we talk about you." He cast me a side glance to see how I reacted. I admit, I was surprised.

"I don't mean we gossip or anything," he went on. "He knows I like you and for what it's worth, I think he likes you, too."

"Now you *are* gossiping." Embarrassed, I returned my gaze to the water below, but Tom didn't want the conversation to end there.

"Come on, Tara. You needn't play coy. Guys are attracted to you. You've got to know that."

"I'm not playing coy, but you of all people should know that guys aren't on my radar right now."

Tom nodded and looked apologetic.

"I'd like things to be as they were at the start of the tour. I was excited about seeing Europe and meeting new people, you especially. But all that's changed. Everything's spoiled."

"Yes, it's like living in a nightmare and not being able to wake up."

Tom grunted his assent.

"When I found myself in that antechamber, talking to your teacher, all I could think of was, 'How did I get into this mess?'"

"It's not your fight," I said looking up at him. "You can walk if you want. I wouldn't hold it against you."

Tom looked at me with his mouth open, as if I'd spoken in Mandarin.

"What are you talking about? I couldn't walk away now. What kind of a guy do you think I am?"

"A fabulous one," I said as I stood on my toes to plant a kiss on his cheek. "Thanks for being my friend."

Tom blushed when he felt my lips brush his skin.

"You better not let lover boy catch you doing that. He might cut off your flower allowance. Where is he, anyway? I thought he'd be dogging us."

"If you mean Antonio, he's arriving by limousine and staying with friends."

"Friends? He has some? Bet they only come out at night."

"Stop being mean. I think you should give him the benefit of the doubt, at least till we know more."

"Oh, I can do that," he snorted. "I've got plenty of doubts to give him."

I delivered a light punch to his arm just as Ellen appeared, coming toward us from the opposite end of the vessel. She hurried forward when she saw us and joined us at the rail, her shoulders pressing against Tom's.

"I've been looking for you everywhere," she said, gazing up at him. "Why don't we do a little sightseeing after we've checked into the hotel? I think it would be fun. You could come, too, Tara," she added as an afterthought.

That she had a crush on Tom and that he was attracted to her was obvious. Under different circumstances, I might have been willing to step aside. But right now, I needed Tom and I didn't much care for the way she was behaving toward me. I told her Tom and I were busy and looped my arm around his in a proprietary way. When Tom didn't contradict me, Ellen's face fell. I confess I took pleasure in her reaction.

Finally, the vaporetto reached our stop. Tom and I were the first to disembark. We were headed for a salmon-colored hotel near the Teatro La Fenice, the opera house where we were to perform. Behind us came Ellen, then Alec and a few crew members. Susan and David brought up the rear. They were throwing daggers at one another with their eyes, so I decided it was time for me to get to the bottom of it once I'd settled in my room.

At the desk, I found a note waiting. The message was from my parents, written three days earlier, to say they missed me and were thrilled by the reviews we'd received so far. For a moment, staring down at my mom's familiar handwriting, I remembered how it felt to be loved and safe. I wanted to cry I missed her so much.

Once in my room, I threw my suitcase on the bed and was surprised when Susan's head popped in through an adjoining door. She said she was tired and wanted to have dinner sent up. Did I want to join her? I could see she was unhappy and wanted to talk so I agreed. I gave her my order and told her to give me enough time to take a nice hot soak in the tub. She said she would. We had plenty of time as neither David or Tom would be joining us. They'd gone off to reconnoiter the city on their own. She didn't look happy when she told me.

After my bath, where I'd sat soaking in hot water for a quarter of an hour, I wrapped myself in a hotel robe and joined Susan in her room. Our dinner had already arrived, but she hadn't touched her omelet. She was sprawled across her bed, crying.

I headed to one of the windows and opened the drapes for a view of the canal. Perhaps remembering where she was might cheer her up a little. The glow from the streetlamps shimmered on the water and heightened the lovely bones of the ornate buildings across the canal. I would have preferred to lose myself in that dreamlike setting rather than deal with the misery at hand. Still, I knew my duty and turning to look into the room, I asked Susan what was wrong.

She shook her head at first, too emotional to speak. She needed more time so I returned my gaze to the window in time to glimpse a gondola gliding across the water. Venice wasn't the place to suffer from a broken heart. Thomas Mann had described the city's allure as a fairy tale. I could see what he meant but from where I stood, the enchantment was more like a draft of opium -- exotic, dense, and laden with mystery that was a trifle diseased.

"He doesn't love me," Susan managed to choke out a few words, at last. "I should have known it wouldn't work. Why am I such a fool?"

I turned back to look at her.

"What do you mean he doesn't love you? Has he said so?"

"Not in so many words. But I want him to announce our engagement and he refuses. He thinks we should wait."

"Engagement? When was this decided?" I moved to the bed so I could hug my friend. She waved me away, refusing to accept my congratulations and went on with her lament.

"Europe has opened my eyes, Tara. This is a big world with lots of opportunities and lots of ways to live. Now that the tour's a success, David and I can go anywhere we like. We don't have to care what our parents think. We can be independent."

"You're not thinking of leaving the company, are you?" The question reflected my concern for myself. I didn't want to lose a friend, but what I said was that Alec would be devastated.

"Oh, he'll get over it. After this tour, he'll be getting more grants than he can use. Of course, if he agreed to pay us more..." She stopped a moment to speculate and then returned to her point. "What matters is that David and I belong together, but he's afraid of his parents."

"That's understandable."

"No, it isn't," Susan snapped. "We can make our own way now. All he has to do is choose."

"And you're afraid of the decision he might make. Is that it?"

Susan's red-rimmed eyes were sullen as she looked at me.

"I've no idea what he's thinking. Lately, he's been behaving like a child. All he wants to do is hang out in bars and nightclubs. I'm sick of his flirtations. He has to make a decision. Either he loves me and wants to marry me or he doesn't. I can't live like this anymore."

Her fear of losing David was palpable, not only by her tears but in her shuddering movements, as if she had little control over her body. I needed strong words to comfort her but I couldn't think of any. I had little experience in this arena. She needed someone like Anne with more experience, but Anne wasn't here. I was, and the words that fell from my mouth were as limp as wet laundry.

"Maybe David's right. We're all exhausted. Why not wait until we go home so we can celebrate properly?"

Susan shot up from the bed and began pacing, leaving no doubt that I'd failed to be of help. I felt miserable for my ineptitude, but to be honest, I'd have traded her troubles for mine in a heartbeat. Nonetheless, I decided to make another stab at soothing her feelings and suggested she might try flirting with him to get his attention.

She looked stupefied when she heard me, as if I'd reached into my ear and pulled out an iguana.

"Do you know how ridiculous that sounds? You're saying I don't give him enough attention? That's crazy. He always gets his way. Why do you think I've been dragging myself to all those nightclubs? Do you think I don't get enough dancing during our rehearsals? She clamped her hands on her hips as she glared at me. "Honestly, Tara, I don't know why I bother talking to you. You haven't a clue about love. If you did, you wouldn't treat Tom the way you do. You're selfish, you know that? You don't think of anybody but yourself."

Now it was my turn to looked stunned. At first, I couldn't believe my ears. The attack was unexpected and, I thought, unfair. But when I saw the fire in her eyes, I knew Susan had meant every word she'd said. She was my friend, but a part of her was jealous.

"I don't take advantage of Tom. That's a lie." I shot up from the bed to tower over her, half expecting her to back down, but her reply was full-throated.

"No it isn't a lie. You know he's interested in you and you string him along, bringing him to heel at your side like he were your puppy. He's a decent guy, Tara, and Ellen's crazy about him. If you don't want him, let him go. Otherwise, you're being a bitch."

She'd landed a verbal blow that hit deep. I was guilty of thinking of Tom as my property; but she didn't understand why. If she'd been a better friend, one I could have trusted to keep a confidence and if she hadn't ignored me to devote herself to David, Tom might never have been a part of the picture. Suddenly, I was angry with Susan. She'd let me down and was blaming me for her problems.

"Attacking me isn't going to help," I snarled. "I'm sorry you're upset, but I came here to help, remember? If there's a bitch here, it isn't me."

I turned on my heels and slammed the interlocking door behind me as I left. I could hear Susan apologizing on the other side, whimpering through her tears, but I was too angry with myself to forgive anyone. I stood with my back to the wall and sobbed as I hadn't done since the day Madame Natilova had died.

Ballet Noir

• • •

Monday morning brought a message I was in no mood to receive. Antonio had arrived and wanted me to join him for lunch at his friends' villa. I really didn't want to talk to anyone. If there'd been a Foreign Legion for women, I'd have joined it, or maybe a cave in the Himalayas would serve. Antonio offered one inducement that was hard to ignore. Joining him, I could avoid Susan. With that thought in mind, I dialed his number and arranged to meet him in the Piazza San Marco at 11 o'clock. From there, we were to take a vaporetto to Lido where his friends had their villa. The weather would be fine, he said, a perfect day to cross the lagoon. He sounded cheerful and so happy to hear my voice that by the time I rang off, I felt a little better.

I called Tom's room to let him know my plans. When he didn't answer, I left a message on his cell phone, asking him to meet me later that afternoon in the same Piazza.

The famous plaza was not far from my hotel so I had no trouble finding my way. I'd seen hundreds of pictures of the place so I knew what I was looking for.

According to my guidebook, the open space was sometimes called the "drawing room of Europe," but that was not my first impression. Nor was my eye immediately drawn to the magnificent architecture -- St. Mark's Basilica for example. What overwhelmed my view were the masses of pigeons occupying earth and sky. They claimed any perchable space, strutting about the place with little deference to the tourists who also claimed the Piazza. Given the number of humans bent on feeding them or taking their pictures, one would have thought that pigeons were a rare species though they spread themselves across the square like a large, feather blanket, defacing the architecture with excrement -- the Campanile, the Basilica, and the Doge's palace, structures of vastly different styles and each magnificent.

I'd barely time to take in the place when Antonio appeared, his eyes on me rather than his surroundings, as usual. He looked elegant in a light blue suit. I, on the other hand, had dressed casually in a black skirt and sweater with only Anunciata's gold cross to relieve the monotone.

"You look beautiful," he said as he took hold of my arm to guide me to a vaporetto. He explained, as we walked, that Lido was an island lying between the Venice lagoon and the Adriatic Sea, with lovely beaches for sunbathers. His friends owned a villa high on a hill that afforded views of both bodies of water. He was

148

anxious for me to meet the couple as he had known them for many years. He sounded a little nervous, as if I were about to undergo some kind of audience.

The boat ride was refreshing, if brief, but I confess my initial view of Lido was disappointing. The beach where we arrived was marred by rows of tacky blue huts, changing rooms, in effect, where tourists could shed their street clothes in favor of bathing attire. By noon, the sand was dotted with numerous bodies, lying like beached whales on the sand.

A car was waiting for us, not the limousine, but a silver Cadillac. The driver was familiar to me, however.

"I didn't know Daniel was in your employ."

Antonio answered as he held the car door open for me.

"He's not. He comes with the limousine service. I've hired him for the duration as he'll be driving us to Tuscany when your tour ends. I wanted to make sure we had enough room for your nanny."

Shaking my head to indicate I didn't know what he meant, he clarified.

"I was referring to Tom."

When I heard him, I couldn't suppress my irritation. The animosity between the two men was growing tedious. For one day, at least, I'd hoped to be spared snide comments. When I told him so, Antonio's face reddened. He climbed into the seat beside me and said nothing, turning his face to the window to avoid looking at me.

I guess the honeymoon is over, I said to myself and in my perverse mood, felt delighted.

The trip to the villa didn't take long, fifteen minutes at most, though it seemed longer as Antonio maintained his silence. I began to regret having accepted his invitation.

Eventually, we came to a stop before a pink, two-story palazzo, Rococo in style, that was perched upon a hill, as Antonio had said, affording a breathtaking view of the Adriatic Sea which no words could describe. As I stood taking in the scene, the front door was flung open and a woman wearing a red caftan came tripping down the stairs. She greeted me with a hug, talking the whole time about how much she'd been longing to meet me and how impressed she was by the reviews the company had received – me especially.

Behind her stood a man in his mid-forties whom I took to be her husband. He was dressed in a white polo shirt and matching pants. His hair was a light, sandy color, his complexion ruddy.

"Welcome, Miss Bentley," he said as he held out his hand. "Jeannie and I are delighted to have you as our guest. I don't know much about ballet, but my wife considers herself an aficionado."

"Please, Teddy, don't embarrass me before we've had our drinks." The woman, whose surname was still unknown to me, laughed and turned her blue eyes in my direction.

"It's true of course. I love ballet but I've never considered myself an aficionado."

By their accent, or rather by their lack of one, I concluded the couple was either from the United States or the west coast of Canada. I didn't ask but waited, assuming I'd learn more as the afternoon wore on. I was right. My hostess had a cheerful, expansive personality.

"I'm Jeannie Morris, by the way, and this is my computer geek husband, Teddy. I hope we can call each other by our first names. Tony's talked so much about you, Tara, we feel we know you already." She turned her head to look back at the men who were lagging behind as we climbed the stairs and entered the hallway. "Come on, you two. Don't start talking computers already."

Jeannie returned her attention to me to explain.

"My husband is one of those electronic geniuses and Tony encourages his obsession. As for me, I barely use e-mail. What we both like to do best is collect art and people. That's kept us together for seventeen years."

My hostess led me into a spacious room lined with windows, its white walls brightened with splashes of red carpets and gold drapes.

"Your house is lovely," I murmured. "Do you live here year 'round?"

"Oh no," Jeannie laughed putting her hand to her lips. "We're here during the summers. Our permanent home is San Francisco. We'll be headed back soon. That's where we met Tony. Years ago. He was studying for some wine degree or other."

As she talked, she ran her fingers through her short, blonde curls, an unnatural, but pleasing shade of platinum. She smiled as if reading my thoughts.

"I've been coloring for years. Teddy has no idea, bless him. I've always been a blonde by one means or another. But I like this new shade; it's a little lighter than my last. They say as you get older, lighter hair is more flattering. You're too young to worry about that, of course. How old are you, Tara, may I ask? Twenty? Twenty-one?"

"I turned twenty-one a month ago."

My hostess took hold of my arm and squeezed it.

"Good God, you needn't blush. Enjoy your youth. It passes soon enough, I can tell you." Her eyes fell upon the crucifix I was wearing and her hand, with its many-ringed fingers, flew to her lips once more. "I hope I haven't offended you by taking the Lord's name in vain. You're a Catholic, I suppose?"

I shook my head as I touched the cross.

"No. This is a gift from a friend. I wear it to remind me of her."

"It's beautiful." My hostess leaned toward it for a closer look.

"My folks are Evangelicals but once I got free of them, I got free of religion. If there is a God, I hope She will forgive me."

We shared a laugh which raised the eyebrows of the two men who'd entered the room behind us.

"Look at that, Tony," our host blustered. "Give women a few minutes together and they'll be up to something. Why do we men imagine we have a chance?"

Antonio offered a half-smile, the first I'd glimpsed since we'd arrived on the island.

Before we settled down to lunch, Jeannie suggested I give myself a guided tour of the place, as she had a few last minute details to attend to in the kitchen. I didn't hesitate to accept her offer and wandered through the spacious rooms on the second floor, imagining what it would be like to live in such palatial surroundings -- six bedrooms in all with a library and a cozy entertainment center which included computer gadgets as well. As I wandered through each room admiring its decor and the original oil paintings on the walls, I thought it was a shame to live here only a few months of the year. My inclination would have been to make it a permanent residence, but then, I didn't think like rich people. *It must be wonderful to have lots of money*, I sighed a little covetously.

When I returned downstairs, I found the others standing on the balcony overlooking the sea. The attending breeze was perfumed with the scent of the surrounding greenery and I sighed again as we sat down to a well laid table, An elegant arrangement of crystal and china all glistened in the sunlight.

"We sit out here under this awning as often as we can," Jeannie confessed. "Teddy found this place. Wasn't it clever of him?"

"But it's you who made it a home," her husband insisted. "I want you to know, Tara, that my wife chose all the decorations."

Jeannie gave her computer geek an appreciative smile then prepared to serve as the butler appeared with a tureen of asparagus soup and crusty bread rolls. What followed was a main course of baked ham and roasted potatoes.

The afternoon would have been pleasant if Antonio, seated across from me at the table, hadn't spent much of the time trying to read my mood. I wanted to stick my tongue out at him just to see what he would do, but being twenty-one, such behavior, especially in polite company, wasn't possible.

Much of the time, Jeannie provided the robust conversation. She explained how she and Teddy went about creating their art collection. She wasn't a self-absorbed woman, however, and sensing a little frost at the table, she wasted no time in getting to the bottom of it.

"You and Tony have hardly opened your mouths the entire meal. Is my cooking that bad or have I said something wrong?" Her blue eyes seemed as wide as the Adriatic as she allowed her glance to bounce between the pair of us.

Both of us hastened to assure her the afternoon was perfect, but she continued to look doubtful.

"Then you're working too hard to be on your best behavior. Tony, you're never this quiet. I'm right, aren't I, Teddy?"

Her husband looked up from his ham and demurred.

"Don't drag me into this, darling. You always say I'm not observant. No reason to change your opinion now."

"No, I suppose not," his wife replied with affection. "But I don't want Tara to be shy on our account. Vouch for us, Tony. Teddy and I are as informal as an old pair of shoes." She turned her blue eyes toward me once again. "Ask me anything you like about Tony, for example. I'm prepared to tell all."

"Jeannie, please."

"Don't worry, Tony. You know I haven't any secrets to reveal. I just want Tara to know what a nice guy you are. It's time you had another girl friend. How long has it been since you were engaged to that pretty dancer? The one with the gorgeous blonde hair. Oh, I remember. Sylvia... Sylvia something. So sad about how she died. I suppose you know about it, Tara. Tony must have told you?"

Antonio turned so red in the face when he heard her that Teddy, as unobservant as he claimed to be, came to the rescue.

"I should probably tell you how the three of us met, Tara. It was at a concert in San Francisco. They were playing Tchaikovsky and Tony sat alone in the seat next to us. Well, you've probably guessed Jeannie loves to talk..."

"Teddy!"

"I only meant you're more outgoing than I am, darling. Anyway, Jeannie got into a conversation with Tony during the intermission and when she discovered his background, she invited him to our place to have a look at our wine cellar. And, as they say, the rest is history."

"Teddy's a bit of an oenophile," Jeannie explained.

"As much as you're an aficionado of ballet," her husband corrected. "Anyway, Tony broadened my understanding of wine and helped improve my cellar. I'm much indebted to you." He raised his glass of Chardonnay to Antonio who sat to his left.

"Oh pish!" Jeannie scoffed. "You didn't tell Tara what else I found out about Tony that night at the concert. I don't suppose he's told you he's a gifted musician, has he?"

"Good Lord! Don't tell her that!" Antonio shot up from his chair as though a gun had been fired.

Jeannie waved him down making it clear to her guest that she intended to ignore his objection.

"Why shouldn't she know? And yes, I can see from her expression that you've said nothing. How terrible of you. Teddy why don't you lend Tony your violin so he can play for us? Honestly, Tara, she said, turning to me. "Tony's terrific."

Antonio shook his head.

"I-I'd rather not, Jeannie. I've nothing prepared."

"Oh come on, Tony," her husband chimed in. "We haven't heard you play in ages. I agree with Jeannie. It's time you sang for your supper."

I offered my encouragement, saying I loved the violin. They were the first kind words I'd spoken to him since we'd arrived, and they seemed to do the trick. Antonio relented.

When Teddy returned to the table, having retrieved his violin, he offered a slight apology.

"Mine's not as fine as Tony's, but it's good enough to give you an idea of his talent, Tara."

"That's what I'm afraid of," the cornered man quipped. Then he stood a moment, deciding what to play. Finally, his eyes lit up.

"For you," he said, looking at me. A composition of beauty and passion."

Jeannie winked at her husband as her guest began the *Allegro* from Tchaikovsky's, *Violin Concerto in D major.*

CHAPTER XVI

"If he's such a great musician, how come he doesn't give concerts like Itzhak Perlman or Sarah Chang?" Tom gave me a milk-curdled look which I ignored.

"Could you be a professional dancer and run a vineyard at the same time?"

"Maybe not. But I only concede the point because I know nothing about making wine."

"Well, it's a full-time job, obviously."

"Obviously? Since when did you become an expert?"

Tom broke off when my lips narrowed. We were seated in the Piazza San Marco outside a small café. The hour was approaching 5 o'clock and the pair of us were waiting for, or rather, hoping, Orlando might show up. Tom had left another message on his cell phone. As we waited, I used the time to tell Tom about my lunch at the villa, and that Antonio had invited me out again the next day. I braced for another of Tom's dour looks.

"I don't know what you see in the guy besides his money."

I ignored his suggestion that I was a gold-digger, but I admit, I did find it difficult to explain the attraction. With Antonio it wasn't always smooth sailing. Of course, the same could be said of life with Tom. In fact, men in general could be difficult to understand. Sometimes, I wondered if their senses were differently tuned.

Nonetheless, the afternoon with Jeannie and Teddy had shown me a different side of Antonio, one I'd have never guessed and found intriguing. I liked the couple and they seemed to adore him. In their treatment of him, they had shown me a man who could be self-effacing and yet possessed of an artist's soul. I wasn't ready to write him off. Besides, for the moment, he was a part of my life whether I willed it or not.

Tom and I ordered a second cappuccino as we sat, our eyes scanning the horizon for sight of a man in black. No one came close to matching that description.

Rather than go on squabbling, I changed the subject to David. I asked if he appeared moody lately.

"No. Why? What have you noticed?"

I told him about my fight with Susan, not mentioning Ellen, of course. When I said Susan was afraid David was losing interest in her, Tom laughed. I thought his response was callous and said so.

"You don't understand," Tom sat up in his chair to look at me. "He's going to pop the question on Sunday, the last day of the tour. I went with him this morning to look for a ring."

"What?" I too shot up as I gave him a pinch on his arm. "Why didn't you tell me? How long were you going to keep silent?"

Tom rubbed the spot where my fingers had dug in, frowning.

"What did you do that for?"

"Oh, don't be such a big baby. You deserved it. If you think I'd go running to Susan with the news, I wouldn't. Why would I spoil David's surprise? I hope he didn't choose a ring with a diamond so small you have to have a magnifying glass to see it. He hasn't got much money, I know that, but for something like this, he should go all out. What's it look like?"

"Hold on, Tonto." Tom held up his hand as if he were a traffic cop. "He hasn't bought it yet. He did see one that looked nice but he wants Susan's opinion first."

"If he wants her opinion, how's the proposal going to be a surprise?"

"Give a guy a little credit. Men aren't as dumb as you think, Tara. It's all arranged. The jeweler is going to put the ring in the shop window and after the matinee on Sunday afternoon, David and Susan will walk by. David will make some comment, or other, and see if Susan agrees. If she does, he'll swing back later and slap down his credit card. Easy as pie."

"You're enjoying this little conspiracy, aren't you?"

"Hey, I can be as romantic as the next guy. You should give me a chance." Tom grinned in that impish way of his which reminded me of why I liked him. Susan was right. He was attracted to me, but he was a flirt at heart. I doubted his heart could easily be broken.

"So how big is the diamond?" I went on. "Bigger than a pin-head, I hope."

"No-o-o, no," Tom shook his head a second time. "We're not going there. It's big enough and he can afford it. Anyway, from what you just told me, Susan would be happy with a cigar band."

He was right about that. Susan seemed to have settled on David some time ago. David was the one who was slow to the mark. If he was going to ask Susan to marry him all along, why did he spend so much time playing the field, going to nightclubs and flirting with other women? When I questioned Tom on that point, he was quick to defend his friend.

"Hey, be fair, Tara. He's a good-looking guy. Girls come on to *him*. I have the same trouble myself, if you've noticed."

I gave him another pinch on the arm, this time for bravado.

"Take me to the shop," I said, rising from my chair suddenly. "I want to see the ring for myself. Come on. Let's go."

Tom refused to budge and looked at me as if I had bees nesting in my hair.

"What is it about engagement rings that make girls go crazy? We haven't been here an hour. We should wait a little longer to see if Orlando shows up."

"But I want to see the ring."

"Yeah, I heard you, but it's almost five. The shop will be closed by the time we get there."

"Where is it?"

"By the Rialto Bridge. Look, let's wait another hour and if Orlando doesn't show, I'll buy dinner. On Saturday. Then I'll take you to see the ring. Promise."

"Why do we have to wait until Saturday? Why can't you take me tomorrow?"

"Didn't you say something about spending the day with Moretti?"

I hated it when Tom looked smug.

. . .

Orlando made no appearance that day or the next. On Wednesday evening, after Tom and I had suffered through hours of torturous rehearsal, we found him seated in the hotel lobby. He looked tired, as if he'd trekked on foot over miles of desert terrain. From his dark expression, I knew he wasn't bringing good news.

Seeing him in his present state, I confess I wasn't ready to welcome him. While he was absent, my days passed for what would seem a normal life. I was enjoying Venice with Antonio and had even patched up my quarrel with Susan. Being plunged back into the abyss of my uncertain future was an unwelcome turn of events.

Tom's reaction was the opposite. He rushed forward ready to greet his friend with a handshake, but when Orlando stood up, he threw his arms around him instead. I admit, the scene was touching, like a younger brother greeting an older one home from war. Swept up in the sentiment, I gave Orlando a hug, too, despite my momentary resentment.

Tom and I had not yet eaten, so we arranged to have our meals sent up to Tom's room rather than risk Susan wandering into mine. I got on the elevator with the two men but stepped off on my floor so I could take a quick shower. Twenty minutes later, I rejoined them wearing a fresh pair of jeans and tee shirt. Our dinner had already arrived, and Tom was slathering ketchup over his hamburger as I entered. He moaned when he saw me smirk.

"Why should I wait? I didn't want my food to get cold."

I sat down on a captain's chair near the bed where Tom was stuffing his face. Orlando sat on the remaining chair near the writing desk. Apparently, he hadn't ordered anything but a cup of black coffee. I offered to share my pasta with him, but he shook his head and when he didn't attempt to steal Tom's fries, I knew what he had to say wouldn't be good. Tom began the conversation.

"Tara and I have been leaving messages for you. When you didn't answer, we were getting worried. Did you find out anything more about Reznikov?"

Tom attempted to be nonchalant, but worry was painted in his expression. His eyebrows pinched together as he looked at Orlando. I could understand his consternation. There didn't seem to be any rules for dealing with a Necromancer. Both he and I were feeling our way in this three-person relationship. One thing we'd learned was never to expect information that wasn't volunteered but on this night, Orlando surprised us.

"I can't tell you where I've been, but I did find out that Reznikov is working on Meta-materials. I'm not sure how far he's progressed in his experiments, but it could mean we're in trouble." He paused to access our responses to his initial statement. He had Tom's attention, certainly, because the redhead stopped eating and looked up in surprise.

"Meta what? You mean like plastics?"

Orlando nodded in answer to his question.

"I think he's been working on a cloaking device, a way to bend light so that objects appear invisible to the human eye. The Romans stumbled on the principal when they learned to make glass. With a little gold, they could turn it green but, if the glass was illuminated from inside, it glowed a ruby color."

"That's not being invisible," Tom remarked before taking another bite out of his burger.

"No, but once the Alchemists discovered that a material's appearance could be altered, the search for invisibility was a natural progression. Scientists are working on the same problem today."

"Like stealth bombers, you mean?"

Orlando shook his head. "Bombers are invisible to radar but not to the human eye. I'm talking about making an object invisible to people."

Tom wrinkled his nose as if wondering how it could be done. I was curious, too, but was diverted for a moment, as I observed how his lanky frame extended over the bed. A cloaking device to fit him would have to be the size of a tent.

Tom sat up looking serious, unaware of my amusing thought.

"Any chance he could have done it, already? I mean, maybe he's the one who's been spooking Tara, like that time at the Vienna Opera House."

"Anything's possible," Orlando agreed. "Tiny objects have already been made to disappear using nano-waves, but that's as far as scientists have gotten. Using Alchemy, Renikov may have accomplished it. Who knows?"

"So-o, theoretically, he could be here now, listening to us?"

"Stop it," I objected. "You two are giving me the creeps."

"Be fair, Tara. We've got to consider the possibility." Tom looked to Orlando for corroboration and got it.

"We have to consider how he might use his power if he has it. It's a simple precaution. Otherwise we can't prepare to defend ourselves."

Tom had an idea and broke in.

"Maybe he robs banks. Maybe that's where he got his money to pay for our tour?"

Orlando shrugged when he heard the suggestion but didn't look impressed. I wasn't either. The winery made pots of money and when I said so, Tom looked deflated.

"Of course it does. Moretti is such a genius."

"I didn't say he was a genius."

"No? Because that's the impression you give."

Before Tom and I broke into another squabble, Orlando offered an idea..

"Maybe he knows about the antechamber. Maybe he wants Tara to take him there without her knowing."

"How could he know about the antechamber? Tara wouldn't be stupid enough to tell Moretti that." Tom narrowed his eyes at me. "You wouldn't, would you?"

"Of course I wouldn't. And not because I think he's in league with his grandfather. I wouldn't say anything because I'd be afraid he'd think I was crazy."

"I think you're crazy for consorting with the enemy."

"Listen Tom…"

"Stop squabbling you two and stick to the matter at hand. Here's what I'm suggesting. Suppose all those times Yelena Natilova tried to contact Tara, she left a trace of some kind, a disturbance in the electrical atmosphere. And suppose, Reznikov picked up on those traces through his dark studies? That could mean…"

Tom finished Orlando's thought for him.

"He's waiting for her to try again so he can use his invisibility cloak to follow Tara. But how can he be sure, she'll try again?"

"By increasing the odds." Orlando focused his eyes on me. "That's why he's after Tara. He's forcing your teacher to reveal herself. It's a working theory, at least."

"Yeah, but how did he know Madame Natilova would know Tara would be in danger in the first place?

Orlando shook his head.

"That's a mystery we'll probably never solve, not on this side of the antechamber, at least. The point is, she did know and when she tried to make contact, Reznikov found her traces. It's a working theory, like I say."

"How do we test it to find out if it's true?"

As if to answer Tom's question, Orlando turned to me.

"See what more you can squeeze out of the grandson, Tara. He's our only conduit."

· · ·

"Why this continuing fascination with my grandfather's hobby?" Antonio and I were having lunch at an outdoor cafe opposite St. Mark's Cathedral in the Piazza. "I've told you, I don't follow his work. I haven't in some time. And as grandmother takes no interest, there's really no one for him to talk to."

I picked up my glass of white wine and took a sip before going on.

"To be honest, Alec thinks I should show an interest. You understand. He's anxious about your grandfather. His financial support is important to us."

Antonio looked relieved when he heard me.

"So, this is Alec's obsession and not yours. Well, tell your Artistic Director that grandfather isn't the only member of the family with money. And you've already left me with a good impression."

His gaze was so earnest that I felt guilty for using him the way I had to, applying flattery as a lubricant.

"Thank you for being so kind to me. You've shown me such a good time and have been so generous. I really should never have accepted the outfit you bought for me in Milan..."

"Please. I thought we agreed to say no more of that."

"Yes, but I am grateful and I want you to know it. It's just that I have to please Alec, too. You understand, don't you?" I reached across the table to place my hand over his.

"Oh, very well," he said as he raised my fingers to his lips. "Fire away with your questions."

CHAPTER XVII

As I expected, I learned little from my lunch with Antonio, except that his grandfather had once talked of a cloaking device. As far as he knew, Reznikov had never pursued the study, however. Having provided that tidbit of information, he'd exhausted his knowledge and shifted his attention to what he predicted would be a triumphant end of our tour and the wrap-up party where he hoped I'd wear the outfit he'd purchased for me in Milan. I promised that I would. My assurance was unnecessary, of course, as I was looking forward to an excuse to show it off.

Antonio's optimism about our success in Venice, proved true. Both performances, from the perspective of the audience, went flawlessly. Behind stage, there was the usual chaos. Friday night, Susan misplaced her headdress for the Pas de trios in Act 1, again. When he heard she was looking for it, Alec swore if he found it, he'd glue in on her head. It wasn't found, so Ellen removed hers to eliminate the difference in their costumes, and the audience was none the wiser. Without their head-gear, Tom towered above his two partners and played up the difference in gestures and pantomime which made the audience roar with laughter. Alec stood in the wings, chagrined at first, but seeing how the house loved the innovation, he insisted Tom repeat it on Saturday night, which he did with similar effect.

All that remained was Sunday's matinee, so no one should have blamed us for feeling giddy, as if an army of champagne bubbles had invaded. We'd appeared in some of the finest theaters of Europe and had been accepted. Even I couldn't expel my happy thoughts with those of Reznikov.

To be honest, he'd been the source of our joy. Without him, we'd have had no opportunity to prove ourselves in a way Seattle would never have granted. My only wish was that on Sunday, I'd be flying home to the Pacific Northwest with my friends.

Knowing the flurry of hugs cand kisses that would go on backstage, Tom and I had made plans to escape the theater in good time on Saturday night. We were to join Orlando at 11 o'clock at a prearranged wine bar so we had to hurry.

Nonetheless, when we met outside the theater, I reminded Tom of his promise to show me Susan's engagement ring. He looked sour at the mention of it and said the detour might make us late. I insisted, however, so he took hold of my hand and began dragging me through the crowded streets as if I were a kite he intended to launch.

At one point, I had to stop to catch my breath and while I did, Tom stood over me, looking twitchy. For the millionth time, he suggested we forgo the shop and head straight for the bar.

I tried to reason with him when I had enough breath to speak.

"We're almost there. What's the harm?"

"The harm is I know you, Tara. You'll want to stare at the other rings, and then you'll strain your neck to read price tags. It won't be quick. With you it never is."

"I just want a peek. I promise I won't make us late."

Tom looked dubious but grabbed my hand again and we were off, plowing our way through the streets until, after what seemed miles, we reached the shop. At that hour, it was closed.

"There it is," he said, stabbing at the window with his finger. "Now can we go?"

Dozens of rings gleamed up at me from behind the dimly lighted glass. Any one of them could have been Susan's. How was I to know?

"Which one?" I insisted, exhibiting my own impatience. "Show me which one."

"There!" Tom's finger pecked at the window a second time like an angry bird, so hard that the glass seemed to wobble a bit.

"You mean the one with the gold swirls around the stone?" I pressed my nose against the pane for a closer view.

"Yes. Now come on. Let's not be any later than we have to be."

Tom tugged at my arm but I refused to budge wanting a better look. Surely, we could spare another minute, I thought.

"Is that a gold or platinum setting? In this light, I can't tell."

"How should I know? Platinum, I think."

"It's beautiful and the diamond isn't as small as I imagined. Susan will love it."

"Good. I'm glad you approve. Can we go now?"

Tom's voice grew edgier but I ignored him.

"I can't read the tag. How much did you say it cost?"

"I didn't." Even in the moonlight I could see his upper lip begin to curl.

"Come on, Tara. You promised not to make us late. You of all people should know how important our meeting with Orlando is."

I knew he was right, but that didn't keep me from feeling annoyed. Why was he being such a nag? Yes, Orlando was important, but I also needed to take my mind off my trouble, sometimes. Here was an opportunity to focus on Susan's happiness as a part of my own, if only for a minute. He should have understood that.

I didn't air my thoughts, of course. I recognized I was taking my feelings out on the one person who least deserved it. Instead, I held out my hand so he could begin dragging me through the streets again. But when I did, he took hold of my shoulders and threw me hard against the window. The pane behind me wobbled like jelly.

"O-w-w. What are you doing?" I reached up to rub the back of my head, certain a lump was forming.

He started to answer.

"Some fool's tried to…" Before he could finish, he broke off his sentence and slumped to the ground in front of me. I watched, not understanding, as his arms clutched at his right side as if to protect it.

"What are you playing at?" I could make nothing of this reclining figure. Was he trying to scare me? To punish me for holding him up? If so, he was succeeding.

"Quit fooling around, please. If we're late now, you'll be the one who's to blame."

He didn't respond, so I bent over him for a closer look. That's when I saw the trickle of blood on the side of his lip. He must have injured himself. But how? His fall hadn't been that great. Maybe he'd fainted. But again, why? Surely, he was too young for a heart attack. I shook him a little to see if he was conscious.

"What's the matter, Tom? Talk to me!"

When he failed to answer, I took hold of his arm and tried to pull him into a seated position. He hung at the end of my arm like a dead weight. I hadn't enough strength to lift his head an inch above the ground. Alarmed, I dropped to the pavement beside him and peered into his eyes. What I saw there was a faint flicker. He seemed to be directing me to look off to the side. His eyes rolled back in his head as if he were using them to point to someone who was moving away. But when I followed his direction, I saw nothing, only a throng of revelers too happy to notice Tom and me.

Desperate to rouse him, I took his face in my hands, forcing him to focus so on me, hoping that with a whisper or by the fluttering of his lids, he could tell me what had happened, but the light in those green eyes, that minutes before could crinkle with laughter or flash with anger, was beginning to fade. I watched, helpless, as a glaze frosted over them similar to the surface of a frozen pond. I knew then that were I to touch my forehead to his, he would no longer see me. He was gone. The curtain between our two worlds had rung down. All that held us together was my searing disbelief, a prelude to the searing grief that was sure to follow.

Instinctively, I moved to shield Tom's body from prying eyes. No one was to look at him. He wasn't a spectacle for the curious and I didn't want to hear someone pronounce that he was dead. He was my dearest friend and in my way, I loved him.

Taking him into my arms, I rocked him as if he were a sleeping child, my hair falling over my face so that the external world was curtained from us both. I could feel his blood pool around me, painting my clothes with the crimson stain of his lost life. I'm sure I ceased to breathe because pain had formed a stopper in my throat.

How long I remained in my solitary anguish, I don't know. Someone must have noticed us, Tom and me. Words began to fall, soft as petals about my ears. Strangers were offering to help. Yet what could I say to them, these people who meant well? Did they not see I had turned to stone? That Tom's body was cold *as* stone? They'd come too late. They must leave me alone and let me grieve.

One pair of arms reached down to encircle me, too strong for me to throw off, though I resisted. I would not be moved even if the ground threatened to crack and open beneath me, but the arms were insistent and when I recognized whose arms they were, I found my voice and uttered a wail that must have cracked the heavens before falling back to earth.

"No-o-o-o. You can't take him. Not yet, Orlando. Please, not yet."

The Necromancer's grip softened and for a time, he rocked Tom and me in his arms. Together, we shed enough tears to flood all the canals of Venice.

Even so, there was no escaping the sound of an ambulance making its approach. Soon, I would be forced to leave Tom who had already left me.

"Look Tara." Orlando whispered in my ear as he pointed to the sky.

My eyes followed his direction and there, among the stars, I saw a door open. On its threshold stood a young woman, her hair rippling like starlight on water. Sylvia Huntington... Sylvia Louise Huntington had come for Tom's soul.

CHAPTER XVIII

A church tower was ringing the early hour of two in the morning when Orlando returned with me to my hotel. We had ridden together in the ambulance that carried Tom's body to the hospital. According to the coroner's preliminary estimate, our friend had died of a stab wound sometime before midnight.

The police came to the hospital to interview me, but seeing I was covered in blood and suffering from shock, they released me with the admonition that I was to report to the police station the next morning.

Alec was waiting for me in the lobby when we arrived. Orlando had called him from the hospital to tell him what had happened. He rushed forward when he saw me and, ignoring my bloodstained clothes, he pulled me to him.

We cried together for a long time before we separated. Alec roused himself enough to thank Orlando for his call, and then the two men walked me to the elevator to escort me to my room. They waited while I showered, and when I'd finished, Alec retrieved my bloody garments from the bathroom floor, intending that I should never see them again. He was holding them in a bundle as I climbed into bed. He said he wasn't sure what the hour was on the west coast, but he intended to call my parents and Tom's too, of course, the moment he returned to his room.

He looked haggard as he looked down on me and my heart went out to him. The last job I would have wanted was to phone Tom's parents to tell them their son had been murdered and was lying in a morgue thousands of miles away in a foreign country. Like me, Alec would get little sleep that night.

Once Alec was gone, Orlando drew up a chair beside my bed, intending to keep vigil. I didn't argue. I didn't want to be alone.

I dozed off for what must have been a couple of hours, because when I awoke, a pale light was fingering its way past the drawn curtains of my room. Orlando had fallen asleep in his chair, his breathing rhythmic and peaceful. The difference between us was so clear at that moment. He could rest, death being no stranger to him, while I kept replaying the events of the previous night over and over in my mind, awake or sleeping.

At some point, I must have fallen asleep again because when I next opened my eyes, Orlando's face hovered above mine, his eyes forming a question.

"I heard you moan."

"I'm all right," I whispered, then contradicted my statement by breaking into tears. Orlando lay down beside me, encircling me in his arms so that I could feel his strength. His warmth was what I needed and for a time I lay listening to his heart as it beat at a slow and steady tattoo. He was my life support and in my need of him, I allowed my lips to find his. My kiss was gentle but insistent and his first response was to resist, but I knew he too, was grieving and held on fast. We needed each other, whether he realized it or not. Eventually he acknowledged his need and I had the satisfaction of feeling him relax in my arms. Morning found us together lying naked and entwined.

. . .

In the early hours of the morning, unbeknownst to Orlando and me, Alec gathered the corps together to give them the news of Tom's death. I'm told cries of disbelief went up, then those of anger and finally tears. In the little time Tom had been among us, he had found his way into our hearts, cheering us and entertaining us with his mischief. That he was dead was no more believable than being told that the sun had fallen from the sky or that the earth had split in two and there were now two planets. The unthinkable couldn't be true and yet it was true. That's why, when Alec announced the matinee would be cancelled, a hue and cry went up among the dancers. To walk away? To fold the tent as if Tom never existed was not to be allowed. The company demanded a final performance. The matinee would be dedicated to Tom's memory. His part, particularly in the Pas de trois, would be adapted so that his place would remain vacant. The intent was to leave a gap in the mind's eye for the audience to imagine him and in its way invoke his spirit.

Alec was touched by the idea and agreed but warned it would mean an extra rehearsal. No one objected. Ellen would refresh her role as Odette and a girl from the chorus would take her place as a featured dancer. The performance might be flawed, he told his crew, but the gesture was wonderful.

Before leaving for the theater, Alec stopped by my room. He looked relieved to find Orlando present and asked if he would escort me to the police station. Orlando agreed as that had always been his intention. Once an agreement had been reached, Alec told me he'd talked to my parents early that morning. They were shocked to learn what had happened but were grateful I was unharmed.

Tom's parents were devastated, naturally, and planned to arrive in Venice on the first available flight. Their one request was for Alec to begin the necessary paper work which would allow them to take their son's body home as soon as possible. He told them he would and as he hurried toward the door on his way to the theater, he said I'd have to leave for Tuscany without him. He needed to stay behind to fulfill his promise to Tom's parents.

"I'll join you as soon as I can, Tara, but please, no arguments about the trip. A change of scene will do you good."

I'd barely time to open my mouth before he had disappeared, closing the door behind him. I called out after him at the top of my voice. I wasn't going to Tuscany. The trip was out of the question.

He didn't hear me or chose not to, I didn't know which, but when he failed to return, I started to scream, loud enough perhaps for Yelena Natilova to hear me.

Orlando moved quickly to calm me, wrapping me in his arms as he had done during the night so that I felt cosseted by him.

"Stay calm, Tara," he breathed into my hair as he held me. "We must get through the police interview. Then we can talk about what happens next. Remember what your teacher said. You must be brave. And remember my promise to her, as well. I'll be with you every step of the way.

. . .

How I managed to satisfy the questions the authorities threw at me remains a mystery. At one point, I'd gone to pieces again when one officer described Tom's injuries. He'd been pierced through the heart and lung with a sharp instrument. When I heard the description, all the memories of the previous night came flooding back to me and it was almost impossible for me to speak. In my current state of mind, there was no more information anyone could get out of me and so I was released to Orlando's care. They told him I should remain in the vicinity while the investigation was underway.

His reply was one I could hardly believe. He told them I might be traveling to Tuscany and gave them the address of the villa in Montepulciano where I'd be staying. The police offered no objection though the location was a two-hour drive from Venice. In fact, they seemed glad to be rid of me and my hysteria.

The moment Orlando and I found ourselves on the pavement, I turned on him like a wild animal. How could he be thinking about Tuscany when he knew the state I was in? Had everyone around me gone deaf?

He listened to my tirade without saying a word and when I had finished, suggested we find a coffee shop where we could talk less publically. I realized I was making a spectacle of myself and needed to calm down, so I agreed.

We found a café nearby and while I sank into a chair, Orlando stepped to the counter to order two Espressos. By the time he returned, I'd regained some of my composure but not all.

"I'm not going to Tuscany," I told him as he took the chair opposite mine. "Nothing you can say will convince me. I might as well slit my throat here and now."

My voice was loud enough to attract the attention of other customers, but Orlando didn't flinch or signal any apologies to them. Again, he let me rant while he sipped his coffee. Before long, the young man from behind the counter came over to see if I was all right. Orlando explained that I'd witnessed a murder and that we needed our privacy. The young man backed away, his eyes owlish as he apologized. After that I lowered my voice, but I kept on sputtering until I'd run out of steam.

Orlando handed me his hanky, for I'd shed several tears, then spoke as if to a frightened child.

"You can't call a time-out, Tara. I wish that was possible, but Reznikov won't allow it. I'm aware that you're in shock and your life is in shambles. For all we know, Tom's death was part of a plan to weaken you, but you can't give in. Not for yourself, not for Tom and not for Yelena. We have to go on. You and I together."

"Together? How? Tell me how. You just can't show up in Tuscany."

"Oh, but I can. I'll say I've been touring Italy and when I read about the murder in the papers, I contacted Alec. He knew you and I are old friends, so he gave me the address of where you were staying."

"That may get you through the door but it won't get you an invitation to stay."

"Don't worry. I'm guessing Reznkiov will recognize me for what I am and will want me to be there." Orlando leaned back in his chair and looked confident.

"You think he's that canny?"

"Don't you?"

"I don't know anything except that I'm afraid. What if something happens to you?"

"It won't." Orlando took hold of my hand and squeezed it. "I know how you feel, Tara. I wish there was an alternative, but the only way out of this tunnel is through it."

I knew Orlando was right. I couldn't escape Tuscany. With no plan of my own, I had to trust his.

We finished our coffee and he offered to escort me back to the hotel. I probably could have used the rest but I felt awkward about the previous night. We'd had no opportunity to discuss our feelings and I wasn't ready to open a fresh can of worms. I suggested we go to the Opera House to watch the rehearsal. He agreed but frowned a little, as if he wasn't convinced my idea was a good one.

As we approached the main entrance of the theater, I was unprepared for the nexus of reporters who had gathered outside. They came swarming in my direction the minute they recognized me, not as a dancer, but as the witness to a grisly murder. Questions came at me from all directions, some in Italian but many in English, and all the while Orlando elbowed his way through the crowd, pulling me up the stairs behind him toward the glass entrance. Inside, a guard saw what was happening and waved to us, unlocking one of the doors long enough for us to slip through. Then he slammed it shut again, barring the reporters who tapped on the glass, making the sound of falling hail.

Safe inside, I thanked the man for our rescue, then escaped the angry reporter's faces by hurrying toward the performance hall where, already, we could hear strains of Tchaikovsky's Swan Lake wafting from a tape recorder. The theater was dark as we entered. From a distance I could see Ellen struggling with Alec's direction. She didn't seem to understand what he wanted, and he couldn't understand why not. The role wasn't too difficult for her. Alec knew that. What he didn't understand was that Tom's death was as much a blow to her as it had been to me. Only Susan and I were aware of the reason for her struggles. If she would have allowed it, I'd have put my arms around her and we would have cried together, but I knew the gesture would be rebuffed. What mattered now was the success of the performance, for Tom's sake and for the company's. I'd have to hurt her again, as I'd done before, this time irrevocably. I would have given the world to avoid it, but there was no time. The theater would open in one hour.

When I headed toward the stage, Orlando made no effort to stop me. My guess was he approved of my decision to dance.

•   •   •

Ballet Noir

Our performance that Sunday was all the success the company could have hoped for. Ellen would never speak to me again, and I felt it was a loss for us both. Where tragedy had weakened her, it had somehow strengthened me. Pain was a welcome distraction from the emptiness of loss. To feel is better than not to feel and I welcomed my grief, allowing it to fill my every movement and every gesture as its avatar.

The audience seemed to understand. When the last strain of music fell in the farthest corner of the hall, a stillness followed. Among the audience, there was some general understanding that to disturb the silence would be a sacrilege. Several seconds past, perhaps nearly half a minute, before one pair of hands did clap, followed by another and another until, in concert, everyone rose to their feet to give unstinting and prolonged applause. Tom Donne, who had been dead for 24 hours, was finally receiving the tribute he deserved.

CHAPTER XIX

Madame Lazaremko had the good sense to cancel the wrap-up party. After the matinee, members of the troupe wandered off, alone or in pairs, saying little, as if wanting to think about all that had happened and about how proud they were to have paid a flawless tribute to their lost friend. Only Antonio was out of sync. He appeared backstage, as he always did, with an armload of roses.

I'd neither seen nor spoken to him since the tragedy and had answered none of his messages. I knew how Tom had felt about him, and at the moment, a part of me held Antonio responsible for what had happened. If the judgment wasn't fair, I didn't care. I wanted to be with David and Susan, friends whom I trusted and, who, like me, were in mourning. The pair had put off their engagement announcement deciding to wait until they'd returned to Seattle. As for the ring, there was no thought of returning to the jewelry shop near the Rialto Bridge.

Only Antonio seemed to think life could go on as usual. I might have taken his flowers and thrown them in his face if Anne hadn't entered my dressing room, together with a few dancers from the corps. He was backed against a wall with no one taking any notice of him as my friends huddled around me.

So many feelings were expressed. We hugged each other and shed more tears, but Anne's words were a great comfort to me. She had danced the role of Odette many times in her younger days and been praised for her interpretation, but on this afternoon, any hint of comparison or jealousy was absent from her voice. She congratulated me on my performance and said that never had she seen the role performed with such pathos. Tom had been properly honored and she thanked me. The others nodded, and another series of hugs began. In the midst of it, Phillip wandered in and gave me a hug, too. Finally, our sentiments expressed, our tears dried, my visitors faded away, like petals blown by the wind.

I waved them goodbye as a lump formed in my throat. These dancers, bound to one another by the hardships and triumphs of dance -- regardless of their ambitions and piques of envy -- were my family and particularly, on this day, as dear to me as my own flesh and blood.

Ballet Noir

Still clutching his flowers, Antonio remained with his back to the wall, gazing at me with a sympathy that seemed new to him. He'd never liked Tom, but drawing upon his own knowledge of loss, I think he began to understand mine. When he spoke, his voice was hoarse. He admitted he and Tom had never really liked one another, but he wasn't insensitive to my feelings. In the intervening hours since the murder, he'd twice visited the police station. There'd been no news of a perpetrator, but he'd insisted that someone call the villa the moment there was any development.

"In the meantime," he pleaded. "Let me take you away from here, Tara. Montepulciano, I promise you, is a different world."

. . .

By mid-morning the next day, I found myself seated beside Antonio with his grandmother opposite me in the limousine. The chauffeur, Daniel, was at the wheel, speeding us along the Autostrade on our way to Tuscany. Antonio was dressed in a white sweater and navy pants, while Madame Lazaremko wore an orchid turban with a matching tunic and floor-length skirt. Her frown when she saw my attire -- jeans and a white tee under a blue woolen jacket -- let me know she disapproved. I ignored her. I didn't care what she thought and how I dressed was my business.

During the trip south, Antonio glanced in my direction several times. Rather than allow him to invade the privacy of my thoughts, I peered out the window as if engrossed by the passing scene. Madame Lazaremko did the same. The silence suited me.

At noon, we stopped for lunch at a small restaurant just off the road. I wasn't hungry but we needed to stretch our legs and give the driver the opportunity to rest.

The room we entered was crowded and the food being served looked appetizing, but I was not hungry. When my order arrived, I spent most of the time moving the fettuccini around on my plate. Antonio watched me peck at my food and behaved similarly. He appeared to be nervous for his gaze perpetually wandered from his grandmother's face to mine and then back again.

How different this trip would have been if Tom were with me. He'd have found some humor in the situation. I could imagine him cocking an eyebrow or curling of a lip, facial commentary he knew would amuse me. His antics would have made the trip bearable. Now all I could think about was Orlando and when I might see him again.

As for the second half of our trip to Montepulciano, I can describe nothing except that it was a long, grey blur. I was stiff as I piled out of the limousine upon arrival but I shall never forget my first impression of the villa. If I'd expected a house of horrors, I was pleasantly surprised. The two-story brick structure with its red-tiled roof, stood on a hill and was reached by climbing a set of wooden steps. From there, one could look out upon the surrounding hills with rows and rows of grapevines crisscrossing the landscape, like a patchwork quilt. Under different circumstances, I would have counted myself fortunate to be in this beautiful setting, but I was too keenly aware of the discrepancy between the outward appearance of the place and the evil residing within.

To the right of the house, its north side, stood a small olive grove. South and down a hill, stood the winery where the red grape, also known as Montepulciano, was processed to make d 'Abruzzi wine.

I learned later the family kept a private cellar in the basement of the villa as well.

The butler who greeted us at the door was an elderly man named Tito. He was thin and slightly stooped. His features were aquiline and his silver hair was thinning. I guessed him to be in his eighties. Antonio told me later that he was 93. He'd worked at the winery before Vladimir Reznikov was born and refused to be pensioned off. No longer fit for grape harvesting, he was given the role of butler, though his frailty left him with few duties. The housekeeper as I was to discover, was efficient and humored him by providing light tasks. Mostly, he served the meals and polished the silver. On no account was he allowed to take phone messages. His hearing was poor and his handwriting unreadable. Nonetheless, he frequently ignored this prohibition with ruinous effect, I was later told.

Upon entering the hall, the old man pointed to the top of the stairs to indicate where I would find my room but made no effort to guide me, perhaps because of his frailty or because he assumed Antonio or his grandmother would see to my comfort.

As for Madame Lazaremko, she left me almost at once, pointing to the same landing as Tito had done and then departing for her room which was on the main floor. Antonio had yet to enter as he was settling accounts with Daniel.

With the scant directions I'd been given, I climbed the stairs, hoping to find my accommodations on my own. I met with immediate success. The first room I entered was filled with fresh flowers, Antonio's signature. The largest windows faced east and provided the same lovely view of the vineyard and the surrounding hills as did the foyer. Two smaller windows faced north, overlooking the olive grove. The ceiling was beamed and the walls were whitewashed. On the four-poster bed against the north wall was a comforter of burnt orange, and hanging along the picture railings, were a number of plein air paintings, pastoral settings, signed by artists whose names I didn't know. The adjoining tiled bath was outfitted with a large, claw-footed tub where a person could comfortably soak for hours.

As I said, under normal circumstances I might have been happy there. But mine was not a normal circumstance, and so, I stood at the open window and, with a sinking feeling, watched as Daniel got into the limousine and barreled down the gravel road, leaving a trail of dust behind him. He was headed for the highway, back to Venice or wherever he'd come from. Soon the car became a speck and when it vanished, I realized I was alone, cut off from the outside world.

I had six hours to fill before dinner which was at eight. I didn't know when Orlando planned to arrive but I hoped it would be soon. In the meantime, I browsed through the bookshelves, hoping to find reading material. The volumes were in Italian, and so, disconsolate, I threw myself on the bed and stared into the satin canopy above it.

It took every fiber of my will to fight my impulse to dash from the room and chase the limousine's tire marks back to civilization. When Antonio knocked at my door with my luggage, I was so tense that I leapt from the bed as though it were a trampoline. If he noticed my taut demeanor, he said nothing. Rather, he set down my suitcase, and like the proud proprietor of an Inn, glanced about the room with a look of satisfaction.

"I hope you'll be happy here," he said, his face plastered with a smile. "At one time, this room was a study. When I was a boy, there used to be a desk right over there." He pointed toward the eastern windows. "I used to do my homework in this room, but much of the time, I spent it watching the men working in the fields. The view is very peaceful and that's exactly the atmosphere you need right now."

He rubbed his hands together as he perused the accommodation one more time, then he apologized, saying he had to leave for a few hours because of some difficulty at the winery. While he was gone, he suggested I take a hot bath and reminded me again that dinner was a eight.

With little else to do, I unpacked my few belonging and followed his suggestion. The claw-footed tub was deep and I allowed myself to sink into it, letting the hot water bury me up to my chin. I'd taken the precaution of leaving the bedroom window ajar so I could hear the first sounds of Orlando's arrival. My vigil proved fruitless. Orlando made no appearance and so, rising from my bath, I burrowed into my bed, hoping for an hour or two of sleep. Apparently, I succeeded because I was surprised to be awakened by the chiming of the downstairs clock. The hour was half past seven. Suddenly I was alert and leapt from the bed with just enough time to throw on my dress and run a comb through my hair before Antonio, punctual as usual, rapped on the door.

His eyes glowed with admiration when he saw me, even though I'd worn my black dress a dozen times. On this occasion, he looked casual in a pair of grey flannel trousers, a white crewel sweater and kid skin loafers.

He held out his arm to escort me to dinner and I couldn't help noting how happy he looked. Despite the difference is our ages and his greater experience in the world, he seemed genuinely in awe of me. Or perhaps his behavior was a ruse and he really was in league with this grandfather. I doubted it was the latter but being on my own, I knew I couldn't let my guard down.

The dining room, when we entered, was unlike anything I'd expected. An oak table, long enough to seat ten, stood at the far end of the room parallel to the three windows which provided the same view of vineyard I enjoyed from my room. A large, sideboard occupied most of the north wall, and an open cupboard dominated the south, where, beside it, was an arched door that led to the kitchen. A few console tables were interspersed throughout and on each and every flat surface, numerous candles burned, though they made a modest display compared to the candelabras at either end of the main table. If I hadn't known better, I would have thought I'd walked into a séance.

Antonio seemed to read my thoughts.

"I should have prepared you. Grandfather enjoys dining by candlelight. He's an old man but a vain one."

Madame Lazaremko, who'd come up behind us, picked up on his remark.

"Are you speaking ill of your grandfather, Antonio? Never mind that it's true. You shouldn't share such things with strangers. Where is he, by the way?"

She looked around wearing a puzzled expression. That evening she was swathed in a garnet- colored gown that matched a necklace of the same hue: three rows of crown-cut gems set in gold.

As usual, she managed a disdainful glance at my attire but continued to address Antonio.

"Your grandfather's forgotten the hour, again. Fetch him will you? If I send Tito down those basement steps, we won't sit down to dinner before midnight. And tell Vladimir not to change. He's late for our guest."

Antonio bowed, apparently used to taking orders from his grandmother, and exited the room. In the interim, Tito appeared, carrying a large soup tureen in his hands. Surprised to see no one was seated at the table, he addressed his mistress in Italian, sounding annoyed. She replied in kind and with a curt wave of her manicured hand, sent him back to the kitchen.

The servant did as he was told though he muttered the entire time of his exit, which was considerable. Faced with an awkward silence, I made a stab at conversation, asking if she knew what sort of experiment her employer was working on.

Madame's eyebrows arched into stiff peaks when she heard me.

"My *employer*? Surely Antonio has explained I am mistress of this house. Even so, I should have thought you might have guessed. Do I look like an employee? Do I dress or act in this house as if I were?"

Though she was older than I was and more accomplished as a ballerina, I bridled at her open disrespect for me. As a dancer, I admit, I was used to a certain amount of disregard. My entire life was subject to correction and the approval or disapproval of others, but I'd had some success now as a performer and was no longer willing to stand in awe of anyone. I decided to repay her remark in kind.

"'Mistress?' Forgive me. I had no idea you were paid for services beyond those of an agent."

Madame's nostrils flared like a horse ridden over a great distance.

"What? How dare you speak to me like that? I have more talent in my little finger than you possess in your entire body. If Vladimir weren't so keen to meet you, I'd send you packing this minute... this minute. Do you hear?"

"Yes, yes, my dear. We hear. Even Tito hears, I suspect. What's set you off, Ludmila? Surely not this lovely slip of a girl?"

The tall man who'd spoken stopped in the archway between the hall and the dining room, his obsidian eyes dancing in the candlelight as he looked at me.

"I presume I have the honor of meeting Miss Tara Bentley?" He came forward with his arms outstretched and took hold of both of my hands. "Welcome, my dear. After reading all those glowing reviews, I have been eager to meet you."

He let go of my hands, then turned his black eyes upon Natalya Lazaremko. They seemed to burn brighter when they came to rest on the necklace she was wearing. Bending down, he examined the gems with care. Then he straightened to his full height and addressed his next remark to his grandson.

"So this is what you chose, Isaac? I couldn't have done better myself. The color is lush and Ludmila looks radiant in them. Thank you for buying them for me."

The mistress of the house smiled, gratified by the compliment, but the rebuke that came next undid that good effect.

"Please, Vladimir, while Miss Bentley is here, call Antonio by his right name. Referring to him as Isaac will only confuse the girl."

"Do you think so?" Reznikov stared at his paramour through narrowed eyes. "I wouldn't have thought her so stupid. Though I find your concern touching as only a moment ago, I could have sworn you were ready to send the girl packing."

Withered by his scrutiny, Madame fell silent. If the man with the military bearing noticed his effect, he made no amends, but turned his attention to me. I gave it back with a like candor and was surprised to discover how little time had weathered his features; a face worthy of the hand of Michelangelo. Only his mane of white hair, luxurious enough to satisfy a man or woman half his age, gave a hint to his years. An earthy scent clung to his presence, nothing offensive, but reminiscent of the smell of grass after a spring rain. Perhaps what I detected was the aftermath of some chemical experiment in which he'd been engaged.

Bowing slightly, he took hold of my hand a second time and led me to the table. His touch was dry, but soft like a pressed flower.

"Sit here, Miss Bentley," he said pointing to the chair on his left. "You shall have the place of honor this evening."

Antonio snapped his eyes in his grandmother's direction in time to see her stiffen, as did I. She blanched slightly, but said nothing as she sank into the chair Antonio had pulled out for her beside his own. Reznikov seemed to enjoy his cruel gesture for his eyes glittered as he watched Madame's humiliation. I should have relished seeing her punished, but I didn't.

At last, the soup was served and, as Tito tottered among us to see that our needs were met, my host spoke effusively about the tour. His overblown praise struck me as further humiliation for the mistress of the house. Her dancing was compared to mine and though the remarks were delivered as a compliment to me, they were no doubt intended as an insult to her. Madame continued to listen but said nothing, her eyes fixed upon the plate in front of her.

At one point, Reznikov seemed about to propose a toast. He started to rise insisting that there be champagne for a toast, but when Antonio caught his eye and saw his sober expression, he understood and settled back into his chair.

"No, no. I forget myself. Isaac informs me you have lost a friend recently, Miss Bentley. I must offer my condolences. Everyone at this table knows the pain of such a loss. Perhaps it's best that we save our celebration for another time. If you need anything, my dear, Isaac will attend to it. He's very fond of you, you know."

"Grandfather, please."

"You mustn't be shy, my boy. If you won't speak up, then I must do it for you."

Reznikov had found another point of embarrassment and was homing in on it. What a cruel man, I thought, and realized that very soon, I would be in his sights. Why was there no sign of Orlando? How I longed to hear the sound of his footsteps along the gravel path, or a sudden knock at the villa's door, but the dinner dragged on without interruption.

Then I heard them, those footsteps I'd strained so long to hear. Or, had I imagined them because as I listened, they stopped? It took every fiber of my being not to fly from the table and throw open the entrance to see who might be standing outside. I remember gripping the arms of my chair until my fingers ached.

At last, the rap came, firm against the wood and loud enough for everyone, including Tito to hear. He was carving the ham at the time and looked up surprised or as if he expected someone else to respond. On the second rap, Madame Lazaremko lost all patience.

"Answer it, you fool!"

The old man blinked and looked confused, but did as he was commanded, his steps a slow shuffle as he headed to the door. Everyone watched and waited, disquiet on their faces as they wondered who might be paying a call at that late hour.

A cool breeze wafted into the dining room from the hall and shortly after it, Orlando appeared, dressed in his familiar costume.

With no further need to restrain myself, I rushed forward and threw my arms around him while those remaining at the table looked on. I clung to him like a barnacle to the hull of a ship and only released him when he encouraged me to do so. Then, he introduced himself to the others and explained how he had come to be among us, giving his audience the prearranged explanation we had agreed upon.

Antonio frowned as he listened. He disapproved of this unannounced visitor, perhaps seeing in him another rival. Madame, on the other hand, looked intrigued. Like my teacher, I imagined she had no objection to a handsome face.

Reznikov's reaction was different from the other two. He reminded me of a cat that had found a new mouse-hole. He sat with unblinking eyes, watching Orlando over his tented fingers, and listening attentively to what was being said.

In due course, Orlando was invited to join us at the table. Tito looked unhappy about having to set another place, but aside from his disgruntlement, the scene appeared normal for a time. Reznikov plied his guest with questions, which the latter parried with his usual deftness -- a skill which, until that evening, I'd never admired.

Both men appeared to be enjoying this game, but I sat on tenterhooks, longing for an end to their sparring. By the time dessert had arrived, I'd had enough. I rose from my chair, explaining that I had a headache, and hoping Orlando would offer to escort me to my room so that we could talk in private. I failed, however, to take Antonio's attentiveness into account. He rose almost at the same time and offered me his arm. Fortunately, his grandfather waived him back into his chair.

"Stop fussing, Isaac. You'll turn into an old man in no time, if you don't relax. Maria will give her one of her miraculous powders. By morning, Miss Bentley will be right as rain." Reznikov tossed me a thin smile, not to console me, I thought, but as if he intended to hide his thoughts.

"Sleep well, my dear. I understand you've shown an interest in my work. Tomorrow, perhaps, you'll allow me to show you my laboratory?"

I hurried up the hall stairs without making a reply, my heart pounding against my ribs. If there was a God in heaven, Orlando would follow me soon. To discourage anyone else from entering, I kept the room dark, allowing them to assume I was asleep. Then I waited, almost holding my breath.

I didn't have long to wait. Orlando appeared like an apparition, his silhouette bathed in moonlight. Had he been a spirit, I wouldn't have cared. He was a welcome sight, and I ran to him to throw my arms around him a second time.

"My room is across from yours," he informed me once we'd separated. "As I expected, Reznikov was eager to extend an invitation for me to stay. If you become frightened, come to me. I don't intend to sleep but to keep watch throughout the night. It's possible, I may catch him at something that will reveal his plans."

"Plans?" I echoed incredulously. "I think he's told us those already. You heard him. He wants to show me his lab. But why let matters go that far? Why not spring on him tonight? This cat and mouse game is driving me crazy."

"We can't 'spring' on him, Tara," Orlando explained patiently. "So far he's done nothing but show you and your dance company generosity. Would you have him imprisoned for that? No, our hands are tied until he shows us his hand. I know how you feel..."

"No, I don't think you do. How could you? Death's your stock and trade. Dancing is mine. We live in different worlds. You can't possibly understand how much I'm afraid."

Orlando took hold of my shoulders.

"Listen to me. Until we figure out what he's up to, both of us are at his mercy.

And I do know about fear, Tara. I've looked into that man's eyes and he's completely insane."

"I don't have to look into his eyes. I've seen how he treats Madame Lazaremko. I can almost pity her. One minute he's kind and the next he takes pleasure in her humiliation. Why she stays with him, I can't imagine."

Orlando cupped his hand under my chin to force me to look into his eyes.

"My concern isn't for Madame Lazaremko. My concern is for you. What we're facing is more complex than I realized. For the moment, we're playing a defensive game."

"I don't know what that means. For me this isn't a game and it isn't a sport." I took a step away from him and he let his hand fall.

"I'm sorry. I don't know what more to do."

Orlando sounded so hopeless, I took his meaning for a death sentence, but I wasn't ready to give up. I wanted to fight.

"All my life, I've let other people make decisions for me. I've been coached on how to stand, how to arch my feet, display my hands, arrange my hair, put on makeup. I'm given schedules and told what to wear and how to be lady-like. I love dance, but I haven't had a life. I want both. I'm twenty-one. I refuse to die without a struggle. If you can't help me, then I'll help myself. I don't know how, but I've got to try."

The more I attempted to rally my courage, the more helpless I felt inside. I knew I sounded foolish, like a cat ready to challenge a pack of dogs, but bravado was the only weapon I had to use against my fear. Angry with Orlando and the world, I could feel my eyes begin to prickle with tears. I held them back because I was sick of crying, too. What I did was pummel Orlando's chest with my fists for release, a punishment I felt he deserved. He'd offered hope and now there was none. Even so, I cried out "Help me, Orlando. Help me, please."

His response was to take me in his arms and kiss me, a gentle touch that made me hunger for more. My arms reached up to encircle his neck just as Antonio, after a quick knock, stepped into the room. Finding Orlando and I locked in each other's arms, he struggled to find his words.

"I-I-m sorry. I shouldn't have barged in. I've brought Maria's headache remedy." He moved toward the bed and placed a bottle of white powder and a glass of water on the nightstand before backing away. He was hurrying toward the door when Orlando cut him off.

"I was saying goodnight. I didn't mean to upset your plans."

"Plans? I have no plans." Antonio's eyes flared at the accusation. His intention to defend himself was of no importance to Orlando. He had already disappeared. My intruder turned back to look at me with his shoulders drooped.

"I've made a fool of myself, haven't I? I knew you liked Tom, but I had no idea there was someone else. This fellow's quite another creature, isn't he? Behaves like a Pharaoh. Who is he?"

"He told you at dinner…"

"Oh please, Tara. You and he are more than friends, much more." Antonio swallowed hard as if to bite back his emotion. "I don't suppose I have a chance, do I? Not against him."

If he expected an answer, he didn't bother to wait for it, but came toward me and took hold of my arms.

"I love you, Tara. I've loved you from the moment we met at the bookstore. We're meant to be together. I know it. This champion of yours is going to have a battle on his hands. He can't love you as much as I do. I'd turn the world upside down for you no matter the cost. Would he do that for you? Would he?"

Having declared himself, Antonio released me and strode from the room.

CHAPTER XX

After my night of bad dreams I awoke to a world that seemed indifferent to them. A heavy rain had cleared the sky and left a dome of cerulean blue. In the vineyard, the distant voices of the workers filtered through my open window. Turning my head, I could see the face of my clock. It was 9 a.m. and I felt rested.

Knowing what was in store for me that day with Reznikov and his plans, I continued to lay among my pillows, wondering how I could evade the inevitable. Perhaps I should continue to pretend I was ill and remain in my room one more day. Alec might arrive soon, perhaps tomorrow, to change the equation. I was clutching at straws, of course. The transport of Tom's body could never be arranged so soon.

Feeling irritable, I decided to throw on a robe and stare out the window at the vineyard below. Almost at once, the discrepancy between that idyllic landscape and the frenzy in my mind created a distortion like a warped mirror. The setting before me was one of a peaceful landscape. Carot might have painted it. Yet I knew this scene to be deceiving and as sinister as any Bosch might create. How could I prove evil existed here? What authority would believe me? My one hope was that during the night, Orlando had come up with a plan. If not, mine was to run as far and fast as I could away from the bucolic hell.

I was deep in my thoughts when I heard a knock at my door and soon after, a woman entered. She was carrying a tray of coffee, eggs and bacon, the site of which reminded me that, whether or not this was the day of my execution, I was hungry. She told me her name, Maria, and placed my breakfast on the night stand. Seeing the empty bottle of powder, she pointed to it and gestured, as if to ask if I was feeling better. I nodded that I was and she smiled, as if pleased by my answer.

I climbed back into my bed and before she left me, I observed she was somewhere in her mid-forties, with a well-scrubbed complexion and her brown hair tied in a bun at the nape of her neck. Hers was such a pleasant demeanor that I knew she was far removed from any dark purposes her employer might have.

Left to myself, I was slathering strawberry jam on my toast and thinking the world right for the moment, when a disturbance occurred downstairs. Madame Lazaremko, in a fury it seemed, had entered the hallway, shouting at the top of her voice, first in Italian and then, for my benefit I presumed, switching to English.

"No. No. No, Antonio. I won't stay. Vladimir has gone too far this time. What more does he want from me? The tour was a success. Yet see how I was treated last night. Putting that silly girl in my place and now he wants to.... No, I won't endure it. It's too humiliating. Inform him I've left the garnets on my bureau. Let him give them to her if he wishes because I'm off to Rome with his credit card. I shall shop for rubies to replace them. You can also tell him he needn't look for the Alfa Romeo. I'm taking that, too."

The front door slammed while Antonio, who must have heard her every word, made no reply. What followed were the sounds of Madame's footsteps quick-marching along the gravel path and, a short while later, a car engine sprang into life as it was gunned toward the highway.

Curious as to what the fuss was about, I decided to get dressed and hurry downstairs. Unfortunately by the time I got there, Antonio was nowhere in sight, not in any adjoining room nor in the immediate outside environs. The single hint of human inhabitance wafted from the kitchen where I could hear pots and pans clattering.

Entering the large, airy space, I discovered it was equipped with modern appliances which included a commercial stove with two ovens. At the center of the room stood a large wooden table. On it, various cooking utensils were strewn, including a cauldron of potatoes. At the sink, with her back to me, stood Maria. Hearing my footfall, she turned round and looked quizzical. I asked if she knew where Antonio was and hearing the name, she shook her head, smiled and returned to the sink where she was peeling carrots. I decided to search upstairs.

The first place to look was Antonio's room. Receiving no answer to my knock, I entered and found his bed unmade but otherwise, the room was tidy. The only other sign of an occupant was a book of Italian verse that was lying open on the nightstand.

Next I knocked on Orlando's door, wondering why he hadn't reacted to the earlier commotion. His room was empty, and the bed hadn't been slept in.

Returning downstairs provided no further discoveries. Maria, still chopping vegetables in the kitchen, seemed to be the only other person about.

I was left to solve my puzzle on my own. The first question was, why did Reznikov want me to have the garnets? For that's what I had gathered from Madame Lazaremko's remarks. Did they have some Alchemic significance, I wondered.

To discover that answer I would need to do research but all the books at the villa were in Italian. My cell phone had little internet capacity, but I thought I'd seen a computer in the pantry which stood off to one side of the kitchen. Perhaps Maria used it to order groceries and if so, it might have an internet connection. I decided to find out.

With the cook bent over her sink, I slipped into the tiny alcove. The machine was a clunker but I could access the internet. Within a few key strokes, I had some answers. The name for garnets came from the word "Granatus," meaning a seed like a pomegranate. In Greek legend, the pomegranate contained magic. Hades was said to have given Persephone a pomegranate to ensure her return to him after each of her visits to the upper world. Alchemists thought the stone had the power to call up past lives. How that power was employed or through what chemical process it was obtained, I was unable to discover. I needed Orlando to fill in the gaps.

I returned to his room to see if he might have left a note for me. He hadn't. Perplexed, I explored the remaining rooms, five in all. The last was a small library. Entering, I observed that three of its walls were lined from floor to ceiling with books, but on the north wall, sandwiched between two large shelves, was a fireplace. The hearth was set with paper and kindling but unlit. On either side of hearth was a Queen Anne chair, upholstered in a soft brown leather.

Browsing among the titles, I discovered a few books in English, works by Edgar Allan Poe, Nathaniel Hawthorne and H. P. Lovecraft, having nothing on Alchemy. Still, I became so engrossed in one of Poe's short stories, that I failed to hear the door open behind me, and only when I saw a shadow cast upon the carpet, did I look up to see Vladimir Reznikov standing on the threshold. He was dressed all in black, except for the white lab coat that fell from his shoulders.

"Only me, I'm afraid." He stepped into the room, his eye glittering as he looked about him.

"A pleasant spot, isn't it? I spent a good deal of time here when I was younger. I don't use the place much now. My working library is in my laboratory." He gave a little shudder to indicate he felt a chill. "Shall I light the fire for you?"

I shook my head and said it wasn't necessary. I hadn't meant to stay.

He looked disappointed but asked if I'd sit down long enough for him to have a few words with me. He took the chair opposite mine when I did.

"If you're looking for your friend, I sent him off with Isaac for a tour of the winery. Neither of them looked very happy about it, but I wanted to talk to you so

I insisted. My guess is they don't like each other very much and I suspect you are the cause, my dear. We men can behave so foolishly over a woman."

Refusing to confirm any suspicions he might have about Orlando and me, I said nothing. He didn't seem bothered by my silence being engrossed in his thoughts.

"I suppose you heard Ludmila's dramatic departure this morning. I apologize for that. She's easily put out. Sometimes I offend her by the mere fact that I breathe. She'll have her revenge with my credit card, of course. My guess is that she loves it far more than she does me. Well, if it buys a little peace, why not?"

Whether it was the shadow cast by the morning light or the genuine frailty of his physique, I don't know, but the man in opposite chair looked worn. A stranger, finding us together and observing my robust state, could easily have mistaken me for the man's nurse. Only his black, luminous eyes betrayed any hint of the chaos of which he was capable.

"I hope you slept well," he went on after a gap in his remarks. "No more headache, is there?"

I shook my head and lied when I told him I'd had a good night's sleep. He seemed satisfied and fell silent again, allowing his hands, with their long fingers, to dangle lifelessly over the arms of his chair.

"One day, I must ask Maria what she puts in those powders of hers," he said after a time and as if he were making a mental note to himself. "I don't suffer from headaches, so it's never occurred to me to wonder until now. Do you suffer with them much? The headaches, I mean."

"No, not often. Most of my pain is in my feet."

Reznikov chuckled as if I'd awakened an old but fond memory in him.

"Yes, yes. I do know about that. Antonio has told you I, too, was a dancer? That was many years ago. What we do for love, eh? But a dancer's pain is different from that of old age. More bearable."

Seeing him crumpled in his chair, he almost made me sad for it was easy to see his mortality in the sharpness of his bones and the hollows of his eyes. How could a man so near the end of life be filled with so much hate? Why not grasp at the joy left to him instead of nurturing old insults? He was like a wounded jackal for whom I could feel empathy but didn't dare help. The best I could do was to engage in conversation.

"Has Tito been with you long?"

"Tito?" Reznkov looked surprised by this question, coming as it did, out of the blue. "Oh yes, a very long time. Maria takes care of him. He lives near her in one of the cottages down the hill. She and her husband walk him to the villa each morning. Apparently, he's slept in today. He does that sometimes. Well, why not? He's entitled."

"He strikes me a little too old to be working."

"Does he?" A pair of obsidian eyes turned in my direction and seemed baffled. "How like the young to find the old irrelevant. I suppose I did, myself, when I was young. It's a mistake, you know. We ancients have other powers to compensate for our withered bodies."

Sensing a threat in his bland expression, I pressed my shoulders back against my chair, as if by that gesture I could put a meaningful distance between us. Perhaps he saw I was afraid. If so, he appeared to take no pleasure in it. When next he spoke, his tone was softer.

"You're a remarkably lovely child, Tara. Forgive me for calling you by your first name, but *Miss Bentley* sounds so formal and I'd like us to become friends. I recall one other to whom your beauty might be compared. A dancer like yourself. She's dead now but perhaps you've heard of her? Yelena Natilova?"

He was baiting me, of course, but this time his question served as a spur, reminding me that someone else's safety was at stake besides my own.

"Forgive me signore, but I believe you know Madame Natilova was my teacher. It's in all the literature. Why do you pretend otherwise?"

My host's face crinkled, not from age, but from a smile which he may have hoped would put the gloss of charm to his deception.

"Ludmila told you that I knew her, as well, I suppose. She hated Yelena, which explains why she's has been hostile to you since the pair of you met. Don't bother to deny it. She's not been kind about you behind your back, but it's really me she resents. She assumes your connection with Yelena is the reason why I've given your company so much money and she's right. Her antipathy is understandable. She lacked Yelena's grace and assurance as a dancer. She knew there could be no comparison between the two of them. But as we are being honest with each other, did your teacher never speak of me? Never mention my name?"

On that point, I could answer truthfully. I told him that she never had. He looked disappointed and then sighed.

"Well, it's of no consequence. Whatever passed between us was a long time ago."

"Not in Madame Lazaremko's mind, I'm afraid."

Reznikov nodded and smiled again.

"But we mustn't blame everything on your connection with your teacher.

Ludmila hates you because you are young and, by all report, a wonderful dancer. Let us hope, for both our sakes, that when she returns from Rome with a fistful of rubies, she'll be in a better frame of mind. She has a good side, you know. She can be tender with Isaac and even with me when we're not arguing. But such a temper. I'm always amazed that she comes back."

"Why does she? I wonder. You say she's interested in your money, but she's not a poor woman, surely. Is it possible she truly loves you?"

Reznikov shook his head.

"I've no idea what she feels for me, but don't call it love. Call it an addiction, or a habit."

"Surely it's more than that."

Reznikov peered down at his long fingers and looked thoughtful.

"She did ask me to marry her once. She was carrying our daughter at the time. I assumed she wanted to salvage her reputation. For me, that wasn't enough reason to tie myself to a woman I did not love.

"Do you know she denies being related to your grandson? She tells everyone she's his godmother. That must be hurtful for everyone."

"Yes, yes. The poor boy has told me. All these years, she still refuses to admit our little indiscretion."

"Except for last night."

Reznikov's brow furrowed as he looked up at me.

"How do you mean?"

"Last night I referred to you as her employer and you heard how she bristled."

"So, that was what the fuss was about." The Alchemist tented his fingers as he sat in thought. "I suppose forcing her to change her place at the table didn't help."

"You must have known that would be her reaction. Did you want to unsettle her?"

"Well, perhaps I tease too much, but she offends me with her pretense of love. She knows nothing of grand passion. How can she? She thinks too much of herself." My host turned a pair of curious eyes in my direction. "This young man who was killed, was he special to you?"

Mention of Tom, in the midst of this conversation, caught me by surprise. My thoughts had been bent on Reznikov's notion of love and wondering how well he knew himself. His distrust of Madame Lazaremko might be justified; but much of that suspicion was the product of his nature. Once he'd felt betrayed by my teacher, he used his misgivings as a device to protect himself from ever being vulnerable again. But by evoking Tom's name, Reznikov reminded me of my own duplicity. Like my teacher, I had accepted a young man's devotion without returning it. Perhaps I, too, had been selfish and shallow.

Reznikov drew in a breath of contemplation when I told him Tom and I were merely friends.

"Nonetheless, I'm sorry for your loss. I'm sure you will miss him for a long time. Still, life must go on, eh?"

As he spoke, he fumbled in the pocket of his laboratory coat and eventually fished out a velvet box the size of a paperback book. The moment I recognized what it was, my body stiffened. He might as well have confronted me with a venomous snake. Reznikov took no notion to my reaction, but laid the gems open to me on their pillow of white satin.

"You can ignore Ludmila's behavior this morning. The necklace was never meant for her. Isaac misunderstood when I asked him to purchase the necklace for me. The garnets are for you, and I hope you'll honor me by wearing them tonight."

My gaze fell upon the stones and when it did, I admit my reaction to them altered. I became fascinated. Even in the soft light, they seemed to pulsate with a warm glow, attracting me to them as if, like a crystal ball, I might see the pathway of my future reflected in them. I asked the Alchemist if he thought the gems had magical powers. His response was to look at me curiously.

"Magic? Magic is the stuff of fantasy. It caters to our desire to control our lives or the lives of others. Alchemy is a branch of knowledge, cut off too soon, by the rise of empirical investigation. I say 'too soon,' because science is limited. It appeals only to reason while Alchemy respects the rational and the spiritual, a more balanced way of looking at the universe in my opinion."

"I thought the spiritual side was the province of religion."

Reznikov threw his head back as he chuckled.

"Religion is nothing more than magic's child. What is prayer if not another form of wishing?"

"Then you aren't a Catholic like Antonio?"

"Heaven's no. That's Ludmila's doing." He paused to squint at me as if he were fleshing out a question. "To be honest, I do wonder why women are such staunch supporters of the Church. The religion hasn't been kind to their gender. Its literature is full of sobriquets describing females as 'sacks of dung,' 'beings unworthy of life,' and 'Satan's Daughters.' Even in this age, a women is believed unfit to be ordained. What solace can there be for them faced with such beliefs, I wonder."

"You are a champion of women, then?"

Reznikov's response this time was not a chuckle but a crooked smile.

"I think not. I think of you as Liliths, all."

"Then you agree with the Church at heart."

The eyes looking into mine took on a strange glow.

"Have you read Dante's *Inferno*, Tara?"

I nodded that I had.

"Then you'll recall Canto V where Virgil describes the fate of lovers whose passions outstrip their reason. Their punishment is to be buffeted by the fierce winds of their desires -- their hearts never at peace but always tormented by that *ill air*. What further proof do you require that men should be wary of women?"

"Or the reverse: that women should be wary of men. But are we talking about love or lust? If, torment is part of love's equation, then you and Madame Lazaremko must be legendary soul mates."

What freedom allowed me to speak as boldly as I did, I don't know. Normally, my range of emotions is relatively small. I laughed, I cried. I was happy or sad. Never have I considered myself a wit. Yet there I was, sparring with the devil incarnate, and in spite of my fear, half enjoying it. Some license to be profligate had been unleashed in me which I attributed, in part, to being in the presence of evil. Did Eve feel similarly intoxicated, when she bit into the apple?

If he had been my tutor, Reznikov couldn't have looked more satisfied.

"Touché, my dear, though you mistake me, entirely. For myself, I welcome the tempest women bring. Far better to burn with passion than to live quietly in some dark corner of the universe. It's natural that you should fail to understand my meaning, of course. You know so little of love, less than a blind man does of color, I think."

His rebuke stung me because it was true. For a moment, I almost envied him his mad obsession with Yelena Natilova. He was prepared to take arms against ordinary life and wring from it a personal destiny. He showed courage and courage was power. I could understand, too, why Natalya Lazaremko might rather suffer his insults than be banished from him.

Reznikov rose and removed the cross that hung about my neck, replacing it with his strands of garnets.

"Blood of earth, tongues of fire... the color suits you. Wear it tonight, child. The evening will be special, I promise you."

As the gems touched my skin, I was infused with a warmth that left me drowsy. Suddenly, I felt as if I was sinking into a deep, narcotic sleep. Certainly, my body no longer felt as if it were under my control. My arms and limbs grew numb, yet I wasn't panicked. I yielded to it the way one might yield to a quiet death after a long and painful illness.

I was so deep in my dream-like state that I failed to hear the library door open. Orlando strode into the room in a single step, his face turning pale as he saw the necklace.

"Someone screamed. Didn't you hear it, Tara? Don't you know what it means?"

Reznikov blinked and looked about him as if to discover what might be amiss.

"A scream you say? Tara and I heard nothing. But I should investigate." He headed for the door but paused briefly on the threshold to address the Necromancer.

"Please stay with us one more night. I've planned a little celebration this evening which I'm sure you will enjoy."

That said, Reznikov glided from the room, heedless of the scowl his invitation received.

Once we were alone, Orlando spun round and took a swipe at my necklace. Somehow, I evaded him.

"No, the garnets are mine. Mine!" Enraged, I ran from the library.

CHAPTER XXI

Violin strains of Tchaikovsky's *Allegro* floated through the open windows of my bedroom as I entered. I wasn't sure what had come over me in the library but I turned the latch of my door to prevent Orlando from following me. I needed time to think and for a while, I stood listening to Antonio's music as it rose from the olive grove. How beautiful and melancholy it was, like a meditation. Hearing it, I grew calmer. Eventually, I was so drawn by the melody, that like a traveler longing for home, I unlocked my door and headed for the olive grove, still wearing the garnet necklace about my neck.

I found Antonio under a tree with his eyes closed as he played, as if the music were carrying his thoughts far away. Certainly, he neither heard nor saw me until I was almost upon him. Then he opened his eyes and observing the necklace, he let his arms drop to his sides as his chin fell to his chest.

"So, he's given them to you, after all. I seemed to have made a mess of everything, haven't I? I thought the garnets were for Ludmila. That's why I took her to the jewelers with me. She was so happy grandfather wanted to buy her a gift. Now, see how desolate I've made her."

"It wasn't your fault." I took a step closer so I could touch his hand. "Anyway, I don't intend to keep them. Your grandfather asked me to wear them tonight. In the morning, I'll give them back."

Antonio looked alarmed when he heard me and shook his head.

No, you mustn't do that. Grandfather will be upset. Besides, Ludmila would never take them back. She'd be too humiliated. You must keep them."

"But, I don't want to cause an argument" I protested.

Antonio's lips parted in a weak smile.

"It's good of you to care about the feelings of a woman who's shown you so little courtesy. But the gems are yours. All I ask is that when Ludmila returns, you put them away so that she doesn't see them."

I agreed to his suggestion. It didn't require me to give up the gems, merely to be discrete. Why I was so attached to the necklace baffled me, however. I wore

Anunciata's crucifix for a reason: to feel close to her. Ordinarily, I didn't fuss with jewelry, not even earrings.

I drew closer to Antonio to look into his eyes.

"You're certain you won't be upset if I keep them?"

"Upset?" He seemed surprised. "I doubt I could ever be upset with you. Surely you must know that by now."

His warm breath fell across my face. I knew he desired me and I admit to the thrill of feeling I had power over him. I moved closer, wanting him to kiss me, but he backed away.

"Don't toy with me, Tara. I'm no good at games. I don't know how you feel about me but I think I've been clear about my feelings for you. I was also clear with your friend this morning."

"You spoke to Orlando about me?"

"Of course! Any fool can see he's in love with you."

Now it was my turn to take a step back.

"He told you that?"

Antonio's lips curled, noting my reaction.

"That pleases you, doesn't it? You like men fighting over you, I suppose. You probably don't care about either of us. You're playing a game."

"That's a rotten thing to say."

"Is it?" He stood with his violin dangling in one hand and his bow in the other, glaring at me. He wanted me to deny his accusation or possibly, he wanted me to choose, but I refused to be manipulated.

"I don't owe you an explanation for how I feel about anyone and you've no right to make demands. Maybe it's time for me to take my bags and leave. This trip has been a mistake."

I started to leave but Antonio dropped his bow to take hold of my wrist.

"Wait Tara, please. I'm sorry. I shouldn't have spoken like that. You don't deserve it. I'm muddled, that's all. I want to know where I stand. Have I any hope?"

Observing the grip that held me, I abandoned myself to my ire.

"Is this how you treated Sylvia? Did you bully her, too? Is that why she refused to marry you?"

Antonio reacted as if I were molten lead and let go of me at once, his eyes still pleading.

"I loved Sylvia, Tara, and she loved me. I know what Tom told you but he was wrong. He was a boy and a jealous one besides."

"Don't utter a word against Tom. Don't you dare." I started to walk away but the desperation in Antonio's voice held me back.

"Hear me out, please. I want you to know that I loved Sylvia and I've mourned for her as I should, but what's going on now isn't about her. It's about you... us. You've accused me of failing to know you, but you're wrong. I've made a study of you. You can be willful and petulant and, yes, selfish. But you can be compassionate and caring as well. Never doubt my feelings for you. No one will ever love more than I. Give me a chance, Tara, Give us a chance. I'll do anything to make you happy. All I want is for us to grow old together and, if at the end of my life, yours is the last face I see before death takes me, then I'll die a happy man."

He dropped his chin to his chest again, unable to restrain his tears.

If by compassion he meant my heart ached to see him so distraught, he was right. I moved forward and enfolded him in my arms.

"Don't be upset, Antonio. It'll be all right. I promise."

I kissed him gently on the lips, even though I was aware that Orlando stood at my bedroom window, looking down.

. . .

That evening, I wore the tuxedo outfit Antonio had purchased for me in Milan as well as the garnet necklace. The men rose when I entered the dining room. Reznikov and Antonio looked at me with admiration but Orlando did nothing to hide his disapproval. I chose to ignore him. At the moment, Antonio's hurt feelings were my concern.

As he'd done the previous night, Reznikov insisted that I sit beside him, but if anyone thought Madame Lazaremko's absence would ease the tension in the room, that assumption would be proved false. Reznikov still posed a danger and Antonio's anxiety didn't help either. As for the Necromancer, I'd never seen him more dispirited. I puzzled over how to read his mood. Was he angry with me for wearing the necklace, for having kissed Antonio, or was his manner signaling something more dire? I was so anxious myself, that I spent most of the meal moving my food around on my plate.

Only our host seemed to enjoy himself. He maintained a steady monologue on a range of topics from modern art to politics during the reign of the de Medici's. Naturally, as his spirits rose mine fell in equal measure.

Sometime during the dinner, I stopped listening. My thoughts had drifted to those of my friends. In my mind's eyes, I could see them making a jubilant return to Seattle. How I wanted to be with them. Then I thought of Tom lying in a coffin in Italy, and about Alec whom I hoped would soon appear. As a consequence of my ruminations, I failed to hear Reznikov address me. Only when he repeated his remarks did I come to my senses.

"Did I startle you, my dear? I'm sorry." My host smiled at me benignly. "What I said was that I've arranged a little demonstration in my laboratory. Isaac won't be interested. Besides, he's needed at the winery this evening. Some problem with the fermentation."

"I could be interested," Antonio objected, but his grandfather waved him to silence.

"Never mind, Isaac. I'm not offended. I have Tara and her friend to humor me this evening."

My eyes flew to Orlando's, hoping he'd raise an objection, but he remained passive, like a cobblestone that is resigned to being trod upon. What was the matter with him? I could make nothing of his silence. Antonio was the one to raise a protest.

"Tara isn't dressed for the laboratory, grandfather. The last time I was down there, the place was filthy, like a zoo with no keeper."

Thank god! Antonio had a tongue.

Our host laughed, making light of the complaint.

"Isaac suffers from hyperbole. What he doesn't know is that I've done a little housekeeping in preparation for this evening. I can assure everyone, Tara's gown will come to little harm."

Reznikov turned his head to address Orlando before I could make a response of my own.

"Do you dabble in the arcane, young man? An air of mystery clings about you. Remind me, please, what is it that you do for a living?"

Orlando put down his knife and fork.

"I assure you, signore, Alchemy is a study in which you'll find me conversant." He spoke with such laser-like intensity that the old man paled upon hearing it. The Necromancer's challenge was undisguised and left no doubt that his meaning was unfriendly. *Hurrah*, I thought. Orlando was his old self again.

Nevertheless, after his initial falter, our host answered in kind, matching that same intensity.

"I should be interested to know if your accomplishments exceed mine. I suspect we shall soon find out."

Blissfully unaware of the tension between the two men, Antonio interposed.

"Why all the mystery, grandfather? Can't you just tell us what you've been up to?"

Reznikov fell back in his chair, his eyes aglitter. "Up to? Dear boy, you mustn't make me sound like a miscreant. I don't plan to blow up the place. What I have in mind is... well, as to that, we must wait and see."

. . .

After dinner, Antonio, grumbled to himself as he left us to attend to problems at the winery. Watching him pass outside the window, Reznikov noted that a storm was brewing. His tone was thoughtful, like a man for whom the weather was a portent. His eyes took on a faraway look as if his mind and his spirit had left us. Then, he recalled himself and spoke cheerfully as he bit into his last morsel of pie.

"Fortunately, we needn't worry about the weather. The basement is dry and secure from the elements."

Pushing back his chair, he stood up and indicated that we should do the same. Orlando followed his direction, pressing his hand under my elbow so that I was obliged to do the same. Despite his firm grasp, my knees felt like water and I clung to him with both arms afraid I might lose my balance. If he sensed how unsteady I was, how frightened, he didn't acknowledge it and continued to urge me forward.

As long as he was with me, I made steady progress. When we reached the hall, however, Orlando surprised me by stepping away. Why he'd left me to stand on my own, I didn't understand and looked at him with a confused expression. He announced that he had some other business to perform but would join us shortly.

I couldn't believe my ears when I heard him. Surely he wasn't so annoyed with me that he'd leave me to my fate. Or was this some plan of his which he'd failed to relate? I didn't know, nor had I any clue as to how I should comport myself in his absence.

My expression must have appeared desperate because he leaned forward suddenly to whisper in my ear.

"Trust me, Tara. And trust yourself."

That said, he walked away without a backward glance, abandoning me to the tender mercies of Vladimir Reznikov.

My body went numb as I watched him exit through the front door. I could no more move nor breathe than a slab of marble carved as flesh could exhibit animation.

Perhaps sensing my state, my host spoke kindly.

"Come along, my dear. Let me show you the way. Your friend, I'm sure, will have no trouble finding us." Then he placed my moist hand in his dry one to lead me down the darkened hall toward the cellar.

In my catatonic state, I was without the power to resist. I allowed myself to be lead like a Judas goat to the large, oak door that lead to the stairs below. Reznikov let go of my hand to tug at the handle. It groaned a little before opening, revealing an interior as black as an abyss.

I watched without objection as the Alchemist reached for a switch inside the entrance. Immediately, a single incandescent bulb sputtered into life. Too small to illuminate the entire space, it seemed to cast more shadows than light upon the stone staircase that led to the cellar below. As there was no railing to cling to, I would be forced to descend with my back hugging the cement wall.

Reznikov proceeded ahead of me and I followed, hampered by my gown as well as my fear. With every step, I could sense the temperature drop. I must have shivered audibly because Reznikov glanced over his shoulder, urged me forward, his voice crackling with impatience.

Eventually, my eyes grew accustomed to the shadows. I could observe several alcoves on the floor below, each lined from floor to ceiling with dusty wine bottles. Edgar Allan Poe's, *The Cask of Amontillado* came to mind and I shivered a second time.

Upon reaching even ground, I noted the dust of many years had settled everywhere, particularly at my feet. It stirred like a fine mist where I walked and muted the light from above as it bounced off the bottles and made them appear like a cosmos of distant stars.

Reznikov pointed to a second wooden door, one that set his laboratory apart from the alcoves. Standing before it, he withdrew a large key from his dinner jacket and inserted it into the lock. The door creaked as it opened. Would this be among the last sounds I would ever hear, I wondered.

Where was Orlando? Why isn't he with me?

Reznikov motioned for me to enter before him. I hesitated, naturally. But as the Necromancer had observed earlier, there seemed to be no way but forward. I stepped inside and the moment I did, the door behind me was slammed with a shuddering force. I was met by a darkness so profound that not even the tiniest sliver of light from the outer room could be seen. Had I been forced to stand in that inky blackness an hour or ten? My eyes would never have adjusted to that total absence of illumination.

I heard the sound of a match being struck, and saw a tiny flame flare which formed a halo around the Alchemist's face. Its illusion was one of a decapitated head floating in midair and I gasped to see it. Next the lips formed words. "Soon all will be revealed," they said.

With the first candle lighted, a few shadows formed around the glow. Then other tapers were ignited so that, by the time the Alchemist had finished his task, I found I was standing at the center of a large room, one that could only be described as medieval. What little furniture existed was made of dark oak, heavily carved with the images of ravens. The walls were lined with books on three sides while the fourth, located at the north end of the room, gave access to the olive grove through a door ornamented by a large a brass ring.

A long table dominated the room, strewn with beakers, tubes and other glassware. A few tattered books lay opened, their pages turned down at the corners or festooned with drops of colored liquid long since dried. Had Dr. Frankenstein or Count Dracula entered these environs, I wouldn't have blinked, but merely wondered what type of experiment might be underway.

Reznikov pulled out a wooden chair from a nearby desk and invited me to sit down. I did as he asked and with some relief as I was near a state of collapse. Satisfied, the Alchemist paused and appeared to listen for footsteps as did I. Sadly, I heard none. The silence was so pervasive, a mouse munching on a morsel of cheese could be heard.

CHAPTER XXII

"You may have heard the name Werner Heisenberg, perhaps?" Reznikov began once I'd settled in the chair he'd offered me. "He was the man who determined that an electron can appear as either a wave or a particle, depending on how one chooses to search for it. Some call it the 'observer effect,' which is to say our interference determines how objects appear in the natural world. His was an astounding idea because for hundreds of years, theorists assumed there was a chasm between mind and matter. But Heisenberg proved they were wrong.

"As electrons are the building blocks of matter, they come under our will, so to speak -- mind over matter, in fact. Of course, I've simplified his theory for you, but even a dancer should be able to see the idea permits intriguing possibilities: invisibility, transfiguration, teleportation and so forth, feats of interest to a student of Alchemy, naturally."

Reznikov stood with his eyes blinking, unsure of whether or not I had the least notion of what he was saying. I didn't. Still, it behooved me to keep the conversation alive in the hope that Orlando would appear. I decided the best ploy was to become argumentative. I told him his ideas might be suitable for Alchemy or science fiction but had no place in the real world. Why did he waste his time on these subjects, I wondered aloud.

After listening to my opinion, he smiled as if I were a poor, dumb animal, one with which he would be unable to communicate. Pursing his lips, he let his gaze wander about the room, giving himself time to gather his thoughts. When he spoke again, he formed his words slowly as if language itself might be foreign to me.

"Have you no sense of history, Tara? Our thoughts are both our past and our future. Five hundred years ago, da Vinci imagined humans might one day fly. An outrageous speculation in his day, but now, a common occurrence. I could say the same for electronic messaging or television. Impossibility is tomorrow's norm."

"You believe invisibility, transfiguration and those other things you mentioned are possible?"

"Why not, if the mind wills it? But I'm getting ahead of myself..."

He stopped to listen for a second time.

"I thought I heard footsteps," he explained. "But no. I was imagining."

Sadly, I had to agree. The surroundings were so silent, one could hear time's decay. *Where was Orlando?*

No sooner had I said the Necromancer's name in my head, than I experienced a moment of blurred visions. Perhaps the Alchemist has experienced it, too, a fuzziness in our environs, because he began to speak quickly as if there were a sudden urgency. Any attempt of mine to interrupt or delay was dispatched by a wave of his hand.

"I think it best to begin our little demonstration. That should clarify my meaning far better than words."

Reznikov stepped to the table and picked up a knife. Its sharp edge flickered as if alive in the candle's glow. Pointing the tip in my direction, he came toward me, leaving no doubt in my mind as to his intent.

Because he stood between me and the exit, I leapt up and placed the chair between us. It proved a flimsy barrier, however. Reznikov easily swept it aside and took hold of my arm.

"Stop struggling, Tara." His nails bit into my flesh as he snarled at me. "There's no reason to delay. The Necromancer can't help you."

My face must have given me away. So, he had recognized Orlando, after all. Certainly, when he saw my shocked expression, his face crinkled, happy with his effect as if he'd dazzled a child by pulling a rabbit from a hat.

"Did you suppose I wouldn't recognize what he was? Or do you insist upon playing the ninny? It won't help. I've already seen your traces leading to the antechamber. Tonight you will take me with you." Reznikov looked round as if to assure himself we were alone. "Where is he, by the way...this fine fellow of yours? Not as powerful as he seems, eh? Or is he a coward? My grandson would never have abandoned you, but you're like that other one, always thinking of yourself. I was right to see that he was rid of that little fool just as he will soon be rid of you."

"Rid of her? What do you mean?" Shocked by his words, I managed to pull away and set the chair between us again. He didn't bother to push it away, this time. A gleam had come into his eyes, one that reminded me of the eyes of a rabid dog I'd once seen before it was put down. He was obsessed by his evil thoughts.

"I mean, I had her killed, of course. I wasn't skilled at Alchemy, then. A crude arrangement, to be sure, but it served my purpose." Reznikov lashed out with the knife, after his confession, missing me by a hair's breadth. The blade sliced through my garment but drew no blood.

"You're mad. You know that don't you?" Mine was a stupid remark to make to someone insane, but I was stalling for time. "If you kill me, how will you explain my death to your grandson? Do you imagine life will go on as before? That he could still love you? That he'll feel nothing?"

"Of course he'll feel something. In the case of that other girl, I counted on it. I knew my boy loved her and would suffer. I thought she would suffer too and reach out to him, just as Yelena reached out to you, but she didn't love him enough. She was too shallow."

By now Reznikov's features were so contorted by his disease that I knew there was no reasoning with him. Still I went on as words were my only defense.

"Listen to me, please. Your plan won't work. Even if you could recreate the antechamber, you'd never get beyond it. Not even a Necromancer can do that."

The Alchemist made a sudden leap in my direction. Toppling the chair between us, he took hold of my arm a second time, behaving as if my remarks had set him on fire.

"You admit it, then! You *have* reached the antechamber. And Yelena was there. Don't deny it. What did she say to you? Did she speak of me?" The pain, as he dug his finger into my flesh made it difficult for me to speak.

"S-she said no one alive could go beyond the antechamber. T-there are natural laws..."

Reznikov's laughter was more like that of a jackal's than of a man's.

"Oh my poor child, how naïve you are. Laws can be overmastered. I have broken so many. Why should the last be different?"

As he spoke, his face drew so near mine that I was forced to look into his eyes, and there I saw a darkness like no other. Midnight appeared to have curled in upon self, as if intent upon banishing all hope of light. The sight of so much despair brought me to the brink of madness, myself. My voice grew tremulous and when I spoke, it was without a trace of humanity.

"Do you want to die? Is that your intent? Then give me the knife and I'll happily send you to hell."

Though I stood trembling with rage, reason clung to a small corner of my mind. Could I really kill this man, it asked. Plunge a knife into his beating heart? The whispered reply was more terrifying than anything I had ever faced or ever would in my life. For a brief moment, the curtain of my darkness opened and I saw that not only could I kill, but I would have rejoiced in the chance to smear myself in Reznikov's blood.

My tormentor seemed to sense the change within me and stepped away. His retreat left me feeling depleted. For one black moment I had lived for reprisal and knew its power. What cataclysm might have occurred had our two storms, Reznikov's and mine, collided, I don't know but the threat of it put fear in the face of my assailant. He shrank from me, his eyes no longer dark but empty. I was looking into the face of a man who was drowning.

"You dare threaten me? You haven't the power. Have you forgotten? I have been rejected once. Death spit me out as unworthy... a minnow too small for attention. That's why I must become its master. And you will help, not as you propose, but by a surer route. Your way is no good at all."

The despair in Reznikov's eyes only goaded me further.

"So you mean to kill me, instead? You foolish old man, don't you see? Even dead I'd never help you. Never."

I could see his spirit falter and took my advantage, digging my Stiletto hard into his ankle. The pain almost shriveled him. He stumbled backwards with the knife still in his hand, his gaze one of confusion, as if he expected an apology for my attack. Despite the blood seeping through his shoe, he had the presence of mind to regain himself. I watched as he wobbled forward, holding on to the chair for balance. The knife remained pointed at me but whether it was intended as a threat or for his own protection, I could no longer be certain. Either way, his eyes glittered with his madness.

"The wheels are turning, no matter what you do. Even now I sense Yelena's spirit is near. She's afraid for you. I've prepared well for this moment. I am ready for her."

"Ready for what, you foolish old man? She's dead. Don't you understand? She's dead."

"I am not the foolish one here. You know nothing of what I can do or have done. I've been manipulating your life since this tour began, at the Hungarian Opera House and in Vienna when you ran, half mad, into the traffic..."

"Those were panic attacks, nothing more."

"Those were hallucinatory powders let loose into the air. And so easy."

"I don't believe you. I suppose you'd have me thinking you were at the bookstore, too?"

"I was. I admit the attempt on your life was crude. I'd no idea you'd be there, but as they say, nothing ventured, nothing gained."

He spoke so confidently that I was inclined to believe him. Nothing he'd confessed was any more fantastic than ghosts and antechambers and

Necromancers.

"What about Tom? Were you on the Rialto Bridge that night? Did you kill him?"

A part of me didn't want to hear the answer. Once I was certain Tom was killed because of me, I didn't know if I could live with that guilt. Yet I couldn't turn away, either. I had to know the full extent of Reznikov's evil.

He seemed to read my thoughts, even appeared apologetic when he answered.

"We both know I wasn't after him. He was an innocent, but he saw the halo around my invisibility cloak and placed himself in harm's way. Neither of us are guilty. He was collateral damage, as they say."

An explosion went off in my head and I lost all control. I kicked the chair Reznikov was using to stabilize himself and grabbed for the knife in his hand, a movement so quick that he was caught off guard. The weapon fell to the ground with a clatter. Seeing it fall, each of us made a dash for it. How long we grappled for control, I don't know. My youth was pitted against his age, but soon I could feel my strength waning. In a desperate gamble, I decided to release my grip and use both my hands to push Reznikov away, far enough, I hoped, to clear a path to the door.

"Help! Help!" I cried as I made a dash for freedom. "Someone, please help."

I wasn't fast enough. My assailant caught hold of me just as my fingers reached for the handle. Clutching me by the hair, he attempted to drag me to the floor, the knife held high above his head. I screamed what I imagined was my last, desperate wail when the cellar door flew open.

I wasn't certain who was standing in the shadows, but I cried out Orlando's name. Reznikov released his grip on me, acknowledging the presence of someone with power over him. I fell to the ground like one of his heavy alchemy tomes.

"I-I'm glad you've come, Isaac," he said, his voice tentative, as if uncertain of what to say next. "Tara's overwrought about the death of her friend. I tried to comfort her, but as you can see, I've failed. Perhaps you can help her. Something has snapped. She doesn't know what she's saying."

"Liar," I screamed, rising unsteadily to my feet. "You killed Tom and Sylvia Huntington and you just tried to kill me." I sounded hysterical, at best, and hadn't a shred of proof for my charges. Still, I wasn't pleading my case in a courtroom. I was defending myself to Antonio. Would he believe me or would he take his grandfather's word for what had occurred?

Reznikov was quick to turn my hysteria against me.

"Do you hear that, Isaac? She accuses me of murdering a boy I've never met.

We were talking when suddenly she broke out into these wild accusations. I can't explain how this "Sylvia" became a part of her delusion as well, but we must calm her down. Ludmila's valium is in her medicine chest. Be so good as to fetch it for me?"

I clutched at Antonio's arm, refusing to let go of him.

"No. Don't leave me, please. If you do, I'll be dead when you get back. He'll say I attacked him and that he had to defend himself. I'm telling you the truth. He paid someone to kill Sylvia and now he's killed Tom. He has some wild idea he can hitch a ride with a departing spirit. He wants to find my teacher, Yelena Natilova. She's been dead for many years but he loved her once."

"Loved her once? Do you think love ends with death, you stupid girl? I still love her and always will."

"There, you see?" I screamed as I pointed to the madman. "I'm not making this up. He imagines he can reach her through me, but I have to die first."

Reznikov took hold of his grandson by his other shoulder, his face not only grave but pale.

"My boy, you are blood of my blood. I've raised you from the cradle. You know I could never harm anyone. This poor girl is ill. I beg of you to trust me."

I was close enough to peer into Antonio's eyes as I awaited his judgment, and there I could see the whirlpools of his torment. Whichever way the truth lay, it promised nothing but tragedy. Either he must judge me insane or believe his grandfather was a murderer.

"Please, Antonio," I murmured, still clinging to him. "You said you loved me."

"Don't allow her to manipulate you in this shameless fashion," Reznikov scolded. "She wants to put a wedge between us. Why trust her? You barely know this girl. She's interested in your money, Isaac. Just like the other one."

In a brusque move, Antonio pushed us both away.

"Stop it," he shouted, placing his hands over his ears momentarily. "I won't listen to either of you unless you calm down. I don't know what's going on here, but I can't believe these horrible accusations both of you have made. Stop speaking until you can talk sense." Antonio's focus drifted toward the old man. "It's true, grandfather. I haven't known Tara long, but I do understand her. She's in shock because her friend has just died. She needs our understanding. Please don't speak ill of her. If you love me then you will help her."

Reznikov stepped away from his grandson, chewing his lower lip in his consternation.

"Of course, dear boy. We must do all we can to help Tara. That's what I'm saying."

"Then drop the knife if you mean it. Drop it!"

I was shaking where I stood, my eyes fixed upon the blade Reznikov gripped in his fingers. Antonio followed my gaze and seeing the weapon held out his hand.

"Yes. Tara's right. We don't want anyone hurt, do we? Give me the knife, please."

The Alchemist looked undecided for a moment, as if he knew he was at a crossroads and was reluctant to choose his direction. Finally, he shook his head.

"I can't do that, Isaac. You are too trusting. As a boy you always were. That's why I've had to look out for you. The women in your life have all been parasites. You mother was a harlot, like your grandmother. And that girl you were infatuated with years ago, she cared nothing for you. Believe me, I know. This one's the same. Though I believe it pains you to hear it, you would do well to be rid of her. I wish I could convince you of that."

Antonio's complexion turned ashen. He'd come to understand the circumstances a little better and in response moved with slow, cautious steps to place himself between Reznikov and me.

"Give me the knife," he pleaded. "You've no need for it. I'm here, now. I'll keep you safe."

Seeing how his grandson had positioned himself, Reznikov looked increasingly agitated. His gaze danced about the room, the eyes sparkling with a wild madness.

""No, no. Isaac. You haven't been listening. You're too besotted with this girl. It's you who needs protecting. This one will break your heart. Give me this wretched creature, and I'll share my powers with you, powers that you haven't begun to imagine." The old man took hold of Antonio's arm for a second time, as if to reel him in. "I can give you immortality. Think of that, Isaac. I can achieve it for you. All that's required is a quick thrust to Tara's heart. She needn't suffer. She won't suffer if you'll help me."

His madness revealed, I let out a long held breath. Antonio had no choice but to believe me now. His grandfather had just confessed to his sinister plan, but if I expected him to react with outrage, to attack Reznikov with an unspent fury, I was wrong. The voice that spoke next was wreathed in filial love, soothing, the way a mother might attempt to calm an injured child.

"Let me take you upstairs, grandfather. It's late and you're tired. We'll talk tomorrow, I promise you."

Antonio drew his relative closer to him and Reznikov responded with cleansing tears.

"It's not that I *want* to hurt anyone, Isaac. Please understand. But I love Yelena Natilova. I always will. She's my reason for being. I told you that once, remember? And Tara is the key. Help me, Isaac. If you know what it is to love, then help me, I beg you."

Taking a firmer grip on the old man's shoulders, Antonio clutched him to his chest.

"Oh my poor, dear Nonno, love seems to be a curse in our family."

The old man looked up at his grandson a second time, his eyes still shining.

"Nonno? You haven't called me that in years. Then you don't judge me? You'll help me bring her back? And this time, Isaac, I'll make her love me. This time there will no obstacles. I knew you'd understand."

Antonio nodded.

"I do. I promise that I do. But first you must rest. Please, let me put you to bed."

Antonio kissed his grandfather's forehead, and feeling him limp against his body, might have assumed the matter was resolved. If those were his thoughts, he was wrong for without warning, his grandfather used his palms to push him hard against the wall. Antonio fell backward and hit his head against the solid oak bookshelf. He moaned as with one hand, he touched the wound at the back of his head, his knees buckling under him so that he sank to the ground. Reznikov watched him fall with a leer of satisfaction.

"No, no, my boy. I can't stop now. Everything is arranged. See those stones Tara's wearing?" He pointed a stiff finger at the garnet necklace about my throat. "They are my pomegranate seeds. Once they're drenched in her blood, they become an offering. I know you don't believe me, that you think me mad, but I *can* revive my beloved Yelena. I can do that and more. I have the power to wake the entire underworld. Think of it, Isaac. We can create a new world order if only you'll help."

Still stunned, Antonio struggled to rise, using the shelves to hoist himself to his feet. Injured as he was, he continued to speak kindly to the old man.

"If you bring back the dead, Nonno, you will be the greatest Alchemist of all time. Even Newton would be amazed."

Reznikov looked pleased, his dark eyes snapping.

"Yes. You can see the possibilities. We could bring back that girl, the first one you loved. Would you like that Isaac? Would you like to see her again?"

Antonio nodded as he steadied himself. The fall, apparently, had done no permanent damage.

"Yes, I loved her, once. But I love Tara now."

The older man curled his upper lip as if he detected a foul odor.

"You think it's possible to love two women? If so, you can't have loved either one well. You're humoring me. I can see that I was wrong to confide in you. I must go on alone."

Reznikov turned and, without warning, lashed out with his knife, missing me by a few inches. He raised the blade a second time and I screamed, for in those obsidian eyes I could see no traces of human habitation. Seeing my danger, Antonio hurled himself against his grandfather and the two of them collapsed against one wall, a collision that sent books of all sizes and shapes flying. Some landed on the ground. Others displaced the vials and bottles that had rested on the laboratory table. The sound was like that of a cannon being fired into a greenhouse.

Breathing hard, the Alchemist struggled to his feet. His eyes narrowed to the size of needles as he glared at me. I was no more to him than a butterfly to be mounted on a wall. Antonio staggered to his feet, exhorting me to escape. Then he heaved himself against his grandfather a second time. The pair hit the stone floor again, rolling back and forth across books and shards of glass, each desperate to control the knife.

"Run, Tara. Run to the cottages below. You'll be safe there."

Gladly, I would have run except the two men, locked in a life and death struggle, barred my way. In a frenzy of thought, I remembered the north door with the brass ring. Turning around, I sped to it like an arrow to its target. No sooner had I reached it than I faced another impediment.

How many years those hinges had been allowed to rust, unused and unattended, I didn't know, but no amount of tugging on my part would cause them to yield. Behind me, more books thundered to the ground, followed by the sound of wood splintering. I continued to yank at the brass ring, but turned my head to see that the oak table had fallen and all the remaining equipment with it. Worse, Reznikov with the devil's strength, seemed about to overcome his grandson. Antonio's ribs heaved with exhaustion and blood flowed in rivulets along the cracks and crevices of the stone floor.

Though battered, the Alchemist looked as if he was about to stagger to his feet, the knife now clutched in one hand. Desperate, I returned my attention to the door, straining so hard against it that my arms threatened to become dislodged from their sockets.

Dear God in heaven, would I never be free?

A wincing pain shot through both arms as I gave an almighty tug for the last time, knowing I had seconds to live. The rusty metal groaned. The door gave way. Miraculously, I'd created a wedge large enough for me to escape.

Reznikov saw my success. As I slipped through the crack, he uttered a wail. A man standing at the edge of a cliff as the ground crumbles beneath his feet might make such a cry. The effect was terrifying enough to propel me like a bullet deep into the night.

A light rain greeted me. It must have been falling for some time, for the leaves of the olive trees glowed with a silvery sheen and my stiletto heels sank deep into the mud. If I didn't remove them, my efforts to find safety were doomed. Reznikov would find me like some hapless creature stuck in a bog.

Leaning against a tree I struggled to release the ladder of buckles that bound me to my Roman- style sandals. What an absurdity if fashion should be my undoing. At any minute, a madman would come looking for me and find me fiddling with my shoes. In my hysteria, I didn't know whether to laugh or to cry.

That I should fail to notice a figure standing in the shadows is understandable. Not until it moved did I stop my futile struggle and attempt to peer into the dark. Finally the silhouette was close enough for me to recognize. I let out a howl in a manner befitting, Media, The Duchess of Malfi, or Tosca. My outrage was pure and strong enough to churn oceans or cause the stars to burn black. Had anyone ever been as deceived as I?

Orlando took me in his arms and held me though my greatest wish was to scratch out his eyes. He had lied to me, betrayed me and left me to face Reznikov on my own. Why did he appear now when I had no need of him? He was useless.

As usual, he seemed to read my thoughts.

"I didn't leave you, Tara. I've been here all along. I don't ask you to forgive me or even to understand. I wasn't to interfere, not unless..."

I threw my head back to look at him.

"Unless what?"

"It doesn't matter. The future is as it should be."

"As it should be?" Incredulous, I pulled away to look at him. "Antonio is in danger and Reznikov will soon be after me again. How can you say everything is as it should be? Antonio could die."

The moment I said the unthinkable, my hand flew to my lips. "My god! I've been such a coward. I have to go back. I have to help. Let go of me."

I struggled to be set free, intent upon retracing my steps whether my Stilettos willed it or not but Orlando held on, forcing me to turn around and look in the direction from where I'd come.

"It's all right, Tara," he murmured in my ear. "Listen. What do you hear?"

I shook my head vehemently.

"I don't hear anything. What are you saying? Oh, dear god. Is he dead? Antonio's not dead is he?"

My body started to quake with the possibility that the worst had happened. If it was true, I couldn't bear it. I'd rather die myself.

The Necromancer, standing behind me, wrapped one arm around my waist and pointed with the hand of the other one.

"Look. Look there. Tara."

My eyes followed his direction and there, staggering through the door from which I'd made my escape, I saw a man. He paused a moment on the threshold, gasping for air, a slack arm dangling at his side like a broken wing.

"Antonio? Is that you? Antonio?" My voice, choked by tears, was barely audible, but it was loud enough to revive the spirit of the one whose name had been called. He came stumbling toward me as if to a beacon, and as he did, Orlando let go of me and backed away.

"Tara, thank God you're safe. Thank God," Antonio cried.

The blood oozing from his many wounds, made me fear I would lose him after all. I took him into my arms vowing never to let go no matter what fate had in store. His weight was too much for me and together we sank into the wet earth. Antonio was barely breathing, so I sobbed for us both.

I could sense Orlando hovering over us and I feared his presence, growling at him as if I were a mad dog.

"It's not Antonio, I've come for," he assured me. "It's the Alchemist. He doesn't understand what's happened. Yelena Natilova has sent me to bring him to her. She'll help him cross, just as he would have wished."

I turned my head and looked up to read Orlando's expression.

"You mean she has forgiven him?"

"Of course. Love requires forgiveness because it's always a little mad."

He leaned forward to press his lips upon mine, a gentle kiss but one full of longing.

"I'll never forget you. Nor you me, I think." A smile parted his lips as he rose and looked down on me. In that instant, a cloud covered the moon, only for a few seconds, but when it appeared again, the Necromancer was gone.

Like my hauntings of old, a wail penetrated the silence, but, this time, I knew it was the sound of an ambulance wending its way toward the villa. I waited for it while the rain fell hard as pebbles. I felt nothing of it. I clung to Antonio, afraid that if he died, I might not live to see another sunrise.

He moaned as his brown eyes fluttered open.

"Tara? Is it you?"

Drawing him closer to me, I wept, "Yes, Antonio. I'm here."

Epilogue

Seventeen Years Later...

We sat outside, under the shelter of the olive grove, the picnic table in disarray after an extravagant lunch of quiche, fruit and endless bottles of wine. The containers, empty now, glowed with the amber glints of the August sun, while from the vineyard below, voices of happy children rose up to greet us. Was there any sound more joyous than that of youngsters at play?

"I think I'm ready for a nap," Susan said. Her belly round with her third child, (the last she swore). She looked beatific.

Beside her, David leaned over to give the protrusion a pat.

"You both should rest and maybe I'll join you." His eyes twinkled as he spoke, causing Susan to blush. She looked at me from across the table, her voice gentle.

'What about you Tara, now that you're retired as a dancer? Lots of women have babies in their late thirties."

Antonio cleared his throat before I could answer. He was about to make an announcement despite my frown. We'd agreed earlier to say nothing until another month had passed.

"You're right, Susan. It's not too late. In fact, come June..."

My friend didn't need Antonio to finish his sentence. Her lips formed a grimace and a smile at the same time, if that was possible. "We've been here for two days, Tara," she snapped as she threw her napkin on the table. "When were you going to tell us?"

"We just found out ourselves," I replied, a little defensively. "It's only been eight weeks and I've been wrapped up in negotiations with the Tuscany Ballet concerning my new role as choreographer. Antonio and I have had no time to make the mental adjustment."

"I didn't need any time," my husband quipped, placing his arm about my shoulders. "Having you underfoot for a bit has been pure bliss."

Susan looked mollified and David offered a toast though only he and Antonio could imbibe.

"Poor Alec," Susan sighed, after their wine glasses clinked. "He's lost most of us now. David's thinking of leaving, you know. We haven't actually decided but he's been approached by the Alberta Dance Company in Canada. They want him to take up the post of ballet master and to do some choreography, as well."

"That's wonderful," Antonio and I spoke in unison, as we'd been doing with frequency of late. David furrowed his brow despite the opportunity before him. "I feel like a traitor, to be honest. Alec's been so good to us."

"And we've done our best for him," Susan corrected. "Besides, he still has Anne and Phillip. They love running the ballet school and Ellen doesn't seem ready to hang up her Capezios. We all have to move on sometime. It isn't as if the company hasn't taken on new dancers."

"I know, I know." David cut her off. "But if I could, I'd like to perform a few more years. The trouble is, this Canadian offer is a good one."

Antonio, a businessman accustomed to searching for opportunities, took Susan's side. "Your wife's right, David. Change is inevitable and can be exciting." He grinned in my direction as he spoke, letting me know he was speaking for himself, as well. I pinched his ribs playfully and he chuckled in response.

Usually observant, Susan failed to notice our private interchange. She sat staring into the distance wrapped in her own thoughts.

"I admit I loved being a dancer," she said, at last. "I thought nothing else mattered, but being a mother? There's nothing like it." She turned her black eyes on me, her gaze soft and almost weepy. You'll see, Tara. You'll see."

As if on cue, a boy of seven came trucking up the hill toward us. His chin was pressed against his chest, affording us a clear view of his jutting lower lip.

"Mo-m-m," he cried when he was near enough for us to hear him. "Anne stole my cowboy hat and won't give it back. She thinks because she's two years older, she can do what she likes. But it's mine. You brought it for me in Calgary."

Susan sighed and stirred in her chair in response but made no serious effort to rise. David was the one to stand.

"Calm down, Tom. Anne's teasing. Ignore her. She'll get bored in a little while and give it back."

"No she won't. I tried that and it didn't work. You have to tell her the hat's mine."

David shrugged, accepting the inevitable. "I'll come down in a minute. Tell her I'm on my way."

The boy looked dubious, as if he'd heard this promise before and been disappointed. He continued to stand with his hands on his hips, his eyes narrowed.

"You promise you'll come?"

"I promise," David nodded. Satisfied, the child turned on his heels and marched down the slope again.

"You better hurry up. She might break it," he tossed over his shoulder as he disappeared.

I laughed with the others but was surprised that a lump had formed at the back of my throat. This child of seven didn't look a bit like his namesake, Tom Donne, but he had the same swagger. I was reminded of the picnic in Milan when *my* Tom refused to acknowledge he'd been spying on me. He thought I'd be angry, but I was touched by his loyalty. He would have done anything to keep me safe. Didn't he follow me into the antechamber and sacrifice his Life-Savers? My Tom was gone and remembering the fact, my eyes misted with tears.

David bent down to plant a kiss on his wife's cheek. "I'll be back soon. Get the bed warm for me," he smiled.

Susan watched with obvious devotion as her husband stepped from the cooling shade of the olive grove and into the late summer afternoon sun. "I do love that guy," she admitted for all to hear. "I hope he takes the job in Canada. Alec won't be happy, but he's faced worse. When he lost you to the Tuscany Ballet, Tara, I thought he'd have apoplexy, but he got over it and he will again if David leaves. Times are different now. The company is successful and Alec has choreographed some wonderful dances."

She turned her gaze, soft as the color of river-washed pebbles, to my husband. "We're all indebted to you, Antonio. Your contributions kept us afloat in the beginning."

My husband chuckled as he gave my shoulders a squeeze. "What choice did I have? I stole the company's prima ballerina. I had to make restitution."

Susan grinned in response. "That's true, but all in the past. Now tell me about the Brancaccio's. You said they retired ten years ago? I can't believe how time flies. I wonder if they'll remember me when they arrive tomorrow."

"Of course they'll remember you. A lovely woman, like a fragrance, leaves a lingering impression."

Susan shook her head, refusing Antonio's gallantry, and let her glance wander to her rounded tummy. "I don't feel lovely at the moment, but it will be over in a couple of months. I have a feeling this one is another girl. Tom will be horrified as he's counting on a brother. If it isn't, he'll probably insist I send it back to where it came from. If I'm right, though, she'll be called Millicent, after my mother. What about you two? I know it's early but have you given any thought to names? If it's a girl, will she be called Natalya?"

Antonio winced at the mention of his relative and shook his head. "No, that won't do. We don't see much of grandmother these days. She blames Tara and me for grandfather's death. Won't hear a word in our defense. Even the police couldn't convince her of our innocence. Our only communication is through the bank. I send her a yearly stipend and she lives royally in Paris. Her life is quiet now. Doesn't travel much. Arthritis has set in, rather badly, I'm afraid. No, if Tara and I are blessed with a girl, she shall be called Yelena. That seems right."

"And if it's a boy?"

This time, Antonio didn't answer but turned his head in my direction, deferring to me. My reply was brief.

"A man did us a kindness once. If we have a son, we'll name him, Orlando."

To purchase other titles written by Caroline Miller, contact at Rutherford Classics, www.rutherfordclassics.com

www.ingramcontent.com/pod-product-compliance
Lightning Source LLC
Chambersburg PA
CBHW031245120726
47905CB00002B/725